PERFECT PIECE

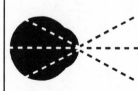

This Large Print Book carries the
Seal of Approval of N.A.V.H.

A SISTERS, INK NOVEL

PERFECT PIECE

REBECA SEITZ

THORNDIKE PRESS
A part of Gale, Cengage Learning

GALE
CENGAGE Learning™

Detroit • New York • San Francisco • New Haven, Conn • Waterville, Maine • London

GALE
CENGAGE Learning·

Copyright © 2009 by Rebeca Seitz.
Scripture references are taken from the New International Version (NIV), copyright © 1973, 1978, 1984 by International Bible Society.
Thorndike Press, a part of Gale, Cengage Learning.

LIBRARY OF CONGRESS CATALOGING-IN-PUBLICATION DATA

Seitz, Rebeca, 1977–
    Perfect piece : a Sisters, Ink novel / by Rebeca Seitz. — Large print ed.
        p. cm. — (Thorndike Press large print Christian fiction)
    Originally published: Nashville, TN : Broadman & Holman, c2009.
    ISBN-13: 978-1-4104-1954-5 (alk. paper)
    ISBN-10: 1-4104-1954-1 (alk. paper)
    1. Sisters—Fiction. 2. Scrapbooks—Fiction. 3. Scrapbook journaling—Fiction. 4. Large type books. I. Title.
PS3619.E427P47 2009
813'.6—dc22
                                      2009023247

Published in 2009 by arrangement with Riggins International Rights Services, Inc.

Printed in the United States of America
1 2 3 4 5 6 7 13 12 11 10 09

As always, this book is dedicated to Charlie, beside whom I will spend all the days of my life.

ACKNOWLEDGMENTS

Writing this series has been such a crazy journey and I can't believe it's come to a close! Thank you, dear reader, for taking time out of your day to spend a few hours in Stars Hill with the Sinclairs. I have loved hearing from many of you and hope you continue to e-mail me with your thoughts and life stories.

I've thanked my family in previous novels and it bears repeating — I could not be me without them.

Ultimately, though, the biggest acknowledgment for the creation of these stories should go to God. If you do not know Him, if you've never met His Son, Jesus Christ, trust me, you're missing out on the most amazing life you could ever imagine. This story that He has written for my life is so much more incredible than anything I could have come up with! It is not perfect. It is not always happy. I don't think the ultimate goal is to be happy this side of heaven. That seems too selfish for a reason to exist. No, far more important than my happiness — which is as fleeting and fickle as the weather — is this secure knowledge that I am loved for no reason other than that I exist as His daughter. I cannot earn more love. I cannot lose love. I can only accept and bask in His love. That provides utter freedom to fully delve into every moment, whether sad or glad, good or bad. I love experiencing life in all its fullness, feeling and breathing the spectrum of existence.

If you know His love, then I look forward to seeing you in heaven. If you do not, why not learn about it right now? Forget what you think you know about Christians — it's not about us or our feeble attempts at reflecting Him. It's about Him. It's about His love for you. And what you're going to do about it. Talk to Him.

ONE

Meg scooted back on the bleacher seat until her backside dipped into space. She stretched her arms along the seat behind and rested her shoulder blades against its cool metal. The May sun shone down, its brilliant glare penetrating her dark sunglasses and lasering through her eyes to increase the staccato pounding in her temples.

"Come on, Tiffany! Watch the ball!" Sheila Regan's voice bored into Meg from the top row.

Tandy leaned into Meg's space. "Sheesh, somebody tell that woman they're *eight,* for goodness sake."

"She spent the past month with Tiffany practicing in their backyard." Meg laid her head back until it met the bleacher's ridged metal surface. A tiny amount of tension eased off. "I'm pretty sure she sees this as a commentary on her mothering skills."

"I just love sports moms."

Meg smiled and enjoyed the cool spring breeze as it danced across her face. If Sheila would hush, and the kids in the dugout nearby would stop cheering for five minutes, she might be able to get rid of this headache. She prayed Tiffany would strike out and the players nearby would take the field.

"Tiffany! That wasn't even over the plate!"

Meg considered the penalties for sports-mom homicide. Depending on the jury members, she might get off with community service.

That could put her working with kids at the softball field.

She sat up and watched Tiffany's bat whiff over home plate a split second after the ball hit James's mitt. She might holler out encouragement to her son — if her head didn't feel like a schizo jackhammer had replaced the gray matter. As it was, she joined the other parents in clapping as the inning came to an end and the teams switched positions.

"You sure are quiet today, Meg." Tandy shifted little Clayton on her lap.

Meg glanced over at the sleeping baby, envying his ability to block out the noise of the ball field. From the corner of her eye, she saw Suzanne get up to take her new dog, Daisy, for a walk between innings. "My head's killing me."

"Did you take that migraine medicine they gave you?"

"Yeah." She took a drink of ice cold water, but barely felt it on her tongue. Weird. "It isn't doing much to stop the pain."

"If you want to go, I can wait until James is finished and bring him home for you."

Meg considered the offer while she watched the kids gather around Daisy but knew she couldn't take her sister up on it. Jamison, Clay, and Darin weren't due back from their camping trip until late tonight. If she left, James would have no parent here to cheer him on.

Not that she felt like cheering, but still. "Thanks, but I better stay."

Tandy's raised eyebrow spoke more doubt in Meg's ability to make sound decisions than words ever could.

Meg tamped down the spark of irritation that flared. She should be grateful for a sister who cared that her head felt like an overripe grape about to split its skin. Why this sudden anger?

For weeks now emotions had coursed through her faster than a Southern woman changed lipsticks. Meg no sooner got a hold on one to try and figure out its reason than

11

another would come slapping itself across her psyche.

She rubbed her head. If this stupid pounding would stop, she would be able to think straight and figure it all out. There had to be a reason for the headaches. She took another sip of water, this time feeling frozen glory snake its way down her throat. It wasn't a dehydration headache. She drank more water than rappers drank Crystal. It wasn't a lack of vitamins, unless Centrum's vitamins for women were somehow missing the vitamin part. Since no one had announced a recall, she doubted the vitamins were the culprit.

Couldn't be lack of sleep. She slept more these days, almost, than Clayton.

Suzanne and Daisy returned to their seats.

Too much sleep? Did too many hours of shut-eye cause migraine headaches?

She made a mental note to check out the possibility as James stepped into the batter-up box and took a practice swing. He looked so much like his dad. Same dark hair, same knees, same elbows, same hands. If she hadn't given birth to him, she'd think he was a clone.

A cracking sound cut across the air and she cut her eyes to the current batter, who dropped his bat and took off for first base like a cow escaping slaughter. James jumped up and down, cheering his friend on to second while half a dozen eight-year-old girls and boys scrambled around the infield trying to get the ball into a glove. Laughter bubbled up Meg's throat and crossed her lips.

"They *are* adorable, aren't they?"

Tandy nodded. "That they are."

James stepped up to the plate for his turn at bat. Meg worried for a millisecond, then decided Jamison's hours of practice in their backyard had prepared their son as much as possible.

The pitching machine punched a ball in James's direction, and he screwed his face up, tucked his chin . . . and swung.

The line drive sailed between first base and second. James had tagged first base and rounded toward second before the ball came to a complete stop. His teammate pushed on toward home while James's little legs pumped him toward third.

"Yay! Go, James, *go!*" Meg stood, ignoring the dizziness that swept through her brain. She would *not* sit silently while her eldest child scored a home run.

By the time James flew past third base, the second baseman finally got a hold on the ball, and Meg saw the boy's eyes focused on home plate.

"Run, honey!" Meg leaned over the seat in front of her even while pain exploded behind her left eye, willing James on to home, praying that second baseman couldn't throw a ball any better than Tiffany. "Run!" Bright starbursts clouded the vision in one eye, but she closed it and kept an eye on James. "Almost there!"

With a mighty leap, James crossed the final two feet and stomped onto home plate.

Meg raised a fist over her head and opened her mouth to yell congratulations through the drumbeats in her mind.

She felt the blackness a moment before it overcame her.

Both eyes went dark, her ears closed to the sound of parents clapping for her child, and one last beat in her brain sent her crashing to the bleachers.

TWO

Tandy spared one glance to the boxy white ambulance roaring from the ball field. Hitching her diaper bag further up on her shoulder, she covered Clayton's ears to the ambulance's sirens and ran for her new minivan, yelling to James to follow her.

The looks on the faces of those EMT workers as they worked on Meg had Tandy's heart in her throat. They told her to hurry. To call family.

She buckled Clayton in, murmuring words of a reassurance she didn't feel, then flew around the van to her own side. James stood waiting at the passenger door, his shoes still covered in a fresh coating of dust from his home run.

"It's going to be okay, sweetie. Jump in." She buckled him into his seat, gave him a quick squeeze, and jumped into her own seat.

Thank God for OnStar. She punched the

15

button for the in-vehicle communications system and swung the van out of the parking lot. Her voice shook as she said, "Dial Clay Cell." The OnStar voice came back, steady as always: "Dialing." Tandy sucked in a deep breath, as deep as possible given that her lungs felt like someone had duct-taped them into a corset.

Meg. Nothing could be wrong with Meg. Nothing serious. Meg, the rock. Meg, the constant in their lives. Meg, the one who stepped into Momma's shoes and mothered them all.

Meg.

"Hello?"

"Clay! Honey, it's me."

"Tandy, what's wrong? You sound frantic."

"Something's wrong with Meg. I have James here in the car with me." He needed to know she couldn't say everything. Couldn't tell him how fear nearly paralyzed her, how she didn't know if Meg would still be alive when she got —

No, Meg would be fine. Meg *had* to be fine.

"The doctors came in their truck and took her to the hospital so she could get there easier than if we took her." There. Simple terms that shouldn't scare James anymore than he already was. "They said the rest of

Meg needs You now. Give her Your presence and tell us what You'd have us do. We bring these words to You in the precious name of Your Son, Jesus Christ, Amen."

Tandy echoed Daddy's amen. She couldn't fathom why God had allowed this to happen, but Daddy was right — everything that came into their lives was something He'd allowed, something for which God had a purpose.

She just hoped the purpose wasn't to teach them all how to deal with loss.

Again.

Jamison stood just outside a thin, blue curtain. A nurse had put him there, her hands firm on his arms, her voice leaving no question about whether he would obey. She'd wanted him to go to the waiting room. He couldn't do his wife any good here, she said. He'd only be in the way of the doctors.

But he couldn't bring himself to turn around and leave Meg lying there. He'd snatched the briefest glimpse before being spotted by the doctors and pushed out. Doctors. Plural. More than one worked on his wife on the other side of this curtain. Why more than one? Did she have multiple things wrong?

Why didn't someone tell him what was going on? He blinked, rubbed his eyes. Better that they take care of her than him. Let them do what they're trained to do. Let them see to Meg. They could take all day if it meant she was fixed and whole and healthy and coming home with him.

The nurse poked her head out. "Jamison, we're going to take her upstairs for an MRI." Only then did he realize it was Sarah, a girl he'd graduated from high school with. "Go on to the waiting room and tell your family we'll know something in a bit."

He looked at her. Sarah the cheerleader, now Sarah the nurse. Sarah the nurse was taking care of his wife.

"Jamison." Sarah touched his arm. "I'll come get you as soon as I can. Go on now."

The idea that she wanted him to return to the waiting room slowly penetrated his mental fog. "Okay." He thought about arguing. About telling them he wanted to go with Meg to the MRI room.

But James's little face flashed in his mind and he remembered he had to go get the Coke his little boy had no doubt found by now. "Okay," he said again, and headed for the double doors to the waiting room.

THREE

Jamison crossed his arms, then uncrossed them. He looked out the window. Saw a car pull into the hospital's parking lot. Laid his right foot over his left knee. Put it down. Left foot over right knee. Put it down.

He checked his watch . . . again. Eleven minutes since he'd been shown into the doctor's office and told to take a seat. Six hundred and sixty seconds not by Meg's side, spent scared out of his mind that the doctor would come in to tell him to prepare to lose his wife.

How on earth would he break that to the kids? The sisters? Jack?

He shook his head, then felt stupid since no one could see him. But whatever IT was that had decided to threaten his family's happy existence, IT needed to know he would refuse its admittance into his life — IT could just go away, IT couldn't have them. Not Meg.

The door behind him opened and he stood. A doctor in a white lab coat smiled what Jamison supposed was a "set-them-at-ease" smile, but what really made him grind his teeth.

"Hi, I'm Dr. Ruskya. Please, sit." The doctor walked around his desk and settled into the wine-colored leather chair on the far side. "I've looked over Meg's MRI scans and, barring your disapproval, we need to take her into surgery today."

Jamison opened his mouth, but the doctor went on.

"She has a small tumor the size of a golf ball that we must remove. Has she said anything about having a headache? Been different than her usual self?"

Jamison nodded. Her complaints over the last few months, the pain he saw in her eyes . . . how could he not have sensed what was going on? "She's had migraines for weeks now. She thought she wasn't drinking enough water."

Dr. Ruskya nodded. "Dehydration is a common cause of headaches, but no amount of water would wash away the underlying cause of your wife's pain. Now the tumor could either be benign or malignant. We want benign."

"Want?"

The doctor's smile held irony. "Of course, we don't want a tumor at all, but it's clearly there. If we have to have one, we want benign because that means it isn't cancerous and won't grow."

"If it's not growing, how'd it get there?"

The doctor shrugged, which didn't help. How was he supposed to trust and believe this doctor when he couldn't explain what was happening?

"It could have been there all her life. It could have grown and stopped. There are a million unknowns with regard to tumors, no matter how much research we've been able to conduct. We have to look at each individual case. With your wife's, we won't know for certain what we're dealing with until we get in there."

"By 'get in there,' you mean go poking around in Meg's brain?"

Dr. Ruskya favored him with an understanding gaze. "I know this must be hard, but she's going to need you a lot in the coming weeks and months. Brain surgery is hard to recover from. She likely won't be the same person when she wakes up and she'll need you to reassure her of herself."

"What do you mean . . . she won't be the same person?"

"The location of her tumor is in an area

of the brain that affects personality. Tell me about the Meg you know."

Jamison leaned back in his chair. At last, something familiar, something safe to discuss. "She's great. A caring mom, loving wife, laughs a lot, loves to spend time with her sisters, scrapbooks."

The doctor nodded. "When she wakes up, you may find that she's the same woman you knew before. Though it's rare, that does happen. But, more often than not, the patient experiences a subtle shift in outlook and mood. She may be angry, defensive, shy, quiet, unsure, rude, or even manic."

"Dear God." Jamison pushed back the terror that grew with each word from the doctor's mouth. "Will she be that way forever?" He tried to picture Meg throwing a temper tantrum, but the image wouldn't materialize.

Again Dr. Ruskya shrugged. "Only time will tell. She may revert to her former self as she recovers. She may be forever altered. We have an excellent counselor on staff who will help with the transition post-surgery. Gina Justice — we all call her Gigi — has been helping brain surgery patients for years. She'll be a big asset to both you and your wife."

"Does she *have* to have the surgery? I

mean, you said this thing could have been there all her life."

"Yes, but something about it has changed to cause these headaches and the seizure that brought her to us today. That means the condition cannot go unchecked any longer."

Jamison felt stupid for even suggesting it. Who cared if Meg changed a little bit? So long as she was still around to hold his hand, talk with him, and grow old with him, he didn't care.

"Can she die in the surgery?"

It was Dr. Ruskya's turn to lean back in his chair. "She could. There is always a risk with any surgery and the risk is higher when we're talking brain surgery. I won't lie to you. We may get in and find things that didn't show up on the MRI. I wish I could tell you we'll do X and Y so that Z will happen, but surgery rarely works that way. I can promise you, though, that we'll do everything we can to remove the tumor and make your wife whole again."

Jamison tried to think through his options, but his brain didn't want to cooperate. Here he sat, a successful accountant whose training and expertise made him in high demand. A man who could manipulate and work numbers with ease, who could oversee massive amounts of money without blinking an eye.

But none of that mattered here.

He was being asked to decide on a course of treatment for his wife's brain tumor. Not that he had any idea what caused it, what made it change, whether she'd get worse if he did nothing, whether she'd wake up still being Meg, or whether she'd even wake up at all! How was he supposed to decide anything without knowing all the answers?

He sighed.

"Mr. Fawcett, this is a hard thing you're doing, but we don't have the luxury of time. The tumor is pressing in on her brain. We need to determine a course of action and, if it's surgery, get her up to Vanderbilt."

Jamison didn't raise his head but cut his eyes up toward the doctor. "And you recommend surgery?"

Dr. Ruskya nodded. "I do."

Meg had told him time and time again to listen to the experts. When they'd added on to the house, she was the voice asking for a contractor instead of drawing up her own plans. When they landscaped the yard, she called the nursery for advice. When she got pregnant with their first child, she read every parenting magazine from here to the Mason-Dixon line.

So, he'd do this Meg's way. If the expert said surgery, then he'd trust the expert. And he'd let Meg rely on this Gina Justice woman afterwards. Meg would like having an expert to talk with. "Okay, let's do the surgery."

Jamison sat by Meg's hospital bed, his laptop warm on his legs, her deep breaths of sleep assuring him of her life. A brain tumor. A selfish, evil mass right there in his wife's brain. No wonder she'd been short-tempered lately. The doctors told him the tumor's location would have affected her personality.

And caused migraines.

He should have paid more attention to the headaches. But didn't all women get headaches a lot? Of course they did. They were always doing fifteen things at the same time. Who wouldn't have a headache from that? He'd told Meg to slow down. Told her and told her.

But it hadn't been the rapid pace of their lives. It had been a tumor. He glanced back down to the glowing screen, rereading information about brain tumors. In just a few hours, dawn would break as a surgeon removed her tumor He'd been told to hope for a benign tumor. They didn't want a

31

malignant one. Malignant meant it could continue to grow, to invade other parts of her body, to end her life.

Lord, please . . . let the tumor go away completely, benign or not. But if it has to be there, let it be benign. He closed the lid on the computer and set it on the table at his side. Leaning forward, he took Meg's hand in his, careful not to rouse her from the depths of slumber.

He reached forward and ran his fingers along the light golden hair splayed out across her pillow. It lay in waves, casting a crown around her head. Her hair had been his undoing the night they met. Their good night kiss that first date might never have been had the evening breeze not floated a lock of it in his direction. All he could do was step forward and do what everything in his being told him was right.

She still gave those sweet kisses to him each morning before he headed off for work. Even if they fought the night before, even if the kids were hanging from the ceiling and every television in the house blared news that the world would be coming to an end by mid-day, she stopped to give him a kiss. Said it was the glue that held her day together.

What would hold him together if she

didn't kiss him any longer?

He followed her hairline down that long, graceful neck that blossomed with color whenever he embarrassed her, which was often in their beginning days. He hadn't known how to handle such a wonderful woman, but she knew enough to see his caring underneath. She'd forgiven him his bumbling attempts at romance, laughing alongside when he sent red roses instead of her favorite sunflowers and saying, "I love you" after his torturous ten minutes of words hadn't let the phrase cross his lips.

The grace of his life summed up in one word: Megan.

He touched her temple, wanting to reach in and remove the invader that lay just beneath her delicate skin. Her soft skin passed beneath his finger as he traced a tiny blue vein that snaked its way into her hairline. She stirred and smiled in her sleep. He sat and stared, drinking in her presence like a man who knows this could be his last sip of all the earth has to offer for beauty and peace.

Megan.

FOUR

Tandy glanced around the waiting room of Vanderbilt Hospital in Nashville. Joy sat in a corner, a sleeping Maddie in her arms. Daddy filled a corner seat, his elbows resting on knees and face toward the ground. Tandy thought he might be praying, but every couple of seconds he tapped Clayton's baby seat and set it to rocking. Clayton slept on. Scott stood staring out the window, where he'd been since walking in the room and announcing they'd taken Meg back to surgery.

The last time she'd been here, Kendra lay in one of these rooms, her leg encased in dressings and a tube down her throat.

Kendra now sat in the corner holding Darin's hand, her leg scarred but healed.

Oh, God. Heal Meg like You did Kendra. Please, I don't think we can live without her. I know I can't.

Clay's hand squeezed around hers and she

looked up into his beautiful eyes. He smiled, filling her with hope that almost blocked the dread that had taken up residence since seeing her sister collapse.

Almost.

She glanced at the big white clock whose hands created a droning sound as they made their inevitable way around the numbers. Over and over they swept. Doctors came and talked to families. The phone at the reception desk rang. People flipped magazine pages. And still, those hands swept on.

They'd been sweeping for three hours now. Halfway through, if the surgery was going as the doctor planned. Tandy stood and paced to the other end of the room. Coming back, she counted the square tiles. Three more hours. At least. More if the tumor was more complicated than they'd seen on all those MRIs.

How could such a thing invade their lives? Hadn't they given enough to medical abnormalities when Momma had breast cancer? Despite that, or maybe because of it, Tandy thought the rest of them should be immune to big things like cancer and tumors. One per family seemed enough of a cross for any family to bear. One let her believe God might have had a purpose in it.

But whatever lesson they should have

35

learned from Momma's death had been learned. What possible purpose could there be in allowing a tumor to grow in Meg's brain? Three children needed their mother. Jamison's eyes had taken on a lost look, as if she'd already left him. Left all of them.

Why did God allow this to happen?

Tandy shook her head. Trying to understand God in the midst of the situation was like trying to eat a cake before the eggs were even cracked. Her perspective and God's didn't come near to matching. He looked at eternity. She looked at getting through the next three hours, hoping that the next three hours would tell her God hadn't decided to let another of their family members go to something besides old age.

She pulled her cell phone out and dialed Jamison's mother.

"Hello?"

"It's Tandy."

"Oh, Tandy! What's the status?"

"Nothing to report yet. She's still in surgery. I just thought I'd call and check on the kiddos. Are they all right?"

"James asks about her every few minutes, but Hannah and Savannah seem content with videos for now. I thought I might take them outside and play in a little bit, hopefully wear them out some."

"That's a good idea."

"Well, I have to admit it's helping me, too. Keeping them busy means I don't sit here and stare at the clock."

Tandy shot another glance at those sweeping hands. "Tell me about it."

"You'll call me as soon as you know something?"

"The very minute. Talk to you soon."

"Thanks."

She flipped the phone closed and shoved it back in her pocket.

Two hours and fifty-four minutes to go.

"Megan Fawcett family?"

They rose as one and looked at the hospital volunteer as she set the phone back in its cradle. "She's out of surgery."

Jamison finally moved from his position at the window and approached the volunteer's desk. "Is she okay?"

"I'm sorry, I don't know anything other than she's through with surgery and in post-op, where she'll be for about half an hour. They'll call me when she's ready to go to a private room."

He swallowed the frustration and reminded himself this woman had no idea that the patient of whom she spoke held his world in her hands. "Will I know what room she's going to?"

"They'll call me as soon as one's been assigned and I promise to let you know." The volunteer laid her wrinkled hand over his upon the desk. "Not long now. You'll get to see her very soon."

So maybe she *did* know.

He mustered as much of a smile as he could, then headed back to his spot in front of the glass. Outside the world spun on as if nothing had happened. As if nothing *could* happen. Cars came and went from the parking lot. Old ones, new ones, shiny or streaked with dirt. Patients and hospital staff stopped on the sidewalk to light a cigarette, an action he added to the list of things beyond his comprehension. Clouds scudded across the sky. The sun shone brightly. The day mocked him with its happiness and life.

He tried to take comfort in the knowledge that Meg made it through surgery. A big victory and one he shouldn't take lightly. He needed to let God know how grateful he was for that. Couldn't risk alienating God right now. Had to do everything right. Had to do his part to keep Meg safe and healthy.

Not that God could be bribed with good behavior. A part of him knew God was above that sort of thing. But another part of

him whispered that he should try everything, no matter how ridiculous, how far
removed from everything he'd ever known
to be true before.

Because if precious Megan could have a
tumor, then everything else must be called
in to question as well.

"Mr. Fawcett?"

He turned back to the receptionist. "Yes?"

"They're going to take her to room 2210.
You can go on there now if you'd like and
wait on her."

"Thank you!"

"You're welcome."

The rest of the family stood as well.

"Oh, is there a waiting room on that floor
for my family?"

"Yes. The nurse up there will direct y'all."

He smiled. That band around his heart
loosened just a bit. In a few minutes he'd
get to see her beautiful blue eyes and hear
her voice. They would make it through this,
they would.

The alternative simply couldn't exist.

The sheets scratched her skin. Wait, they
scratched her arms and one leg. Her other
leg felt like it was asleep.

Meg pushed through the dense fog and
reached for reality. Somewhere her leg lay

sleeping and sheets that had never seen fabric softener had been put on her bed. Things were wrong. All wrong.

Experimenting, she lifted one eyelid. When the only light seemed dim and unobtrusive, she chanced opening the other eye.

Jamison sat on a couch against the wall, a magazine in his hand. Unlike her, his eyes were closed, dark lashes resting across his cheeks. Meg worked to figure out where they could be. A television hung from the wall. Steel bars were on either side of her bed.

She sniffed, but the smells weren't quite right for a hospital.

Think, Meg. You were at the ballpark.

She'd been cheering despite a raging headache and then . . . nothing.

Her head felt like someone had rolled it in duct tape. Reaching up, she felt layers of a soft material and guessed it to be gauze. So . . . something had happened to her head. Something bad enough to land her in the hospital. Because, even though the smells weren't right, this had to be a hospital.

She fought a wave of panic. No sense in getting all riled up. Think. But her brain didn't feel like it could. Like something had been stuffed in the spaces of her brain and

40

was blocking all the signals. She closed her eyes.

Think, Megan.

A button at her fingertips would call a nurse, but that would wake Jamison. Should she wake him? How long had he been asleep? Surely things couldn't be too wrong with her if he was calm enough to be sleeping. *There, that's a nice, rational thought. See? Your brain is fine.*

Unless more time had elapsed than she realized. What day was it? What time? She could hear the hum of a clock over her head and strained to see it, but there was too much gauze on her head. What idiot had put a clock where the patient couldn't see it? There had to be a reason, but her mind couldn't conjure one.

Taking a deep breath, Meg forced herself to try and calm down. If one of the sisters was lying in a hospital bed, she'd tell them to — shoot, what was the word? — *chill.* There, see? Nothing wrong with her mind. The fact that it took her a few seconds to come up with a word meant nothing other than she was getting old.

Anger crawled through her, but she couldn't figure out why. Maybe — she grit her teeth — because she was sitting in a hospital bed and had no idea how she'd gotten there or what was wrong with her.

As another wave of panic began building, Meg made a decision. "Jamison?"

He stirred but didn't wake.

"Jamison? Hon?" This time he opened his eyes and looked around the room, seeming as disoriented as she felt. "What happened? Are we in the hospital?"

Recognition and awareness dawned on his face and he rose from the couch, came to her, and took her hand. "Hi, sweetie. How do you feel?"

She batted his hand away from the gauze. "Confused. What happened?"

The look on his face gave her pause. Maybe she didn't want to know. *Ignorance is bliss.* Truth lay in those words.

But you couldn't face what you didn't know, so she took another deep breath and watched Jamison struggle to find words. Good, at least she wasn't the only one.

Her relief died the instant he spoke.

"Meg, honey, you had a brain tumor."

She blinked. His lips kept moving. She knew words kept coming, but nothing made it to her ears past that first sentence. The stuffing in her brain swelled and filled her ears, blocking her from anymore words.

And, just like that, her whole life changed. Forever.

FIVE

Tandy set her glue runner on the table and grabbed her bottle of Diet Mt. Dew. Time to jump on the big white elephant in the room. "Y'all think she's ever going to be the Meg we knew before?"

"I don't know. It's only been a week since she got home from surgery. That's two whole weeks since somebody sliced into her brain. We should give her time." Kendra pulled her hair back and tied it with a bright red ribbon.

"That Justice woman and the stuff I've been reading on the Internet says we should expect permanent personality changes and learn to love the person she is now."

"But I loved the person she was before." Tandy tried not to pout.

Joy looked toward the scrapping room window, where raindrops slid down the glass like lonely tears. "I did, too. But we can love her no matter what happens, right?"

A rumble of thunder rolled across the sky. Tandy waited for Kendra's voice. Finally, she looked up. Kendra had frozen midway through applying a length of ribbon to her layout. She looked like a beautiful African mannequin in a high-end department store.

"Kendra?"

Kendra blinked and met Tandy's eyes. "I want to say I love her enough to keep on loving whoever she becomes. I really want to say that and mean it. I *should* be able to say it and mean it. She's my sister. But y'all have spent as much time with her this week as I have. Our sweet, mild sister has developed a mean streak."

"She's simply frustrated, Kendra," Joy admonished. "Wouldn't you be if you were put in her shoes?"

Kendra's spiral curls swayed as she shook her head. "I can't imagine being in her shoes and, like I said, I want to be supportive and loving no matter what the future holds. But when that mean part of her comes out, I worry about her kids. I worry about Jamison. I don't know if I should accept that part of her or talk about it with her or just hope it goes away over time."

Joy folded her hands atop her layout. "Well, I think we should give her some time. It *has* only been a week since she came home, and I'd guess at least a month needs to pass before we start worrying about permanent personality changes. Some of those Web sites said she may continue to change for up to a year."

"A *year?*" Tandy thought of the long days before them. Before Jamison. "Surely not. Meg is healthy. I mean, except for this stupid tumor, she's always *been* healthy. She'll bounce back from this."

Lightning cracked beyond the window, thunder tumbling upon it before the burn had gone from her retina. Sheets of rain pounded the pane, desperately seeking escape from the howling wind. Tandy shivered and rubbed the goosebumps from her arms. "I think we better get downstairs. That storm isn't letting up and the top floor of this house is the worst place we could be if a twister comes through."

The high-pitched beeping of their weather radio sounded from the hallway below.

"I'll bet we're under a tornado watch now." Kendra scooped up her supplies and carried them to her spot on the wall shelf. "I need to call Darin and tell him we're all fine."

Joy and Tandy put their paper, inks, and tools away as well. Tandy glanced outside and saw dark clouds roiling in different directions. "That doesn't look good."

Kendra and Joy followed her gaze.

"Come on, let's see what the weather radio has to say. I'll bet Daddy's already got the popcorn in the microwave."

Tandy led the way down the stairs, her mouth watering when the scent of butter wafted up the staircase. "Ooh, I smell it."

"Me, too."

The drone of the emergency management bulletin sounded from the weather radio as they filed through the hallway and down the last flight of steps to the main floor of the old farmhouse.

"Daddy?"

"In here, honey girls."

They trooped into the kitchen. Daddy stood at the counter dumping the contents of a popcorn bag into the big multi-striped glass bowl that Momma had used to make countless cake and cookie batters. He nodded toward the porch. "The lightning's still far enough off. We can go watch the storm from the porch."

Kendra shook her head. "I will never figure out this family's fascination with storms."

Joy picked up the now full bowl. "Oh, Kendra, you should be ashamed."

"Why in the world should I be ashamed?"

46

"You're an artist. Don't you want to see the beauty of a stormy sky and experience the power of the thunder and lightning?"

"All things I can see from *inside* where sane people stay in the middle of a storm."

"Since when do we prize being sane?" Tandy snagged cans of soda from the refrigerator.

Kendra rolled her eyes. "Of all the families in the world, I had to be adopted into a bunch of loony storm lovers."

Daddy chuckled. "I think God knew exactly what He was doing."

Tandy led them toward the front door. "Yeah, who else would put up with your weird artist side?"

They settled into chairs on the porch as the wind kicked up bits of cut grass in the yard.

Kendra reached into the popcorn bowl. "Wow, it's dark out here."

"Always darkest before the dawn," Daddy comforted.

Tandy eyed the growing storm cloud bank and watched the distant tree line dance with the wind. A few birds still flew, so no tornado yet. Streak lightning split the sky, shooting horizontally across the dark expanse. The rain came sporadically. Small drops diving under the porch roof's edge,

47

then fat drops splatting the ground. Cooper was probably whining his heart out at home.

"I should've brought Cooper with me."

"Clay will check on him." Kendra tucked her feet under her.

"Yeah, but he'll worry about me."

"Clay?"

Tandy wrinkled her nose. "Cooper. Clay knows I can take care of myself."

The disquiet of the surroundings crawled beneath Tandy's skin. With the uncertainty of the past week, she wished the storm would just blow itself out and let the sunshine come back. They needed a few blissful days. Meg needed the bright light during the day. Maybe it would shake her from the funk of her post-surgery self.

"Joy, in all that stuff you read on the Internet, was there anything we should be doing to help Meg? Did her counselor have any suggestions?"

A stiff wind scattered tiny drops of moisture across their faces and legs. Joy hugged her arms to her chest. "Not really. Ms. Justice said to be patient, to let Meg heal on her own time. The Web sites echoed that and admonished family members to be as understanding as possible, and to not expect her to be the person she was before."

Daddy's hand paused in the popcorn

bowl. "What?"

"What what?"

"What was that part about her not being the person she was before?"

"Oh. Well, they were in her brain, Daddy. There's been a lot of research in the past few years, but we still have no idea what all the different parts of the brain control. They may have touched something that alters her personality or her sense of taste or even how she views the world."

Daddy shook his head. "Our Meggy will be just fine. All she needs is time."

"She probably will be fine. But maybe not the fine she was before."

Daddy's lips tightened into a thin line, but he said nothing.

Kendra slapped her hands onto her lap. "I think we should hope for the best. It sounds like nobody really knows what to expect, so let's choose to expect something good."

Tandy nodded, though uneasiness still gripped her heart like iron bands. "I agree. And I think we ought to figure out a schedule for going over there to take care of the kids so Jamison doesn't go nuts."

Joy looked out across the yard. "Tomorrow's Saturday, so I'll be up to my elbows in hair color all day. But I can do tomorrow night if one of you can take the day."

"I'll do during the day. The diner doesn't get crazy until nighttime on Saturdays anyway, so Clay won't need me."

"Then I'll do after church on Sunday."

Daddy still sat with his brow furrowed.

"Daddy? You think Zelda would want in on this?"

Daddy blinked. "Um . . . sure. I'll talk to her about it when she gets back tonight."

"I hope she didn't get caught in this storm up in Nashville. What was she doing up there anyway?"

"Just shopping. I don't expect her back until an hour after the mall closes."

The girls chuckled.

"Maybe she had the right idea. Being in a mall where you aren't aware of this weather would be a good place to be right about now."

Tandy set her soda can on the table at her side. "I'm with Ken on that one."

Distant thunder rumbled. Tandy looked up and saw the break of the front. "Looks like the storm is moving on."

Kendra and Joy followed her gaze.

"Thank goodness. We live through another one despite sitting in the middle of it."

"Oh, Kendra. You're so dramatic."

Kendra stuck her tongue out at Joy.

"Very mature."

"Thank you."

Tandy noticed Daddy still stared at nothing, worry creasing his brow. "Daddy? You okay?"

He didn't look up.

"Daddy?"

His head turned. "What?"

"I asked if you were okay. You're sure quiet."

"Got a lot on my mind, honey girl."

"Something we can help with?"

He stood and gathered up the popcorn bowl and soda cans. "I'll let you know."

They watched him walk back inside, the screen door popping closed behind him.

"What was that about?" Kendra brushed popcorn kernels from her broom skirt.

Tandy shook her head. "I think that bit about Meg changing rocked him."

"Well, it's the truth," Joy defended. "Ms. Justice said it's rare for a brain surgery patient to *not* be altered in some way."

"Calm down, baby sister. I wasn't saying you shouldn't have said it."

"Stop calling me baby. I'm a grown woman with a child of my own."

"Speaking of which, I should go check on Clayton. He's been asleep long enough."

Joy sighed. "And Scott's probably wondering what's taking me so long."

"Boy, am I glad Darin and I decided to wait on the kid thing for a while."

"Don't mock. It's not like Clay and I *planned* to have a baby in our first year of marriage. Those honeymoons have a way of blindsiding you."

Kendra shook her head. "TMI, Taz."

"Oh, please. We're all married here. It's not like we don't know what happens on a honeymoon."

Joy stood and held out a hand. "I beg of you, stop there."

"Okay, okay. I wasn't planning on going any further anyway."

"And we thank the Lord above for that." Kendra rose and untied her hair. She shook it out and stuffed the ribbon into her skirt pocket.

Tandy followed as the sisters walked back into the house. She walked through the living room and back up the stairs toward the bedroom where Clayton lay sleeping. Something niggled at her. Something off-kilter in her conversation with the sisters. Something not quite right, but she couldn't put her finger on it. As she gathered Clayton's things and then scooped him from the crib, it hit her.

Meg. They didn't talk the same without Meg around.

Six

Meg sat down at her breakfast table and tried to be happy that another day had dawned. She'd never been an unhappy person before this *thing* came into her life. Moments of unhappiness, sure, but nothing she couldn't overcome. Nothing that didn't go away.

She eyed the plate of blueberry muffins at the center of the table. Her sweet husband had gotten up early to make breakfast and get the kids out of the house so she could have some peace and quiet.

The house sat in depressing silence. She wished he hadn't taken the kids to the park. The sound of their laughter bouncing off the walls, their feet pounding the hardwood as they ran from room to room, would be nice right about now.

But it wouldn't help the pounding in her head. She touched the bandage on her head. Ironic that the surgery to remove the cause of her headache caused a headache. Her doctors assured her this pain would go away as she healed, but she couldn't remember a time anymore when her head didn't hurt.

I'm with you, Garth. I'm much too young to feel this old. The country tune wound its way through her brain, the pounding giving a perfect beat backdrop. *Great, now my headaches are keeping time to country music. I think we're close to rock bottom around here. At least I can still remember lyrics.*

Lately the struggle for words had taxed her patience. Words — always her friends before — now hid around shadowy corners of her mind. The sisters kept up their banter, but she didn't contribute. Their words simply came too fast for her to keep up.

Why couldn't she feel hopeful? Positive? Happy? The tumor was gone. And benign. It wasn't coming back. Why couldn't she feel good about that? Forget good, ecstatic ought to be in play by now.

But the surgery had messed up everything else. She plucked a muffin from the plate and bit into it. As she'd come to expect, it tasted like plastic. Everything tasted like plastic. She hadn't tasted a single food since the surgery.

"Which could be a great way to lose

weight."

Great, now I'm talking to myself. She *had* to find a positive side somewhere. Get a grip on this negativity washing over her like a tidal wave. A good mom knew how to point out the good things in life. She'd been a good mom before.

"I will be a good mom again."

She prayed speaking the words would make it true.

Well, almost prayed. She wasn't quite ready to talk to God about some aspects of this particular detour. His reasons for allowing this to happen eluded her as much as her old happiness. Why did He let this thing slip into the wonderful life she led? She believed what she'd been taught — that nothing happens to God's children without Him first knowing about it and giving it permission to enter. So why this? What could be learned from this?

The brain-injury support person at Vanderbilt said not to try figuring that out until she had some perspective, some time. But if she could figure out the lesson now, she could learn it and be done with this, right?

The doorbell rang as she took another bite of muffin. Might as well eat, even if no pleasure came from it.

She didn't get up to go to the door. If it was another well-wisher from church, they could leave the casserole on the doorstep and Jamison would find it when he came home. No sense letting people see her walking with a steel walker because her stupid right leg didn't cooperate.

She looked down at it and pounded the top of her thigh. The doctors said this, too, would probably heal over time. Oh, goody. *Eventually* her leg would work again. Would that be before or after her kids graduated from high school, met a wonderful person, and wanted to walk down the aisle? She pictured walking down a white path, Jamison propping her up.

"I *hate* this!"

"Well, emotion is good."

Meg jerked her head to the kitchen door, where Tandy stood with Clayton on her hip.

"What are you doing here?" She didn't mean to sound so snappish, but everything came out with a snarl these days.

Tandy shrugged and entered the kitchen. "I thought you might want some company."

"You came to babysit the invalid."

"Oh yeah, that's definitely it. Can't trust you alone, you know?"

"Stop patronizing me."

"Then stop acting like a kid." Tandy

56

snagged a muffin. Clayton swiped at it, but she pulled it away from his chubby little fingers.

"Help yourself."

"Thanks." Tandy bit into the golden top. "Mmm, these are good."

"I wouldn't know."

Tandy glanced at the half-eaten muffin on Meg's plate. "Really?"

"I still can't taste anything."

Tandy shoved the plate of muffins away. "Then let me get you some broccoli and spinach for breakfast."

"This is *not* funny."

"No, but you might as well stuff your body with good things until you can taste them again."

"I may never taste anything ever again."

"Or you could start tasting things with your very next bite."

"Are you going to be this chipper the whole time you're here?"

"I haven't decided yet." Tandy offered her finger to Clayton, who sucked on the blueberry filling smeared there.

"Then let me decide for you. Stop."

"You'd rather I be as churlish as you?"

"Churlish? I'm a brain-injury patient, don't use big words." She struggled to figure out the meaning of the word.

"Okay, snotty."

"Thanks, that's much better."

Tandy sighed. "Look, I know this is horrible for you right now and I have no idea what all you're going through, but I'm here until Joy gets done fixing all of Stars Hill's hair, so we might as well find a pleasant way to spend the day together."

"So you *are* babysitting the invalid."

Tandy threw her free hand up. "You got me. I'm here to babysit." She looked around. "Where are the kids?"

"Jamison took them to the park. Which I'm sure you know or you wouldn't have come over. I wondered why he left me alone."

"Maybe he needed a break from your sunny disposition."

"He wanted to be away from me?"

"Oh, for heaven's sake, Meg. I get that things are awful right now, but do you hear yourself?"

"My hearing hasn't changed, if that's what you're implying."

Tandy stood and went to the refrigerator. Meg tried to get a grip on the anger that threatened to boil over at any second. Why was she so mad? Tandy had only come because she cared. Nothing wrong with that. So she couldn't do everything she'd done before the surgery. Most of that would come back. She simply needed time. "I'm sorry."

"No problem. I've got thick skin." Tandy returned to her seat and bounced Clayton on her lap.

Meg rubbed her throbbing head. "I don't know why I can't look at the bright side of life anymore."

"You just had major brain surgery. Guys dug into your gray matter. I think you're allowed a little time to adjust."

"Yeah, but I hate this out-of-control feeling. Like I can't even get a rein in on my own emotions."

"Did you talk to Ms. Justice about it?"

"Of course I talked to Gigi about it. I even called that brain-injury support line she gave me."

"And?"

"And was told to give myself 'room to grieve,' whatever that means."

Tandy arched a brow. "What would you be grieving?"

"The loss of the old me, I guess. Did you know they took away my driver's license?" Meg picked at the browned edges of a muffin. Outside, a whippoorwill sang its tune.

"Scott told us. That's another reason we're taking shifts. No sense in leaving you stranded at home."

"Not that I'm going out in public until my leg starts working."

"Still giving you fits?"

Meg slapped it as she'd done before. "I don't understand. I tell it to move, and the stupid thing completely ignores me. As if I have no control at all."

"That's twice with the control thing."

"Well, you try having people mess with your brain and see if you don't want some semblance of control back in your life."

"I wish I could get through this for you."

Meg looked up. She didn't deserve such good sisters. "Thanks."

"You're welcome."

They listened to the music of the birds for a while. Meg considered being grateful for the ability to hear. She could have lost that sense altogether. Instead, sounds somehow seemed amplified. Every bird had its own unique song. Just like the kids, each one expressing individuality — even Hannah, at two years old.

But what happens when someone else changes your tune? When you can't remember how to sing it or even what it sounded like? Gigi didn't have a lot of answers for that other than to wait it out, take each day one at a time, blah blah blah. Whether it was the upbeat Gigi or the folks at the other end of the brain-injury support line, the message was always the same. Try to stay positive. Give yourself time. She sighed.

"Want to talk about it?"

"No." Tandy wouldn't have any more answers than she'd come up with. No one had answers.

"In that case, let's go sit on the patio. It's a gorgeous day outside and I'm betting your hyacinths smell wonderful, and Clayton likes to sit in the grass."

"I wonder if I can still smell them." She pushed up from the table and took her walker from the chair beside her.

Tandy stood and lifted the plate of muffins. "No time like the present to find out. Head on out there. I'll put these up and join you in a minute."

"Okay."

Meg felt Tandy's eyes on her shuffling gate as she did her best to walk through the kitchen. "I know you're watching me."

"It's a Mom thing. You grow eyes in the back of your head."

"Exactly."

"You're not doing too bad."

"Tell that to my self-esteem."

"Your self-esteem and I will have a chat just as soon as I get these muffins put up."

Meg smiled and focused on getting out to the patio, anxious to see if hyacinths still smelled right.

Jamison sat on a park bench beneath a giant elm enjoying the slight breeze and sound of his kids' laughter. Other children ran around the playground, tossing balls and flying down slides or soaring into the air from swings.

He envied their ability to enjoy the moment. Before last week, he hadn't given much thought to the future other than to put money back in a 401k and plan for retirement. It never once occurred to him that he wouldn't enter the final years of his life with Meg by his side.

That happened to other people. To other couples. Not to them.

But he'd nearly lost her. The thought stole his breath. A world without Meg. Everything would lose color and meaning. Not that she was his god. Of course not. God was God in both their marriage and their family. But she was the singular romantic love of his life. The one human being he wanted to spend every waking moment with, talking about each day's occurrence and arguing and laughing and just being.

This new Meg, though . . . this angry,

upset woman who had entered his marriage left him baffled. Where was Meg's ready smile? She'd always been the one to tell him to let the kids get by with the little things. It was her voice that calmed him when he wanted to yell at them to pick up their toys or eat their dinner. Her cool hand on his had made him dial back his harsh disciplined tendencies more than once.

Yet this past week had left two over-disciplinarians in the house. He tried to compensate. The look on James's face when Meg yelled that she needed some peace and quiet had been enough to convince him that he'd have to step up while she recovered.

But would she fully recover? He'd called the support line, so he harbored no delusions about the reality facing them. Meg's personality might be forever altered. She might never be the fun-loving, happy-go-lucky person he married.

He would still love her. Maybe his love could remind her of her old self. In the long run, it didn't matter. When they said for better or worse, in sickness and in health, they both meant it and he wouldn't back away from that vow.

For eight years he'd lived with the constant fear that something might happen to James. The fear had increased with each new child's arrival. He never once thought of worrying that something might happen to Meg. Bad things didn't hit people like her. They just *were.* Always there. Always present. Always taking care of the details of life.

He rubbed his eyes and checked on the kids. James had befriended another boy and they stood to the side of the playground, tossing a football back and forth. Savannah swung contentedly, her little face upturned to the sunshine that lit her hair and created a halo of gold. Hannah climbed the ladder to the tiny tot slide.

They were fine. All accounted for and happy. For a brief moment he felt satisfaction with his life.

And then he remembered Meg.

SEVEN

"Honey, we're home!" Jamison called out through the house.

"Honey, I'm home!" Hannah echoed. Savannah and James ran through the kitchen.

Tandy came through the patio door. "Hey, you're back!" She picked Hannah up and threw her in the air. "Did you have fun at the park?"

"I went down the swide!"

"Oh, I bet that was fun."

Hannah bobbed her head. "Now we came home 'cause it's nap time. I don't wanna take a nap."

Tandy tweaked her nose. "But you'll have more energy when you wake up. That makes it easier to play."

"I wanna play now."

"Hannah Rose, that's enough." Jamison tried to be firm but kind. Meg was so much better at this stuff. Or, the *old* Meg was so much better at this stuff. He squelched the fear that the new, angry Meg was here to stay. "How about you go give Mommy hugs while I make you some chicken nuggets?"

"Mommy's mad."

His heart twisted. "She's not mad, sweet girl. She's just got a boo-boo that hurts really bad."

"I can kiss it, make it feel better."

"You go do that." Tandy sat Hannah on the floor. "Mommy's outside on the patio."

They watched Hannah scamper through the doorway and over to Meg, who sat watching Clayton finger blades of grass. Wonder lit the seven-month-old's eyes.

"How's she been today?"

"Okay."

"Really?"

Tandy grimaced. "She's having a rough time, not that I have to tell *you* that."

"Yeah, she's not exactly sunshine and roses right now."

"She told me she feels out of control."

Jamison nodded as he pulled nuggets out of the freezer. "She said the same thing to me. I wish I could fix it for her, but the doctors say she just needs time."

"I hate it when they say that."

"I think she hates it more."

Tandy nodded. "Joy is planning on coming when she gets off work."

"Y'all don't have to be here every waking moment. Getting a break this morning was enough to last me a few days."

"Yeah, but who's going to take care of the kids when you go back to work this week?"

"I'm going to work from home for a while."

"Seriously?"

Jamison shrugged and put a plate of nuggets into the microwave. "There's no reason I can't be here for a while. I may even find I like it."

Tandy glanced outside to check on Clayton. He lay in the same spot she'd placed him, running his hands back and forth across the grass. "Yeah, but how will you work with three munchkins running around?"

"James and Savannah are in school all day for another week. All I really have to worry about is Hannah, and I've got nap time and VeggieTales for that."

Tandy stuffed her hands in her pockets. "Sounds like you've got it all taken care of."

"Not really, but it's a start. I mainly just want to give Meg room to heal so we can get on with our lives."

"Joy says she may not get back to the normal we knew."

"I know." Jamison pulled the plate from the microwave and dumped a container of pears into one of its compartments. "I'm praying otherwise. It's only been two weeks. Feels like two years, but I keep telling myself it's only been two weeks and that she can get a whole lot better if I just give her time."

"Me, too."

He filled a cup with juice and snapped on its lid. "Can you run this outside to Hannah, please? She'd probably eat better out there than forcing her to come back in here."

"Sure." Tandy took the plate and turned toward the door. "Hey, Jamison?"

"Yeah?" He looked up from the second plate of nuggets.

"Thanks for being here for my sister."

He smiled. "I don't belong anywhere else."

Tandy nodded and went onto the patio.

He turned back to preparing James and Savannah's lunches. Normally Meg took care of this. He hoped he wouldn't completely kill all nutritional values she'd instilled in them up until this point. Chicken nuggets and pears weren't exactly a well-rounded meal. His mother had always had something green with every single meal.

But he was tired and wanted a nap himself.

"Just get them fed," he muttered. How Meg did this all day every day eluded him. He'd so much rather be behind a desk crunching numbers. Numbers didn't talk back or have meltdowns. They performed consistently with a beautiful elegance he'd admired since learning addition in first grade.

Child-rearing offered so many opportunities for failure that he often wondered — more in the past week than at any time since the birth of their first child — why people attempted it. Because, despite his best efforts, children could still end up criminals. Plenty of people sitting in jail were raised by loving parents.

Although more sat there who *didn't* have loving parents, he guessed.

He quickly finished getting the other two lunches ready and carried them into the living room. James and Savannah sat working on the puzzle they'd begun with Meg before she'd collapsed.

"You guys have made good progress on that."

Savannah sat with her arms crossed on the table, staring at the pieces. "It was easier with Mom."

"Well, as soon as Mom is all better, I'm sure she'd be happy to help again." He set the plates down on the table. "In the meantime, how about a quick break for lunch?"

James picked up a nugget while keeping his eyes on the pieces. "How long is that gonna take?"

"What?"

"For Mom to get better." Savannah dipped a nugget into ketchup. "For her to not be mad."

His heart twisted at the lost look on his eldest daughter's face. She shouldn't know about things like brain tumors at five years old. Why couldn't she have been shielded from this? Why couldn't Meg?

"I don't know, pumpkin. But I do know that Mom wants to get better as fast as she can."

Both children munched their food and kept their faces pointed toward the puzzle. He waited to see if any more questions would come, but none did.

"Speaking of Mom, I'm going to go check on her. You guys good for a few minutes?"

"Yeah, Dad. It's not like we're babies or anything." James rolled his eyes.

"Of course." Jamison hid his smile and turned. Since being faced with the possibility of losing Meg, he found himself wanting to hang on to all the kids every waking second. Like he could keep them from

70

danger if he just didn't let them out of his sight.

He'd let Meg out of his sight. A lot. He'd spent thousands of hours at the office — hours he could have spent here with her, laughing while they cooked dinner together or sat on the couch. They used to do that before the kids came along.

He thought back to one Sunday morning when they'd awakened to soft drizzle outside and decided to stay home together. Sitting in front of the fireplace, looking into her eyes, he'd gotten lost in her. Hours flew by and before they knew it, their stomachs were growling and they'd talked all the way through lunchtime.

The treasure of those days no longer seemed lost on him.

Overcome with an urge to hold her, he went out onto the patio. "Hey there." Tiny lines around her eyes told him of the exhaustion the past two weeks had caused. She passed a hand across her brow, and he saw the effort behind her smile. He crossed the flagstone and dropped a kiss onto her upturned face.

She leaned her head against his hip. "Hey, yourself."

His hand automatically went to her shoulder. In her presence, his heartbeat slowed and peace settled upon his shoulders. He felt the balm of being with her soothe the worry that battered his soul.

Tandy smiled at him. "I was just telling Meg that Clay and I are having a boring night at home tonight. We'd be happy to take the kids off your hands if you'd like. You two haven't had much time together lately."

He sent up a prayer of thanks for a considerate, sympathetic sister-in-law.

"And I was telling her she didn't have to do that." Meg tapped the table with her fingertips. "I'm totally capable of handling my own children."

"I didn't mean you weren't, Sis. Just thought you might like a little peace and quiet. And having them over is fun for Clay and me. We get to act all silly and have a good excuse for a messy apartment when they leave. I don't clean up for weeks."

"Sounds good to me." Jamison thought again of that long Sunday in front of the fire. Maybe simply being together and talking would help ease the strain that had followed her from surgery.

Meg looked up at him. "You *want* this?"

He sensed a land mine in there somewhere, but reading her mind was nearly impossible *before* the surgery. This new Meg left him completely bewildered. "An evening at home with you is a great way to end a Saturday."

"Yeah, but do you think the kids need to be away from me right now? I mean, it's not as if their world hasn't been turned upside down enough. Now we're carting them off to my sister's."

"It's only for a few hours," Tandy reasoned. "I don't think it would unsettle them."

"How would you know? They're *my* kids."

Jamison cast about for something to say. Meg had never questioned the wisdom of allowing the children to visit any of the sisters. One day not so long ago they'd enjoyed a wonderful afternoon together while Joy kept James and Hannah and his mother kept Savannah. So what was her problem?

Tandy stared at Meg.

Fear began tapping again on Jamison's heart. He didn't know which caused it more — the fact that he didn't recognize the attitude of this woman he'd called wife for a decade — or the thought that he could feel such fear in her presence.

Her rigid shoulders suddenly drooped beneath his arm. "I'm sorry." She rubbed her temples. "I don't know what that was about. Just ignore me. Take the kids. They'll probably be thrilled to go somewhere without their crazy mother."

"Hey." Tandy reached across the table. "You're not crazy."

"Don't be too sure."

A small frown teased Tandy's brow. "You're not. Jamison, tell her."

He squeezed his wife's shoulder. "Of course you're not crazy. You're just recovering. You'll be fine. This will all be fine."

He hoped the words sounded more certain than he felt. His need for her to believe in the ability to heal, to be whole again, to be *Meg* again, strangled him.

She patted his hand on her shoulder. "You're right. I'm tired and emotional."

"How about a quick power nap while I pack up the kids' stuff for Tandy's?"

"Sure."

He watched her rise, take the walker from where it rested on a nearby chair back, and walk toward the door. Her right leg seemed a little better, but he had enough self-awareness to know that could be his hope talking.

"She *is* going to get better."

He looked down to find Tandy's eyes upon him.

"The thing is, I don't know that."

74

"It's only been a couple of weeks since the surgery."

"Yeah." He glanced over at Clayton and saw that Savannah had fallen asleep by his side. "Look at those two."

"Adorable, aren't they?"

"When she's asleep like that, it's easy to forget the tantrums and yelling."

"Ah, parenthood. Ain't it grand?"

He sighed. "Some of the time."

"But not when you're left to do it on your own with a wife recovering from brain surgery?"

"Yeah, not so much then."

"She *will* get better, Jamison."

He met her eyes. "I really hope so."

"I know so." Tandy pushed her chair back and stood up. "I'll call Joy and let her know I'm taking the kids so she doesn't need to come over this afternoon."

"Thanks, Tandy." He'd never liked taking help from people, but he certainly had appreciated it these past weeks.

"Anytime."

EIGHT

"You volunteered us for *what?*" Clay's voice boomed through Tandy's cell phone.

"You didn't see his face, sweetie." Tandy checked her rearview mirror. All four kids fought sleep. "He's so tired he can't see straight and his worry for Meg is about three times the size of Mount Everest."

"So you said we'd take all three kids? For how long?"

"Just tonight. I'm supposed to bring them back around bedtime. It's only a few hours. What's the big deal?"

Clay sighed. "I thought we were spending a quiet evening at home alone. I'd planned to get Clayton down and have some time with you."

"Oh." She swallowed. "Sorry."

"It's fine. You're right. We should help out with the kids, and Jamison needs a break. You and I can spend tomorrow together."

"We've got church in the morning."

"We could have Joy stop and get Clayton, take him to church, and spend the morning together."

She braked at a red light and considered playing hooky from church. If she went, everybody and their brother would be asking all the sisters about Meg. She'd be forced to listen to the gossips pretend care and concern when really they were just digging for information to blab all over town through the week. The few who truly cared had come by the hospital or Daddy's farm.

"You're corrupting me, Mr. Kelner."

"Every chance I get, Mrs. Kelner."

She laughed. "Okay, I'll call Joy and see if she can get Clayton. *You* get to explain to Daddy how you persuaded me to backslide and not go to church on Sunday morning."

"Not a problem. You're dad believes in the sanctity of marriage and understands the wisdom of not taking each other for granted."

"Hey, I think I'm going to drive around for a while before I come home. The kids are either asleep or near it, and if I stop this van, you know Clayton will wake right up and not go back down for hours."

"Yep. Take your time. I'll be here when you get home."

"Love you."

77

"Love you, too."

Tandy flipped her phone closed and looked in the mirror again. Four sets of eyelids rested on four little cheeks. She checked the gas gauge and debated whether wasting pricey gas to keep them asleep was worth it. An image of Clayton — exhausted and red-faced from crying his way down to sleep after an interrupted nap — made up her mind.

"Time to keep the gas stations in business."

Jamison unfolded a quilt and spread it out before the fireplace. Despite the even temperatures they'd been having, he had his heart set on an evening in front of dancing flames. He wanted to see them shine in her eyes hear her voice. He didn't care if they talked about the past few weeks, if only they talked.

So he'd done what any sensible husband bent on creating a "moment" with his wife would do: cranked the AC up, created winter in his home, and built a fire. He snatched pillows from the couch and arranged them for maximum comfort. The bubble bath he'd drawn and escorted her into should be cooling off right about now. He needed to get upstairs and help her from the tub. Once her leg started getting all the signals from her brain again, she wouldn't need so much of his help.

He both longed for that time and dreaded it. Having Meg dependent on him let him know he was needed. He felt guilty about feeling good.

Checking the room once more, he noted the dimmed lights, flickering candles, and steady fire. As perfect a setting as he could make it.

He left the living room and walked through the kitchen where dishes from dinner still sat in the sink. How Meg had kept the house clean, the kids fed, and all the family balls up in the air still eluded him. The dishes would simply have to wait until morning.

The Berber carpet on the stairs beneath his feet needed to be vacuumed. Little bits of Otis fur had gathered in the creases between steps. Did Meg notice these things? Had they been here before this nightmare began but escaped his attention? No, he doubted Meg had allowed dog fur to build up to this extent. He hadn't been *that* caught up in the day-to-day that a mound of black fur would go unnoticed.

He turned into their bedroom. Flickering candlelight played off the double wedding ring quilt on their bed and the soft gold paint of the walls. The room looked as if it danced with delight. Sheer curtains swayed in the slight breeze coming from the sliver of opened window. Perhaps he should forego the living room and stay up here with her. The stairs wouldn't be easy for her to navigate anyway.

It startled him, this longing to simply be in her presence and hear her voice. Oh, he'd love to put his arms around her, hold her, remember the physical ways in which they'd always fit together so well. But it was too soon for that. Tonight, all he wanted to hear were her words. He yearned for Meg's wit to float effortlessly across those lips and assure him that her brain hadn't changed so much that his heart wouldn't recognize her.

Images of the fire downstairs and all of his preparations flitted through his mind. He could clean it up before morning. She would never know about it, thus having no reason to regret her difficulty in getting to the bottom floor of the house.

He crossed the bedroom floor, the hardwood under his steps giving off a chill. If they were staying up here, he'd need to adjust the air conditioner. He stopped in the bathroom doorway.

Meg lay beneath a mound of bubbles, her

head resting on the lip of the tub, one hand draped over its edge. Water droplets had fallen from her fingertips and pooled on the tile just beside a bath mat. Her eyes were closed and the tiniest of smiles played at her mouth.

His heart eased at the sight of that smile. Even the beginnings of a smile meant his Meg was still in there somewhere. He leaned against the doorway and crossed his arms with as little noise as possible. Drinking in the relaxed image of Meg, he could believe all would be right in their world one day soon. Even if she changed a little, deep down inside he knew that his Megan would never leave.

He shifted and the sound caused her to stir. "Hey." Exhaustion and contentment laced her voice.

Not moving from his position, unwilling to mar the peace that lay upon her face like dew on morning grass, he smiled. "Hey yourself. Good bath?"

Her lids came down over the blue eyes in which he'd gotten lost more times than he could count. "*Excellent* bath." The small smile blossomed into an almost full-scale version. "This is exactly what I needed."

"Happy to be of service."

"Did you tie the kids up and duct tape

them to chairs?"

He kept the laugh as low as the candle-light. "Even better. They've gone ahead and left with Tandy." At her opened eyes, he hurried to clarify, "But she'll bring them back later tonight. It's only for a few hours."

Again, the lids relaxed and her shoulders eased back into the bubbles. "Thank you for that. I don't know why I can't stand to be away from them."

He did, but a thousand horses stampeding toward him with fire in their eyes wouldn't make him say it aloud. Of course a mother faced with the distinct possibility of not seeing her kids safely to adulthood wouldn't want to be away from them over-night. He'd watched her anxious eyes follow them around the room and seen the numerous instances in which she reached out to run her hand down one's hair or pat one's shoulder, as if to reassure herself they all still lived. Hatred for life's unexpected turns coursed through his veins, but he ignored it. Nothing to be done but keep living.

"I thought you might have become a raisin by now."

She held up the hand that had been draped over the bathtub edge. Candlelight infused the warmth of life into her long, slender fingers. "I'd say I'm about at prune stage."

A decorative towel hung on the towel bar to his right. They never used the pretty towels, the ones that were monogrammed with their initials and given to them as wedding presents. Tonight, though, it felt as natural as the breeze at his back to pull the towel from its rack, take two steps to her side, and offer it.

Her eyebrows raised.

He shrugged. "I think the folks who gave them to us meant for us to use them." He held her gaze and watched uncertainty play in the pools of blue.

Finally she stood and took the towel without a word.

Tension seeped into the room and he cast about for its cause. Desperation quickened his heartbeat. Had he said something to remind her of her condition? Of her frailty? He inwardly cursed, then rebuked himself for even thinking the word. Losing his morals wouldn't help him deal with the situation.

She held out a hand and he moved quickly to help her from the tub. Her weight was slight as she leaned on him before stepping onto the bath mat. Her second leg didn't come as easily as the first, but he noted that she got it over the lip without having to assist with a hand. Progress.

As she removed her weight from his side, she unfolded the towel and skimmed it over her skin.

Her shoulders bowed, her face was cast toward the floor. All this from simply giving her one of the good towels? Did that somehow emphasize something negative? All he'd wanted was to give her the best.

"Megan?"

She didn't raise her head. "Hmm?"

"Did I say something?"

"No."

"Did I do something?"

Her sigh was so small it could have been only his imagination. "Not really." She wrapped the towel around a frame grown more slight since the surgery.

He dared to put an arm around her and lead her toward the bedroom. She allowed herself to be directed, dropping onto the bed beside him when he gently pulled her down. They sat, shoulder touching shoulder, letting the whisper of wind swirl around their legs and across their bare feet.

He said the only thing that came to mind. "Was it the towel?"

She laid a hand wrinkled from exposure to the tub water upon his knee. "Not really.

It's what the towel made me realize."

"And what was that?"

She took her hand back, folded her arms across her chest. "We have a lot of things I keep put away for a special day."

He thought of their wedding china wrapped in bubble wrap and tucked into boxes, only brought out at Christmas. The Tiffany platters his parents had given them for their anniversary every year lay hidden in the same cabinet as those boxes, only seeing the light of day when it came time to celebrate the birth of the Christ child. Monogrammed towels hung in each of their bathrooms, with towel hooks on the backs of the doors for their "every day" towels to dry unseen.

"It occurred to me that no one has promised us special days." A tear slid down her cheek. He watched it travel across her skin, marking a path now achingly familiar to his eye. He knew where tears liked to fall on that lovely face. He'd watched enough of them now to have memorized every centimeter.

She didn't turn to meet his gaze.

Words wouldn't come. No, they hadn't been promised a certain number of days. Heck, they hadn't even been promised their next breath. But did that mean they should live like every single second could be the last? No one could live like that. Living required planning. He taught that to every client that walked in the door. IRAs and retirement plans and 401k options — those were about preparing for the future. A wise man prepared for the future.

He struggled for a way to explain the balance of living for today while planning for tomorrow. Every sentence seemed imperfect somehow and so he sat in silence — until she leaned her head upon his shoulder.

That small act infused him with courage. This was Meg, and she obviously had a lot of fear to deal with. Heaven knew he had enough fear for the entire state population as well, but right now she needed a man who could hold her hand and tell her they'd be together for a thousand tomorrows. Whether it was true or not didn't matter as much as him simply saying it, letting her know that one of them believed in the future.

He needed to be man enough to let her lean on him.

Slipping an arm around her shoulders, he pulled her close. "Every day I have with you is a special day. I gave you the towel not because I'm worried we won't have special days, but because I don't think we've been enjoying the days we have. You and I have a lot of days, of years, left together. I know that in my heart. This is a rough time, but we're going to get through. And we're going to do that while using our good towels and our good dishes and recognizing that we can plan for the future even while we enjoy the present."

He stopped to take a breath. Was that little speech right? He didn't know, but *something* had to be said. Frustration welled up inside. The ease of their relationship was lost and he wanted to hit somebody for it. For years he'd watched buddies gripe about their home lives, their nagging wives, and every other detail of being married. He and Meg had fought, of course, but there was an ease about the whole thing that he'd never appreciated until he couldn't find it.

In its place were two people scared that life could be so harsh and that they might not be able to face life — or what was left of it — together. He tightened his hold on her shoulders. No need to think that way now that they were through surgery, though. Her tumor was gone. It wouldn't be back. All he had to do was get through recovery.

Sitting there on the bed, though, he considered the setting he'd so meticulously prepared downstairs. In days past Meg would have known almost with a sixth sense that his drawing her a bath meant something more, meant that he needed to *connect* with her again. To let the volley of their wordplay stitch them together. She would join him downstairs, and they would sit in front of the fire talking, laughing, and sharing love as only married people should. She would have known that course of events the second she saw the bathwater.

Yet tonight they sat having a discussion about the limit to their days. He pulled in a deep breath and fought a sadness that rolled over him in gray waves. There would be no intimate conversation tonight. No laughter. No watching her eyes dance.

Tonight he'd have to settle for that small smile on her face before he'd opened his mouth.

NINE

A week after her visit to Meg's house, Tandy pulled her van into Kendra's driveway and marveled at the changes in this sister's life. Gone was the apartment in a converted antebellum home. Kendra now called a two-story townhouse home. Bright red and purple petunias waved at Tandy from their window boxes beside a plum-colored door. White porch railing encircled the small stoop and a mat out front welcomed visitors.

Tandy smiled at the outward changes that reflected the love of her sister and Darin and knocked on their door. She waited a second, then turned the knob and walked in. "Yoohoo! Anybody home?"

"Upstairs." Kendra's voice drifted down from above. Tandy passed through the small living room and kitchen to the stairway at the back.

She found Kendra in the hallway at the

laundry closet. "Hey, you."

Kendra looked up from the towel she'd been folding. "Hey, yourself. Ready to pick some strawberries?"

"Yeah. I haven't called Wells though to see if they've got any to pick."

"Tandy!" Kendra shot a reproachful glare. "If I got out of bed at six in the morning for no reason, you're in big trouble, lady."

Tandy waved a hand. "They were out picking yesterday, I'm sure it'll be fine."

"You're not going to call at all?"

"Like I said, they were out yesterday. Zelda told me she picked a ton."

"She's probably not the only one. Better call and see if there are any berries left."

"If we get out there and they're closed, we'll just go to some yard sales."

Kendra tossed the last towel into a basket with several others and carried it down the hall. Tandy followed her into the bathroom. "I don't understand why we can't just call."

Tandy blew out a breath. "Because I don't have the number and I can't remember his first name to look it up."

"Well, why didn't you just say that?"

"I did!"

"No, you didn't. You said you hadn't called and that we weren't going to. That's not the same."

Tandy transferred her look to the floor. "Okay, I *meant* —"

Kendra smiled. "Yeah, yeah." Picking up the now-empty basket, she balanced it on a hip. "Let me grab the paper in case we're forced to spend the morning at yard sales."

"Great."

Tandy went to the top of the stairs and looked down. When had Kendra become such a . . . *mom?* Before Darin she'd never have pushed the issue of calling before leaving. Kendra lived by the seat of her pants — the carefree artist. Unsure if she liked this new development in Kendra's personality, Tandy nibbled a lip while descending the stairs.

"Okay." Kendra waved the paper in the air as she caught up with Tandy. "All set."

"Perfect. Where's Darin, by the way?" They made their way back through the house. Tandy noticed what she hadn't before — perfectly ordered stacks of magazines and barely a tchotchke out of place. Strange.

"Still asleep. He thinks we're absolutely nuts to be up this early purely for the sake of picking strawberries."

"Did you tell him to go to the grocery store and check out the price of food these days? If we don't pick it ourselves, I'm not

91

sure we're going to have it at all anymore."

They stepped onto the porch and Kendra turned to lock the door. "I told him to roll over and go back to sleep."

"Probably a wiser choice."

"I thought so."

They sprung down the steps and over to Tandy's van. The morning sunshine already shone brightly across a bright blue sky studded with big, puffy white clouds. On days like this, she missed the sunroof of her old Beemer.

"Penny for your thoughts?"

Tandy frowned and put the van in gear. "I'm afraid they're not worth a plug nickel."

"At least you haven't lost your grasp on reality."

"Very funny."

"You gonna tell me what has you so lost in thought?"

"I'm . . . adjusting."

"To?"

"Life."

"Specifically?"

"All these changes we've been making. I mean, think about our lives just two years ago and look at them today. I'm married. You're married. I have a kid and drive a van, for goodness sakes. Joy has a kid. Daddy's married. You're in a townhome where everything looks like a set from *The Stepford Wives*. Meg's recovering from brain surgery. Isn't it all just a bit much?"

"*The Stepford Wives?*"

The van bumped over loose pavement as they left town and headed for the country. "Yeah."

"Why does my house look like *The Stepford Wives?*"

Her voice didn't hold offense, just curiosity, so Tandy answered. "Your magazines are in stacks whose edges I could hold a ruler against. There's not a speck of Miss Kitty fur anywhere. I checked. Every glass surface gleamed and your kitchen counters didn't have a smudge on them. For a while, I wondered if Joy had been by but she's as busy with Maddie as I am with Clayton, so that couldn't have happened."

"Tandy, my apartment was always clean."

"Not like that."

"Well, no, maybe not as clean as I keep the house, but I lived by myself then. I kept it as clean as I wanted. Darin happens to like it a little more clean. What's the big deal?"

Tandy sighed. "I don't know. It's not a big deal, really. It's just another change, and I'm about to my change limit."

"How about a dollar?"

"You're a riot."

"I try."

Tandy worried her bottom lip as the county road zipped under the tires. Truth be known, she wished she knew why all the changes left her feeling so out of sorts.

"You know this is just the control freak in you coming out, right?"

"I am *not* a control freak."

"Mm-hmm. Keep saying it, honey. Somewhere, somebody's going to believe you."

"Okay, I like to know what's going on. Doesn't everybody?"

"Oh, please. You like to *control* what's going on and a whole bunch of stuff has happened outside your control but inside your world, and it's throwing you for a bit of a loop. Perfectly understandable."

Tandy mulled over that a moment. She *did* like to plan or know an outcome before it came. Kendra had always been the more spontaneous one, dragging her out of bed in the middle of the night to sneak out of the house only to hang out in the barn talking until the sun came peeking over the hill. It hadn't been about breaking the rules so much as trying something different to see what would happen. It drove Tandy crazy then, but a whole lot crazier now.

Except now Kendra was the one calling

before leaving and grabbing the paper as a backup plan.

"I think you're becoming a control freak too." Tandy nodded toward the newspaper.

"I am as far from a control freak as a June bug from a horse fly."

"Says the one who can't believe I didn't call the berry patch first?"

"That's just common sense."

"And grabbed a newspaper so we had a backup plan?"

"Again, good sense. I don't want to waste my morning."

"But you would have wasted it two years ago! We'd have taken off and if our plan didn't work out, we'd have figured something out then. But now we think everything through and make contingency plans and pack diaper bags and buy parent cars and it's just a little much."

"Parent cars?"

"I offer you Exhibit A." Tandy swept an arm around the van.

"Is this because you're missing the Beemer? I told you not to get rid of it."

Kendra's sensible tone did nothing to calm Tandy's nerves. "I *had* to get rid of it, Ken. I wasn't bending myself into a pretzel ninety gazillion times a day to get a car seat into the back of a little sports car."

"You could have kept it for things like today."

"And where in that car would we have put flats of strawberries?"

"You're right. Somehow, when we weren't looking, we became *adults.*"

"Now tell me why that bugs me. I was an adult before. I had a career, a life, an apartment. I was adult."

"Yeah, but not adult like Momma and Daddy. No husbands. No babies. No other people in our life to have to live with, compromise for, love. It's different now."

Tandy swung the van onto a gravel driveway with a big strawberry sign at its entrance. "That's my point. We've got a lot of different right now." She braked to a stop and unbuckled her seat belt.

Kendra laid a hand on her arm. "You're right, T. It's a lot. And this thing with Meg has us all on edge. But different can be good. We've had a lot of the good kind of different, right?"

"Right."

"Then let's focus on that."

Tandy sucked in a breath. "You're right. I know you are. I don't know why I'm so out of sorts lately."

"Well, get back in sorts because we've got berries to pick, sister."

Tandy grinned. "Beat you to the patch."

"You know, some things *never* change."

"And praise God for that."

Tandy pushed open the door and raced across the grass over to the stacks of baskets under a green awning.

It wasn't long before the sisters chose two rows side by side and began pulling plump red berries from plants. Other women were spread out in various spots along each row, bent over plants and intent on their work. A silence broken only by the sounds of birdsong and rustling plants blanketed them and Tandy let it soothe her frazzled senses.

She had almost gotten back to a point of peace when a voice from a couple rows over floated to her.

"I heard she's completely different than she was before the surgery. Angry all the time."

Another voice *tsk*ed. "That poor Jamison, having to live with a totally different woman than the one he married."

Tandy considered turning around and telling these two gossips to leave her family out of their conversation. She loved Stars Hill, but the part about having everyone know her business chafed a lot of the time. She stopped at the first woman's continued words.

"Billy told me he saw Jamison down at Cadillac's Saturday."

"Really? Drinking?"

"Nope. Just sitting there, staring into space, hand wrapped around a glass of water."

"At least she hasn't driven him to drink yet."

"Somebody better tell that woman to get her act together before she loses a good man."

Tandy clamped down on the anger threatening to spew out all over these biddies. What made them think Meg and Jamison were any of their business? What gave them the right to judge? Like they'd never had to deal with a difficult thing in life. If they hadn't, then they hadn't had much of a life in the first place. Tandy glanced up to see if Kendra had heard.

Kendra stood stock-still in her row, staring behind Tandy in the direction of the voices. Tandy stepped over the plants and joined her sister. "Guess you heard."

"I think half the berry patch heard. It's not like they're trying for secrecy, talking in voices they can hear all the way on Lindell."

"What do you want to do?"

"I *want* to go smack them upside the head

and toss those full baskets all over the place."

"But instead we're going to . . . ?"

"Stand here like good Christian girls whose Daddy preaches the forgiveness of Jesus and trust that God will take care of the likes of them."

"I really don't like this option."

A muscle in Kendra's jaw worked. "I don't either."

"We could at least let them know we're here. Maybe shame them into shutting up."

Kendra turned back to the plants in her row. She bent and began picking berries again. "One thing Momma taught me that stuck — you can't change the behavior of adults."

Tandy looked at Kendra's back, then over at the gossiping women. She'd always thirsted for vengeance and justice. That's why becoming a lawyer had held such appeal and arguing in court had given her a thrill like nothing else. She stepped back over to her row and knelt down at the plants. This wasn't Orlando. She couldn't just rail at those women and think the entire town wouldn't be talking about it by dinnertime.

She sighed. What she should really be focusing on here — what an *adult* would

99

focus on — was Jamison and why he'd been at Cadillac's. The thought appalled her more than the gossip. What could he be thinking? He knew Stars Hill's grapevine as well as any of them. Did he think he could sit at a bar and not have anyone in the family find out? So what that he'd only been drinking water. He could have gotten a glass of water at his own kitchen sink.

Unless what he really needed was to get away from Meg.

Tandy's fingers paused on the strawberry plant. She hadn't been by to see Meg in nearly a week. The sisters' idea of taking turns being with Meg hadn't exactly been followed through. That left Jamison handling the bulk of the recovery time. If Meg still walked around in the same angry funk she'd been in last time Tandy sat with her, Jamison had as good a reason for a break as any high school senior in May.

She pulled the berry at her hand, tossed it in her basket, and stood. "Hey, Ken, I think I've got enough. You about ready?"

Kendra turned and eyed Tandy's basket, then the others in the flat at Tandy's feet. "That's all you're picking?"

"I thought we might go out and check on Meg. It's been a few days since I saw her."

It took only seconds for Kendra's eyes to

take on a knowing gleam. "Gotcha. Let's go."

TEN

Jamison snatched up a stuffed turtle from the living room floor and tossed it across the room toward the toy bin. Today, he promised himself, he would find a housekeeper. Taking care of a wife whose temper tantrums seemed as close at hand as his next breath was exhausting enough. He simply didn't have the energy to pick up after three kids.

He thought through their family budget. Paying a housekeeper, especially if he asked her to stay half a day every day to get him out of cooking meals as well, would require a severe tightening of their belts. Medical bills had begun pouring in and, even with insurance, Meg's surgery costs ate away at their savings faster than a deer on fresh corn.

Still, he could either hire some help or find himself sitting at a bar again. He shook his head and pitched another toy. It landed

102

on top of the turtle.

What had he been thinking? By now, the entire family probably knew he'd been to Cadillac's. Seeing Billy Baird there had secured his spot on the Stars Hill grapevine more certainly than the sunrise tomorrow morning. It wouldn't matter that he'd been drinking water the entire night. It would matter that he'd been drinking water at Cadillac's.

He could have had a nice glass of wine at home, but it wasn't the numbing effect of alcohol he'd been after. It was the silence. The anonymity. The joy of being left alone for a few minutes with his own thoughts. Here at the house the only things he did were listen to Meg, help Meg, wait on Meg, cook, clean, and take care of the kids. Sitting at his desk he answered call after e-mail for clients, making certain their financial needs and concerns were met in excellent fashion.

Before the surgery his sweet Meg had given him a half hour of wonderful silence when he came home from work. It was as if she knew he needed a buffer between the office and the family and she'd given it to him without his having to utter a word.

He missed his wife. Because he had to

admit it to himself now: She wasn't his Megan.

She still smiled sometimes. She still loved to have her feet rubbed, even though she couldn't feel it as well on her right side. But she'd taken to criticizing him and the kids with every other sentence. She didn't approve of his clothes choices for the kids, she didn't like the way he cooked their chicken, she thought he took too long at the grocery store, she couldn't understand how he could live with dust on the tables — the litany began each morning as he opened his eyes and didn't stop until sleep overtook her.

He didn't know how much longer he could go on like this.

A better man than he would last longer than a few measly weeks. He wanted to feel bad about his own lack of patience, but he wanted her to get better more.

The doorbell rang. He kicked a small car under the couch and went to see who had come to witness his horrendous housekeeping habits now. Tandy and Kendra came through the door just as he approached it.

"Yoohoo!" Tandy called.

"Hey, we're here." He cringed. His voice sounded like an old man's. The sisters eyed him up and down and he mustered up enough energy to paste on a smile. "What brings you two out this way?"

"We were at Wells picking berries when we heard about your . . . um . . . visit downtown." Kendra ran a toe along the floor.

He'd hoped it would take a little longer for the family to find out. But, like pretty much everything else in life right now, things weren't going his way. He let his shoulders slump. "Wow, news travels fast."

Tandy closed the door behind them. "As you well know. What's going on, Jamison?"

He spread his hands wide. "I wish I could tell you. I just needed a little time to myself and I knew that was the one place I wouldn't run into anyone I had to talk to."

Silence met his statements and he felt a spurt of anger. Of course they wouldn't understand. They hadn't even been by to see Meg for days. They had no idea what he was going through.

He startled at Tandy's hand on his arm. "I'm sorry we haven't been by. We should have come. *I* should have come."

"Me, too." Kendra's hand joined Tandy's.

Jamison blinked and looked up. He'd seen the sisters take care of each other plenty of times over the years. But he'd never been on the receiving end of their care. Neither he nor Meg had ever had a need for it.

Maybe that's why the sisters didn't seem to be doing such a good job of caring for Meg — it was as new a concept to them as it was for him. "Well, you're here now."

The girls took back their hands and Tandy glanced up the stairs. "That we are. Is she up there?"

"Yep. Reading books or watching television. Or she may be asleep by now."

"Asleep? It's barely midmorning."

"I wouldn't advise reminding her of that." He smiled and was surprised by the unfamiliarity of the skin as it stretched across his face. He needed to smile more often. The kids shouldn't have to deal with two parents in the doldrums.

"Where are the kids?"

"With your dad and Zelda. They spent the night last night."

Again, he'd tried to create a mood of intimacy. He longed for their lost conversations and had hoped to have a night full of discussion of nothing that mattered. Instead, he'd listened to a vitriol of his shortcomings and gone to bed with an anvil compressing his heart.

"Good." Kendra tucked her hair into the purple handkerchief tied around her head. "You go have some time to yourself and leave this to us."

"Oh, I'm fine. I've got to clean up anyway."

"Leave that to us." Tandy started for the stairs. "You take the time while you can."

Kendra followed her sister but winked at him over her shoulder. "Just don't go taking your 'me' time anyplace we're going to hear about, okay?"

He nodded. "No problem."

Tandy tried to wrap her mind around Jamison's image as she ascended the stairs. He looked as if he'd aged ten years in the past three weeks. Guilt ate at her. She should have been here more often.

They all should.

Seeing Meg — strong, resilient Meg — brought down by her own health, though, just rocked her too much. Tandy squared her shoulders. She was done with that now. Jamison should not have to bear this alone, and obviously Meg hadn't been making it easy on him.

She paused outside the closed bedroom door and looked at Kendra. "You ready?"

"We could stand here until dinnertime and I don't think I'd be. Jamison looks like roadkill."

"I know." Tandy paused, certain only of the fact that she wasn't prepared to walk through that door and find a woman who looked like Meg but didn't act like her.

"I was kidding about waiting until dinner."

She blew out a breath. "Right."

She opened the door and squinted into the darkness, confused by its presence. "Meg?"

No response came.

"Meg?"

The reply came back muffled. "Hmm?"

Tandy crossed to a window by memory and reached for the cord to open the blinds. After fumbling around a few seconds, she found it and pulled. Sunlight poured through the panes.

"Ugh! Stop that!" Meg's voice made Tandy's blood run cold. Never had she heard such anger coming from her eldest sister. She heard Kendra's gasp.

Tandy finished adjusting the blind — Meg didn't need to be sleeping in the middle of the morning no matter what kind of mood she was in — and turned to see her sister.

Meg lay sprawled among a tangle of bedsheets. Her wrinkled gown sat bunched up around her knees and a look of annoyance lay upon her face. "What are you two doing here?"

"Thought maybe you could use a little

sister time." Tandy forced cheer into her tone.

Meg flopped her head back onto the rumpled pillow. "What I need is sleep. Go away."

"What is *wrong* with you?" Kendra sat down on the bed with a thud.

Meg opened one eye. "You're kidding, right?"

"No."

"I had brain surgery, moron."

"Did they do a lobotomy while they were at it?"

Meg's mouth gaped open like a fish jerked from the river. "Excuse me?"

"I said —"

"I heard what you said, you inconsiderate idiot."

"Then answer me, you rude twit."

Tandy waited. This new Meg overflowed with rage and bitterness. It was almost as if someone had thought up the exact opposite of her sister and traded their personalities in surgery. Meg would never have spoken to them this way in the past. Tandy marveled at Kendra's ability to roll with it.

"I don't have to answer to anybody." Meg dropped back into the pillow.

"Oh, but that's where you're wrong, sister dear." Kendra pulled the pillow out from under Meg's head. Tandy winced, hoping it was okay to do that to a person recovering from brain surgery. Kendra could be a little overzealous sometimes.

"Hey!" Meg swiped at the pillow, but Kendra tossed it on the floor.

"Time to get up. The day is wasting away and you're lying here doing the same. Come on. We've got errands to run."

Meg motioned toward the walker resting against the bed's footboard. "In case you hadn't noticed, I'm not quite able to *run* anywhere right now."

Kendra shrugged as if Meg had said she didn't have clean clothes to wear. "So we'll walk. Hobble. Drag. Whatever. We'll do something besides *wallow in our own self-pity.*"

"Oh, I'm sure Stars Hill would love to see that. Meg Fawcett Hobbles Her Way Through Darnell's. They'll have pictures on the front page of the *Press*'s Tuesday edition."

"About time you made it into the paper for something besides your kids' accomplishments anyway."

Tandy bit her lip to stop the smile. She'd been handled by Kendra before and knew that, sooner or later, Meg would give in. Kendra's relentlessness left no other option.

Evidently Meg remembered that as well because she closed her eyes. "Fine. You want to embarrass the entire family by parading a cripple all over downtown, who am I to stop you?"

"That's the spirit. You need me to help you into the bathroom? Because, cripple or no, we're not taking that face out of here without makeup on it. No need in scaring the citizenry."

Meg shot a glance at Tandy. "Can't you rein her in?"

"Now who's kidding?"

Kendra looped Meg's arm over her shoulders and walked with her to the bathroom. Tandy followed, ready to grab Meg if she so much as stumbled.

"You know, I can make it just fine if you'd hand me my walker."

Kendra glanced at the steel aid and sniffed. "And have you getting around here like Old Mrs. Witherspoon? No. We're finding you a fashionable cane today. A hip, cool, awesome cane that doesn't look like something from a hospital supply closet."

Meg leaned against the counter and took her arm from Kendra. "I don't want a 'cool' cane. I want to be left alone."

"And, in the absence of that, we'll get you a cool cane."

Meg sighed, but she didn't fight back. Tandy decided to take that as a good sign.

"You know, I've never tried woodworking, but I bet I could make you an awesome cane."

Meg ignored her and continued applying makeup.

"Or we could drive up to Nashville. There's a store in Opry Mills Mall that has unique stuff and might have a cane. Ooh, or we could put Sara on it. She loves finding different stuff for us."

Meg finished rubbing foundation into her skin. "A cane definitely qualifies as different, but I don't think a dress shop owner has such things in her catalogs."

"Oh, please." Tandy waved that away. "Sara can find anything she puts her mind to. I think we should ask her. She's been asking about you all the time. You know she'd love having something to do for you."

Meg pursed her lips. "I'm sure she only asked so she'd have the latest bit to share with everyone."

"Megan Fawcett, you know as well as I do that Sara Sykes does not feed the rumor mill around here. She's genuinely concerned."

Meg sighed. "You're probably right."

"I'm most certainly right."

Meg adjusted the handkerchief around her head. Tandy wondered how long it would take her hair to grow back and wished again they hadn't had to shave all of it off to make an incision on one side. Meg had always had such gorgeous blonde hair.

Meg washed her hands, rubbing off the extra makeup there. "Okay, that's as good as this face can look given that it's owner is —"

"A sour puss." Kendra grinned. "Don't worry, we understand."

Meg rolled her eyes and allowed Kendra to once again help her into the bedroom. Tandy kept an eye on Meg's right leg, noting that it seemed a little stronger than it had a week ago.

"You know, I think your leg may be getting a bit better."

"Stick around." Meg removed her gown and pulled the shirt Kendra offered over her head. "In an hour or so, it'll decide to ignore me again. The strength and feeling come and go faster than my mood swings."

"At least you know you have them."

Meg smiled. "I *do* know. I'm sorry I bit your head off before."

"I'm just happy to know you're not possessed and that somewhere in there lurks my sister." Kendra knelt at Meg's feet and

113

helped her pull on a pair of elastic-waist pants.

Meg placed her hands on Kendra's shoulders for balance. "I don't know why it keeps happening. One minute I'm fine and thinking I'm on the road to recovery. The next, I hate my life and everything around me. The doctors say it's my brain trying to recover, but I wonder if I'm not losing my marbles."

Tandy came to stand beside Meg. "You're not losing your marbles."

"I *am* losing my husband, though." Meg's voice wobbled.

"Jamison?" Kendra rose. "You tell whatever little voice in that head of yours is whispering these lies to just shut up. Jamison's tired and this isn't easy on him, but he would never leave you."

Meg brushed a tear from her cheek and put her feet into the shoes Kendra laid out. "Oh, I didn't mean he was leaving me. You're right. He wouldn't leave. He's not that kind of man. But I know he's exhausted, and I can't seem to quit yelling at him or criticizing or correcting him. It's like, I know he won't leave, so it's safe to take out my anger on him. Does that sound dumb?"

"No, but you *are* going to have to give the man a break sometimes. He looked like death warmed over when he answered the door."

Meg shook her head. "I know. *I* did that to him."

"The situation is doing that to him. It's doing that to you as well." Kendra led them toward the bedroom door. "What you need to do is stay mad at the situation and let him join you in that anger. Don't be turning that temper of yours on him. Y'all come together in your fury and see what you can conquer together."

Tandy's eyes widened. When had Kendra gotten so wise?

Meg nodded, while tears continued to slide down her cheeks. "Here I go again. If I'm not yelling, I'm crying."

Kendra patted Meg's hand that draped across her shoulder. "If I get a vote, I choose the tears. Your temper isn't anything I want to mess with again."

Meg gave a small laugh.

Tandy followed them down the stairs, a chore that now took ten minutes instead of ten seconds. Meg placed one foot down, then the other beside it, imitating the descent of a toddler instead of an adult. One arm stayed looped around Kendra's shoulders while the other had a death grip on the banister. No wonder Meg chose to stay upstairs all day. Just getting to the lower level probably tired her out.

Not that she would get better by sitting in bed all day, Tandy reminded herself. This may not be the *easiest* thing for Meg to do, but it may be the most necessary thing to do right now. Meg needed to be reminded that a world revolved outside her front door. The surgery hadn't brought about the end of life, though maybe the end of the life she'd known.

They finally made it to the bottom of the stairs. Meg licked her lips. "Can we rest a minute?"

"Wimp," Kendra teased.

"Guilty."

"Okay, but only for a minute or two. The faster we get you into the car, the sooner we get to shop."

"I can't wait," Meg deadpanned.

Kendra and Tandy laughed.

ELEVEN

A bell tinkled overhead as Jamison walked through the door of Clay's Diner. He'd driven the back roads for half an hour to clear his mind, just breathing in the clean air and letting his eyes focus on the clouds overhead. Clay always knew who in town needed work, and he hoped someone had mentioned the need for a housekeeper position lately. He caught Clay's eye on his way to a booth and nodded.

Clay came from behind the counter and over to the booth just as Jamison slid into it.

"Hey, stranger. Hungry for an early lunch?"

Jamison glanced at the clock on the wall and saw that it was a little after eleven. "Yeah. A burger would be great. And some tea."

"You've got it." Clay scribbled on a pad. "How's Meg?"

Jamison shrugged. "She's recovering. We get good days and we get bad."

"And today?"

"Today your wife and our sister-in-law are over there giving me a break. I'd say it's a good day."

"Kendra or Joy?"

"Ken."

Clay nodded.

"Hey, I think I need to hire a housekeeper for a little while. Do you know anybody who's looking?"

"Jenny Sanders came in here a while back asking if I knew about any houses that needed cleaning. That the kind of thing you're looking for?"

"Yeah. I need cleaning and help with cooking. I think the kids might mutiny if I fix hot dogs with mac and cheese one more time."

"Jenny's a good cook. She worked here for a while, before I had Spencer. Makes a mean chef salad." Clay tapped his pencil on the order pad.

"Salad — green, leafy stuff with vegetables thrown in, right?"

Clay grinned. "I'll go get her number."

"Thanks, man."

"No problem. Should have thought of it before now but I can't get my head out of baby world long enough to do anything but keep the diner going."

"No worries. I remember when we first had James. I don't think I slept for a year."

"Did it get easier the more kids you had?"

"That depends — does Tandy want more kids?"

"She says no for now, but maybe one more in a year or so."

Jamison unfolded his silverware from its napkin. "Then I'll refuse to answer on the grounds it may incriminate me."

"Message received."

Clay headed back to the kitchen and Jamison gazed out the plate-glass window with "Clay's Diner" painted across the front in navy letters. So much had changed in his life these past few weeks that the normalcy of Lindell Street struck him as odd. He half-expected everyone to look different, to be as shell-shocked as he felt inside. But, no, there went Corinne Stewart, walking down the street in her suit and pumps, handbag swinging from her arm, breeze rustling her white curls, and a smile upon her face.

Jamison shook his head. Life could be so absurd. Going along, happy as a clam one minute, racing like a madman to the hospital the next. Married to a content woman who mothered your children with wonderful tenacity and ability one day, then yelled at them for no reason the next. He watched Ms. Corinne enter the antique store across Lindell and envied her day.

What was he doing? Envying a widow woman? He shook himself. This had to stop. Self-pity never got anybody anywhere, and Meg didn't need a husband more focused on his own problems than hers. He had to shape up. Be the man she needed him to be right now.

Though, if he gave up all pretense of machismo, he had no idea what kind of man she needed. Strong? Of course. But strong how? Stand up to her when she yelled? Tell her she acted the part of a raging banshee and needed to get control of herself? Or strong enough to let her be whatever she felt at the moment, to give her space to work through the tumult of emotions?

Considerate? Sure. But considerate of what? Her feelings, no matter how crazily they fluctuated from second to second? Or considerate of their children, who did not need to see their mom in that condition?

Patient? No doubt. But patient in what manner? Patiently bringing her back to a sense of her old self or patiently accepting the new Meg? Patiently counseling the kids that Mommy is going through a rough time or telling them that Mommy has changed?

He sighed. Maybe he didn't have enough strength for this. A truly strong man would know what to do, wouldn't he? Before this nightmare, if anyone had bothered to ask, he would have affirmed he had strength. He knew the Maker of strength and could lean on Him if anything horrible ever happened.

But now he knew better. He knew that just because the world turned upside down, God didn't drop what He was doing and come running to your side with advice. Oh, he didn't doubt for a second that God was there. He just wasn't *there*, physically beside him, discussing the situation and telling him how to be, what kind of man Megan needed.

Clay sat a plate in front of him, pulling him from his reverie. "Grub's on." He tossed a slip of paper onto the table beside the plate and took the seat across from Jamison. "That's Jenny's number."

"Thanks."

"Don't mention it. Tandy called while I was cooking up your burger."

"Is Meg okay?"

"She's fine." Clay paused. "Now."

Jamison sighed. "She'd been having a bad morning."

"From the way Tandy described it, I hope this was a horrible morning."

Jamison shrugged. "Like I said, some days are good, some not."

"Okay, look, you've got to tell us when you need some help. I know this stuff can't be easy, what you're dealing with right now. Heck, if something like that happened to Tandy, I think they'd have me in a white padded room by now with all sharp objects out of my range of vision."

Jamison smiled and bit into the burger.

Clay kept on. "And you know I'm not about to go on about feelings and all that junk. The sisters do enough of that for me, you, and every other male walking on this planet. But I'm for real here. You need help, you call, okay?"

Jamison nodded. "Thing is, Clay, I don't know how any of you would help. I don't know what to do for her myself, much less what to ask you guys to do."

"I'm sure after today Tandy will have plenty of ideas. I'll talk to her tonight and see what I can come up with. You up for some golf tomorrow? We could leave from church and go right to the course."

The thought of hours on a golf course wiped a smile across his face. "That'd be awesome."

"Consider it done. Spencer can hold down the fort here for a few hours and I'm sure

Darin and Scott can take off for a little while."

"Don't mention it. I'll send Tandy over to stay with Meg and the kids. She won't mind. That okay?"

Jamison focused on chewing his burger and keeping down the lump in his throat. Strong men didn't cry in diners with their brother-in-law sitting across the table. Normally the thought of crying wouldn't even occur to him. He was just so blasted tired right now.

He swallowed the bite and cleared his throat. "Seriously. Thanks."

Clay slapped the table. "Nothing I shouldn't have done days ago, man." He went back to the kitchen.

Jamison dragged a French fry through vinegar and renewed his people-watching. The day looked a lot brighter than it had when he walked in here. Right now he had a good half hour to sit and do nothing but eat and watch people walk down the sidewalk. Tomorrow he'd be on a golf course with a club in his hand and the sunshine on his back. Yes, life looked much better than it had ten minutes ago.

"Good to see you out and about, old boy." Roscoe Hutchins slapped a big, beefy hand on Jamison's shoulder. He wondered how he'd missed Roscoe's approach. He looked up to see the farmer standing by his table, plaid shirt and navy suspenders in place.

"Hi, Roscoe."

"How's the missus doing?"

"She's coming along all right, thanks for asking."

"I've been praying for her something fierce."

"Thanks for that. I'm sure we'll be back in church here soon."

"We hope so, son. Y'all take your time, though. No need to rush things. Grace Christian's been there this long, it ain't going to up and disappear anytime soon, I suspect."

Jamison smiled. "No, sir."

Roscoe patted his shoulder and ambled away.

Guilt washed over him. Here he'd sat, looking forward to the escape of the golf course, when the whole town sat praying for his wife's recovery.

Some strong man he'd turned out to be.

TWELVE

Later that night a tired Kendra and Tandy pulled into Joy's circular driveway. The fountain out front, lit by three spotlights, shot water into the air in a display of abandon that Tandy wanted to take deep into her soul. After watching Meg struggle through Something by Sara, the library, and Darnell's, she felt weary of the world. More like a grown-up shackled to a ton of bricks than a woman with a handle on life.

She turned the key and the engine died into silence.

Kendra unbuckled her seat belt. "It's not going to get any easier the longer we sit here."

Tandy turned her head to watch the fountain's display. "I know."

They sat a moment longer, listening to the splash of water and ticking of the cooling engine.

"You think she's going to be okay?"

"She's okay now, T. Maybe not the okay we knew before, but she's alive and functioning. I'm sure there are thousands of brain tumor patients out there who would be grateful for that status."

"Consider me ungrateful. I want my sister back."

Kendra took in a deep breath. "I know. Me, too. But I don't think what we want matters a whole lot right now. I think we have to wait this out and be happy with what we're dealt."

Tandy dragged her gaze from the splashing water. "Let's go. Maybe Joy will have some ideas."

They exited the van and climbed the stone steps to Joy's massive mahogany front door. Tandy pushed the doorbell and stepped inside. She pressed the intercom button. "Joy, it's us."

"In the kitchen," came the reply.

They crossed the marble-floored entry and entered the gallery hallway whose walls were lined with Vettriano originals. Tandy paid them little heed, her pace urgent. She hoped the calm, cool, collected Joy would have a workable solution to the madness that had entered their lives with that stupid tumor.

They entered the kitchen and found Joy

elbow-deep in flour, rolling pin in hand. Her shiny black hair had a streak of the white powder as well. Butterfly barrettes held back the ebony strands. "Hi, girls. To what do I owe this pleasure?"

Joy's well-modulated and perfect speech seemed so incongruous with her flour-covered self that Tandy burst out laughing.

"What?" Joy lifted an eyebrow.

Kendra joined Tandy in the laughter and pointed at Joy. "I didn't know there was a flour fight in town."

"Ha ha. Very funny." Joy ran her rolling pin across the dough, flattening it into a giant, thin circle. "I'm making a pie to take over to Meg's."

Tandy pulled out a bar stool and plopped down. "That's what we're here about. We just left her place."

"And?" Joy blew a wisp of hair from her face.

"And it's pretty strange over there." Kendra sat down beside Tandy.

"Strange how?"

Tandy snagged a shiny apple from the bowl on the counter. "She's not herself, Joy. Everything sets her off and she goes from happy to sad to angry in about three seconds. I nearly got whiplash trying to keep up."

"She's been doing that ever since she got home from the hospital. Why is it a big deal at this point?"

Kendra crossed her arms on the granite countertop. "Because it's not getting any better. If anything, it's worse."

"So, the darkest night comes before the dawn, right? Maybe this is the worst part before she starts getting better."

"I wish I had your optimism." Tandy bit into the apple.

Kendra's dangly earrings clinked as she shook her head. "I don't. It's unrealistic. I think she's worse because nobody's been around to push her out of this. You saw how she reacted with just a little prodding from us, T."

"She's right about that." Tandy kept crunching.

"Prodding? What did you do?" Joy lifted the crust into a nearby pie plate and began crinkling the edges.

"We forced her out of bed and out into the land of the living. You should have seen her when we first got there. Middle of the morning and she was in bed with the blinds drawn in a gown that I don't think she'd changed for a few days. She looked awful."

"Well, she *is* recovering from brain surgery."

Kendra rolled her eyes. "That's almost exactly what she said. But how is it recovering to shut yourself off from the world? I'm worried about the kids, too. Before all this happened, Meg doted on them. If she's anything with them like she was with us, they have to be wondering what alien invaded their mother's body."

"What does Jamison have to say about all this?" Joy moved to the stove and stirred a bubbling mixture.

Tandy swallowed. "He looks like death warmed over. I think he's at his wit's end. Did you hear where he was the other night?"

"No, where?"

"Cadillac's."

Joy's head snapped up. "Excuse me?"

Tandy nodded. "Yep. Sat right there at the bar drinking water."

"Who told you that?"

"Some women out at Wells were talking about it. I don't think they knew we were there."

"When did you go to Wells? And why didn't someone call me?"

"We figured you'd already been there at the first day of picking. You mean you haven't gotten any strawberries yet?" Kendra stood and walked over to the refrigerator.

"Of course I have. But I could have gone with you two and gotten some more. You didn't have to leave me out."

Tandy took another bite and spoke around the apple in her mouth. "We weren't leaving you out. We were trying to keep up."

"Can we get back to Meg?" Kendra retrieved a bottle of water from the fridge and returned to her seat. "We need to do something or she's going to end up a raving lunatic."

Joy gave a withering look. "I highly doubt it's that extreme, Drama Queen."

"You didn't see her today. Ask Tandy."

Tandy shrugged. "She seemed pretty bad, Joy."

Joy turned back to stirring the pot but said nothing.

"So?" Kendra swigged her water.

"I'm thinking."

"We're better at solving life's problems when we're around Momma's scrapping table." Tandy finished the apple and got up to throw the core away.

"Why didn't you call a scrapping night then?"

Kendra held up her fingers and ticked off the reasons. "Because we'd have to invite Meg and it's awkward to talk about someone when they're in the room. Because we invited Zelda to the last scrapping night, which might mean we have to invite her to all the future ones and I don't think Meg would appreciate her business being discussed in front of Zelda."

"She *is* our stepmother now," Joy reminded.

"I don't care if she adopts all four of us. She's not our mother." Kendra returned to her list of reasons. "Because Momma's studio happens to be in the home that Zelda now inhabits with our Daddy, so even if we wanted to have a scrapping night without her, we couldn't. And because I need to hit Emmy's for some supplies before I scrap again."

Joy lifted the pot and poured its contents into the pie shell with a practiced hand. "Okay, so no scrapping nights for a while until we figure out the Zelda mess."

"Which we don't have time to do while we have the Meg mess," Tandy declared.

"Right." Joy scraped the sides of the pot, then set it in the sink. "It's a little difficult to come up with a plan of action when I'm having a hard time understanding the depth of the situation. How about we wait until I see Meg tomorrow and then reconvene tomorrow night? I'll have a better idea then of what we're up against."

Kendra and Tandy shared a look. Tandy nodded. "Sounds logical."

"Good. Now, have you two had dinner?"

"I'll grab something at the diner." Tandy pushed back from the counter. "Speaking of which, my husband might be wondering if I've been kidnapped by now. I should get home."

"Me, too." Kendra stood. "Tomorrow night around 7?"

"Seven it is. I'll have a late dinner ready."

"Ooh, my mouth is watering just thinking about it." Tandy swallowed. Joy's meals were always delicious.

They left the way they came. Tandy felt marginally better as they walked back into the night air. They didn't have a plan, but Joy would soon see what she and Kendra hadn't been able to describe. She breathed in the smell of cut grass.

That'd have to be good enough for now. She had a husband and baby to get home to.

Meg's image in the hall mirror made her stop and backtrack. When had she become so haggard? She leaned into the glass and noted the presence of new lines and wrinkles. As if brain surgery wasn't enough, it had to stamp her face with the vestiges of time as well.

Nice.

"Mom! James took my donut!" Savannah's plaintive wail stopped Meg's inventory of her reflection. She still couldn't believe Jamison had left her with all three children to go *golfing*. Ugh. The nerve of the man. Didn't he know she couldn't handle them all yet? That it was hard enough to keep up with three children with two functioning legs? That no method existed for a mother to adequately parent when her brain resembled the scrambled eggs he should have fixed for breakfast instead of shoving donuts at them on his way out the door?

She huffed and made her way to the kitchen as quickly as she could, knowing if she didn't get there soon, the small skirmish could escalate into World War Three in two point seven seconds. Where were the sisters? Weren't they supposed to be here?

"James, did you take your sister's donut?" The harshness in her tone wasn't called for, but the kids needed to learn to cool it one way or the other.

"She said she was finished with it."

"Did not! It's mine! I want it back!"

"Savannah, lower your voice. We do not yell in the house."

Hannah's sweet two-year-old voice cut through the tension. "You do, Mommy."

Meg saw red but dialed it back. Hannah didn't mean malice. She was two, for crying out loud. If she said Meg yelled, it had to be because Meg yelled, even if she couldn't remember doing that lately.

Then again she couldn't remember much of anything these days. Getting from one moment to the next required Herculean efforts of which she felt sure she'd been deemed incapable by God somewhere long ago.

"Give me!" Savannah, tired of waiting for Meg's intervention, reached out and snatched the pastry from James's hand.

"Hey, that's mine!"

Meg shot an arm out to block James's intended head butt of his little sister. "James Fawcett, calm down this instant. I will get you another donut. Under no circumstances do you hit your sister."

James slumped back in his chair. "Fine, Mom."

"Thanks for that loving response." Meg retrieved a donut from the box on the counter and handed it to her eldest. Why did she have to have brain surgery at the end of the school year? It would be so much easier if she could take them to school and

134

preschool for the day. What could she possibly do to keep them entertained until Jamison came home?

Which, she knew from experience, wouldn't be until lunchtime at least. She prayed they were only playing nine holes but assumed Jamison would choose eighteen given that he hadn't golfed since her hospital stay.

Not that she blamed him for that. Okay, she *did* blame him for that. She hadn't gotten to scrapbook in months. The house looked like the Clampetts lived there. Her children were so full of sugar and junk food they'd probably become part of the obesity problem overtaking the country. Her clothes sat in the dryer so long they were hopelessly wrinkled by the time they arrived in her closet or drawers.

She didn't expect perfection from Jamison but knew he could do better than this if he really cared. Things were a shambles because he didn't really *want* to be picking up the slack so she could be free to recover. He probably wanted her to just suck it up and move on, act like nothing had happened, keep on being the wife he'd always had.

But something *had* happened and he needed to get used to it. She wasn't the same old Meg, the one who cooked and cleaned and mothered and expected nothing in return. Let him get a taste of her life for a change. Maybe he'd appreciate her if she ever took her duties back on.

The idea of *not* working toward reassuming her old way of life made Meg pause. She sat down at the table by her kids. What if she just quit? Decided to be one of those uninvolved moms? Laid in bed until nine or ten every morning? Left it up to Jamison to do the grocery shopping and child-rearing?

She looked at the kids, munching happily and getting sugared up. She still loved them. Had loved each one the second she found out they were growing in her womb. But their exhausting ways, their constant demand for her attention — she could live without that. Couldn't she? Did she need to feel needed by them? Could that be why she'd doted on them all this while?

Unhappy with the direction of her thoughts, she shook her head.

"Does your head hurt, Mommy?" Savannah's eyes held worry a five-year-old should not know.

"No, baby." Meg smiled. "Mommy's feeling much better."

"Then can we go to the park?"

James's ability to take advantage of a situation had to have come from his daddy,

Meg decided.

"No, James. Mommy isn't well enough to drive yet, so we'll have to stay home." Not that Jamison had given that a thought when he went jaunting off with the guys before the sisters got here. Tee time or no tee time, what if they had an emergency? She couldn't drive the kids to the hospital. She'd have to sit and wait on an ambulance.

Which, in Stars Hill, could take anywhere from three minutes to thirty. Thanks heavens she was due to get her license back soon.

"But I don't want to stay home! I want to go to the park!"

"And I want an eight-year-old who controls his temper. Guess neither of us gets what we want this morning, hmm?" She stood and went to the sink. Outside the window birds flitted from limb to limb with nary a thought. She envied their wings. Their ability to get from here to there so easily. She'd been able to do that a month ago. Hadn't given it a second thought.

Now, she dragged a leg along like a ball and chain. Tandy had been right — the leg was getting better and responding more to her will. Still, she didn't rely on it as she once had. Couldn't, really. No telling when the thing would go on revolt again.

"Mommy, will you get to drive again one

day?" Savannah's round eyes implored her to grant the security of the stable Mom they'd known before.

"One day, honey. Maybe even this week." Overcome with a need to rid her children's lives of the fear of uncertainty, she followed that with, "How about we call Aunt Joy and see if she can drive us to the park?"

The kids screamed their approval. Meg pulled the wall phone from its cradle and dialed her baby sister.

"Lasky Residence."

"Hey, Joy, it's me."

"Hi there. I was about to leave for your house."

"Then you must be psychic because I'm calling to see if you've left yet."

Joy's laughter traveled the line. "Scott's on the golf course, too. I meant to be out there before Jamison left, but Maddie isn't being the most agreeable of children this morning."

"Maddie doesn't even talk yet. She's nothing. These three, on the other hand, are demanding the park and we all know their invalid mother can't drive them."

"Oh, stop. You are not an invalid. You're a recovering patient who will drive again one day very soon. Tell the children Auntie Joy will be there to save the day in about fifteen minutes."

"Thanks, Joy."

"Save your thanks for my pie."

"You made pie? What kind?"

"Now it wouldn't be a surprise if I gave you all the details, would it? Get the children ready. I'm on my way."

Meg replaced the receiver, feeling a surge of happiness unlike anything since her surgery. The day shone brightly outside, her kids were full of sugar and could, very soon, run all of it off on the playground. And a pie baked by Joy was on its way to her even now.

All in all, a pretty good start to the day. She considered hating her swift mood swing but decided to be grateful for it — for once.

Meg clapped her hands. "Okay, kids. Let's find shoes and backpacks. Aunt Joy and Maddie are on their way over."

"YAY!" Three sets of hands flew into the air.

Meg's heart lifted further at the outright joy on their faces. She really did have a lot to be thankful for and needed to not lose sight of that. "Come on, now. Shoes and backpacks."

Chair legs scraped against the floor as they left the table and darted out of the kitchen. Meg listened to their little feet pounding down the hallway. "James, help Hannah find her shoes and bring them to me!"

"Okay, Mom!"

See? She could do this. She had a very capable eight-year-old to help her out. Life didn't have to be a building storm cloud. She could choose a white, fluffy cloud instead.

Meg hummed as she cleaned up the breakfast mess scattered across the table. Today, for this minute anyway, she would choose to be happy.

Jamison climbed the tee mound and looked down the fairway. A strong wind kicked up the tree limbs, which waved a welcome back to him. He felt like waving in return. Getting onto the golf course soothed his frayed nerves like nothing else these days. The peaceful carpet of grass, busy squirrels darting here and there, whine of golf cart motors, and *snick* of golf club to ball calmed him like aloe on a burn.

He inhaled the clean air, filling his lungs and allowing nature to wash away the tension coiled in his soul. He'd thought to play nine holes and rush back to Meg. Now he considered staying out for eighteen.

"You going to play in this lifetime?" Clay chided.

Jamison grinned. "Yeah, yeah." He addressed the ball, took a last look at the fluttering flag about three hundred yards away, and swung.

His muscles burned from disuse. Only a month away and already he'd lost a bit of his form. Perhaps placing a golf ball under his right foot — an old Annika Sorenstam trick — would fix his swing. He knew his hips weren't aligning with his arms and shoulders.

Darin slid off the golf cart seat and walked toward the mound. "My, how the mighty have fallen." He glanced down the fairway to the place just this side of the rough where Jamison's ball had come to rest.

"Hey, cut a guy some slack. I haven't been out here in a month."

"Excuses, excuses." Darin pushed a tee into the ground.

Jamison shook his head, enjoying the ribbing. He took his place in the cart, waited in silence while the other three took their swings. Contemplated calling Meg to see how she fared at home. But what if she said she needed him to come back right away? He knew his feelings were selfish, but he needed some time away from her. Time to remember that he loved her, that he had a life, that he had friends, that this was just a small time in their lives and they *would* get through.

He looked down the long carpet of grass and noted the three lays. All had out-stroked him. Terrific.

He tried to feel bad about being out-played. A month ago he'd have obsessed over each stroke, every tidbit or nuance from the wind to the bit of dirt on his club.

Today he was just happy to be on the course.

"So you decided on nine or eighteen?" Scott steered the cart around a bend in the path.

"I'm leaning toward eighteen."

"Might as well. Joy's with Meg, so that's taken care of."

Jamison settled back into the seat, his happiness quotient expanding by leaps and bounds. "Then definitely eighteen."

"That's my man." Scott pulled the cart to a stop at the next hole.

They played twelve more holes. Gradually, Jamison found his swing again and by the time they headed for the clubhouse, he had happily found his groove.

"Thought we had a chance at beating you for a while there." Darin parked his cart behind Clay's truck and hopped out to unbuckle his bag.

Scott unloaded his own bag and slid it into his car. "Please. Might want to keep those dreams in the realm of reality."

Clay pulled the flap on his glove and the ripping sound of Velcro cut through the air. "Then they wouldn't be dreams, right?"

"Touché."

After putting their bags in the vehicles and parking the carts in the cart bay to recharge for another day, they ambled to the Nineteenth Hole.

Clay held open the door. "Who's hungry?"

"Me." Scott walked through the entry.

Darin lifted a finger. "Count me in."

Jamison considered calling home to check on Meg. But Joy was there, so everything had to be fine. No sense in cutting the day short. "Famished."

"All right, then. To the dinner spot, boys."

They settled in at a table overlooking a small garden. The sight reminded Jamison that Meg hadn't planted any new flowers this year. He hadn't tended her existing ones, either. Wonder if Jenny Sanders did gardening? He'd have to remember to ask her tomorrow during her interview.

Clay gulped down half his iced water and set the glass on the table. "Okay, man, spill. How's Meg?"

Jamison looked at the faces surrounding

143

him. Here was a chance to be real, to get some feedback and find out if they had any better ideas than he about how to deal with Meg. But these guys were married to her sisters and Meg might just kill him if she found out he talked about her.

He sighed. "Fine."

"Yeah, I'm sure." Darin threw a wadded up straw paper at him. "Come on, give. Kendra's wandering around the house muttering under her breath like she does when she's got a problem she can't figure out, and I'm guessing that problem is your wife. That means I've got a vested interest in getting Meg on the road to recovery before my wife drives me insane."

Jamison chuckled. "When you put it that way . . ."

"I do."

"Okay, truth be told, I don't know what to do with her." He described the mood swings, the lack of logic to her actions, the out-of-character tantrums, and the sense of dread in their house. "I feel like I'm walking on eggshells scattered across nails laying on broken glass most days. One wrong move, and I'm shredded."

Scott whistled low. "Wow, that's pretty bad."

"Tell me about it."

Darin toyed with another straw paper. "You thought about counseling?"

Jamison shook his head. "The doctors say to give her time and wait it out. Any counseling we get now wouldn't help long-term because she might be a totally different person a week from now."

"I meant counseling for you."

Jamison's eyes widened. "No." Counseling? Definitely not. That's all he needed were the town gossips not only telling everyone where he chose to drink a glass of water, but that he'd lost his marbles as well. "You know this town. They're having enough of a field day with this. I can't give them more to discuss."

"You can if it keeps you from losing your mind."

Darin shot him a knowing glance. "Or visiting dark bars."

Jamison averted his gaze. So the whole family knew. "Not a big deal. I only wanted a few minutes to myself."

"Hey, nobody's judging here. Right, guys?" Darin looked around and waited for Scott and Clay's nod. "Still, you've gotta admit that sitting down at Cadillac's is going to stir the gossips a whole lot faster than a trip to a head shrinker will do."

"Yeah, but I don't need counseling. I need

145

to go to sleep and wake up six months from now when Meg's decided who she is." This talk killed his happy mood faster than baking soda on a grease fire. "Look, guys, I've had a good day here. First good day I've had in a month. How about we skip the bonding time and just eat?"

He watched them exchange glances, only then realizing the entire outing had been more about the chance to talk to him than golf with him. He told himself that was a sign of caring, not manipulation.

Which didn't help it feel any less like manipulation.

Darin finally spoke. "You've got a hard thing going. We only wanted to know if we can help. You want us to butt out, we're gone. You'd rather spend time swinging a club than dissecting your woman's motives, that's cool by us." He leaned forward. "But if you change your mind, you got six ears here and three brains that mostly work." He looked across the table. "Though I wouldn't count on burger boy over there."

"Hey," Clay splayed a hand across his chest. "You break my heart. No more burgers for you."

"I'm just saying your mind ain't been right since Clayton came home from the hospital. I'm chalking it up to sleep deprivation and praying you get over it in a few more months."

Jamison couldn't resist. "Maybe you and Meg are on the same timetable."

They enjoyed a laugh. The conversation paused while a waitress set their plates down. Jamison's mouth watered at the aroma of steak. With the family relying on church casseroles at first, then his cooking skills, he hadn't enjoyed a steak in a month, either. He picked up his fork and knife, determined to wring as much enjoyment out of the day as possible.

As he cut the meat, he thought about Meg. Maybe Joy's presence put her in a good mood. Who knew? Perhaps he'd arrive home to find a wife who could smile for longer than two seconds.

The steak tasted delicious, exploding in his mouth in a riot of tastes, peppercorn definitely among them. He could work a grill. Why hadn't he grilled for the family? He'd fix that soon. They could grill — hmm, something easy — chicken for him and Meg, hot dogs for the kids. They'd love it. Meg might even sit out on the patio with him and talk. He still longed for conversation with her but knew her mind might not be up to the verbal sparring that had made their relationship special before. He prayed that wouldn't be a lasting effect of the surgery.

"Earth to Jamison." Darin snapped his fingers in front of Jamison's face. "Want to join us back on this planet?"

Jamison swallowed the bite of steak. "Sorry. You were saying?"

"I was saying —" Clay relaxed back into his seat — "what you need is a date night with Meg."

"Great idea, except that she hates going out in public because of her leg."

"It's not any better?"

"It is, but she says she never knows when it's going to give out. You know Meg, she doesn't want the town seeing her as anything less than what she was before the surgery."

Darin harrumphed. "The sisters worry too much about what this town thinks."

"Spoken by a man who hasn't lived here all his life," Clay said.

"Who cares what people are saying? You're telling me she's just going to hole up in your house to keep people from talking? *That's* crazy, if you ask me."

Jamison shook his head. "I can't say I completely disagree with you, but it doesn't matter what I think. It only matters what she thinks and right now she thinks she doesn't want folks in town looking at her."

"So take her up to Nashville. Get lost in the crowd."

Jamison considered that, surprised he hadn't thought of it himself. A night in Nashville would exhaust her, sure, but it might also give them some much-needed time together.

"That's not a half-bad idea."

Darin straightened and adjusted a non-existent tie. "Thanks. I aim to please."

"Tandy and I can keep the kids," Clay volunteered. "Anytime they come over, Clayton sits in his playpen, mesmerized. They're like babysitters for us."

"Can you watch them tonight?"

"I don't know. Spencer has had the grill this morning and he's my only backup. I doubt he'll want to stay all day. But he's doing lunch and dinner tomorrow, so that would work out."

Could he keep his good mood going that long? If Joy had successfully cheered Meg up, would she still be in a good mood by tomorrow afternoon? A month ago the question wouldn't even have occurred to him. These days, though, he knew better than to count on a sunny disposition from his wife.

"How about I call you tomorrow to confirm? If Meg's having a bad day, I don't want to drag her all the way up to Nashville."

Clay nodded. "Works for me."

Jamison went back to his steak, letting the guys' conversation flow on without him. Pretty soon, he'd have to start spending more regular hours at the office again. The clients had been understanding thus far, but everyone had a limit to their patience and he worried he might be reaching theirs. Now would be a really bad time to lose their source of income.

He pushed the thought from his mind like a debtor avoiding collection calls. A volatile wife gave him enough to worry about. So today he'd choose to focus on the golf course and a possible date with a happy version of Meg.

Thirteen

The next morning Jamison opened his eyes and turned his head. Meg lay curled on her side, sleeping, her face a beautiful mask of tranquility. One hand lay beside her on the pillow, those long, delicate fingers half-curled in relaxation. The other lay fisted beneath her chin. Savannah slept in that exact position.

Meg's long, pale eyelashes rested against smooth skin. Her full, peach-colored lips were partly open, like a rosebud just beginning to flower. He hadn't looked at her in a long time, he realized now. But if anyone had asked, he'd still swear Megan was the most breathtaking woman on the planet.

As he let his eyes roam across her face, he tried to figure out just what made her so gorgeous to him. Even with the crazy mood swings and the scare of the last couple of months, she still lay there like a goddess. How did she do that? How did that loveliness stay constant even though their world had slipped into chaos?

He hadn't known she was awake until her lips formed a smile. One ocean blue eye peeked out at him. "Good morning."

He smiled, loving that her morning voice came to him on a husky tone. "Good morning."

Both jewel eyes came open. "Taking in the sights?"

"Something like that."

"Do I want to know how long you've been staring at me with my mouth open? Was I snoring?"

He slid his hand into hers on the pillow. She'd never known the depth of her own beauty. He loved that, too. "It wasn't long. And, no, you weren't snoring."

"Thank goodness. Are the kids up?"

"Listen." He let his gaze roam the ceiling.

"I don't hear anything but the birds outside."

"Exactly. So all three must either be asleep or much better at stealth mode."

She chuckled and he squeezed her hand. "So I was thinking . . ."

"Did it hurt?"

So she hadn't forgotten at least some of their conversational rituals. "A little. I thought we might go up to Nashville this afternoon, just the two of us."

"I'd love to, but I'm pretty sure leaving an eight-year-old, five-year-old, and two-year-old on their on, alone, all afternoon and evening, still isn't acceptable in this country."

"Good thing I found us a sitter then, hmm?" He scooted a little closer to her.

"And who might we be dumping our children on today?"

"Clay and Tandy. And Clay promises it's a gift to them."

"A gift? Did he say that with a straight face?"

"He did. Says our kids are entertainment for Clayton, like watching cartoons only better."

Meg grinned — she looked so much like Savannah that he couldn't help but grin back. "So he's using our kids to make his happy."

"Yes, which I find awful in the abstract and downright wonderful in the specific."

"Hmm, I think I'm with you on that."

"Does that mean you want to go to Nashville with me?"

"Why not? I've been cooped up in this house too long anyway."

Gratitude for her continued good mood welled up in him like a tidal wave on a desperately dry beach. He drank it in, knowing the ebb would happen at some point but only able at the moment to appreciate the flow.

Jamison walked back down the stairway at Tandy and Clay's. The kids were so excited about visiting their aunt and uncle he'd barely gotten a good-bye hug before they scampered off to Clayton's nursery to play with their "cool cousin."

He joined Meg in the van. "Okay, three kids effectively abandoned for the evening by their parents."

"Roger that." Meg pulled down her visor and slid a finger along the CDs secured to the other side by a CD case. "How about some Martina McBride for the drive up to Music City?"

Right now, he'd listen to Black Sabbath if it made her happy. "Sounds good."

Meg put the *Greatest Hits* album in the CD player as Jamison steered the van toward the interstate. He glanced at her. "Have you thought about where you want to eat dinner tonight?"

"Yeah, but I haven't decided on anything yet. I thought I'd see where we ended up first. Do you want to go shopping?"

"Yep, it's right up there on my list with

'Run Car Off Road Into Ditch.' "

"So it made the list."

"Definitely."

"Because I thought maybe we could hit Cool Springs, then see a movie, and then have dinner. With a trip to the bookstore thrown in there somewhere, since I'm out of stuff to read."

"How can you be out of books to read? People have been bringing you books constantly so you'd have something to do while you got better."

Meg wrinkled her nose. "Yeah, except they think I like prairie romances. Which I do, but everything in moderation, you know? I need some mystery, some intrigue, some international spy running all over the place with enough money to bribe officials, make gadgets that explode on impact but not a second before, and buy planes and cars."

"Ah, fiction fans. Such a fickle lot."

"We're not fickle!" Meg crossed her arms, mock indignation plain on her face. "We simply want a story that brings us in and refuses to let us go until the end."

Jamison glanced at her, then back at the road. "Don't ask much, do you?"

"Nope."

He smiled. "I hear there's a new Cornwell book out. Dead bodies, morgues, mystery, science, and Kay Scarpetta all rolled into one. Will that satisfy your story craving?"

"Ugh, I don't think I can take Cornwell's depression right now. Did I tell you about her last book? All the characters had gotten so introspective they'd lost complete sight of the rest of the world."

"Okay, how about a Koontz?"

"Now *that* sounds like something I could get lost in."

He smiled.

"I didn't know you paid such close attention to my reading habits."

"I pay close attention to all of you, habits or otherwise." He wiggled his eyebrows.

"Careful, I'll start to think you're only taking me to dinner for one purpose."

"And what would that be?"

"To satisfy your hunger."

"You might be right."

Her laughter entered his ears like a perfect shot from the professional tee on a par 5. Sweet. Perfect. Satisfying.

They talked the entire hour ride to Nashville, playfully debating the merits of Martina McBride over Faith Hill or squash over zucchini. The subject didn't matter as much as simply sharing words. Their conversation flowed over and under and all around, wrapping them with the warmth of its familiarity and reestablishment.

He considered driving right on through Nashville and on up to Kentucky, then calling Tandy and Clay to say they'd pick up the kids in the morning. But he shouldn't push it. Their first real time together with him seeing the old Meg, the memorable smile, the recognizable gleam in her eye, the way she tilted her head to think about his words rather than coming back with some barb . . .

He didn't want it to end.

Still, he knew he needed to take sips from her fountain because, right now, it was all she had the energy to give. Even if she didn't realize it.

"So, the mall first or did you have a particular store in mind?"

"Mall is fine." She'd been turned in her seat, facing him. Now she straightened herself toward the front of the van, all business with the thought of shopping on her mind.

"Are we looking for anything in particular?"

"Shoes. I need flat shoes."

"*You're* going to buy flats?" As long as he'd known her, Meg refused to wear anything without a heel. Even her tennis shoes had a sole an inch thick. He hadn't under-

157

stood at first. Why should a woman as tall as Meg need a heel in her shoe? But Meg explained that too many tall women tried to "make up" for their height by wearing flat shoes and slumping. She didn't want to be that way. She wanted to stand tall, embrace her height rather than "make up" for it.

He couldn't imagine not loving her for that.

"The heels are a little hard to walk in these days." Her voice had gone small.

Why didn't he think before he shot his mouth off? "Oh, honey, I should have realized —"

"No, I'm glad you didn't. It means you don't think of me as a cripple or unable person. You know, changed."

He reached across the space between them and grabbed her hand. "I could never think of you as those things. You're amazing."

"Thanks."

"You're welcome." He let go to turn the steering wheel and park in the garage under Dillard's. The sound of tires squealing against the smooth concrete swirled around them as he searched for a space among several other cars doing the same thing.

"You know, maybe I should look into getting one of those handicap signs and we could park nearer the door."

He couldn't tell if she was joking. "Nah, we'll leave it for the folks who really need it."

The thankfulness in her smile told him he'd chosen the right response. Finally spotting a space, he whipped the van into it and killed the engine. "Ready to find some shoes?"

"Let's do it."

They left the van and walked to the escalator that would take them to the main floor where women's shoes were. Jamison watched closely but didn't detect any hint of a limp from her. Maybe the leg had decided to come back to life as well.

They arrived at the shoe section and Jamison looked around for a seat, knowing when he wasn't needed.

"Hey, what are you doing?"

"Finding a good spot to wait on you. And wishing I'd brought a Clancy novel with me."

"You don't want to look with me?"

"I could look, but if all these years together have taught me anything it's that I don't know the first thing about picking out shoes for you."

"But this time it's easy." She pulled him away from the chair he'd scoped out. "Think flat and you can't go wrong."

He snatched up the nearest flat. Beige with cutouts in the leather, he felt fairly certain his grandmother owned a pair of these. "How about these, honey?"

She looked at him, then at the shoe, then back at him. "You're not being real."

"And with that, I'm off to find a chair."

She relinquished his arm and he deposited the God-awful shoe back into its place on his way. He settled in, prepared to watch Meg flit from table to table, pick up about four dozen shoes, try on half that many, and walk out of the store with — maybe — one pair.

Half an hour later they exited the store hand in hand.

"What's the smug look for?" She adjusted her purse strap.

"Just thinking about how well I know you."

"How well is that?"

He held the bag up, one finger under its string. "I present to you Exhibit A."

"Oh, please. Those shoes were around the corner from where you were sitting. There's no way you saw them before I did. I didn't even think you saw them on my feet when I tried them on."

"I didn't."

"Then I'm confused."

"I think I like it that way." He squeezed her hand, a hand he knew better than his own.

She lifted her eyes to the sky. "I don't care if we live to be eighty, I don't think I'll ever understand you."

"Well, we all have our limitations. Half the battle is admitting them."

"Good thing you're cute."

"And mad for you."

"That helps, too."

They strolled past ten stores before Meg saw a pair of dark brown leather sandals in the window of Coldwater Creek. "Ooh! I like those. And they're flat! This will only take a second."

"Sure, take your time." Coldwater Creek knew enough about humans to provide comfortable chairs for the men. He settled into a leather club chair and set the bag of shoes down beside him. No way would they be in here for only one pair of shoes. He checked his watch. He gave her twenty minutes and he doubted she walked out of the store with the shoes that first caught her eye. Slumping down in the chair, he leaned his head against the chair back and closed his eyes.

Nineteen minutes later he woke to someone nudging his foot.

"Hey, sleepyhead, I thought we were spending the day together."

Jamison straightened up, coming out of the nap as fast as he'd gone into it. "We are. Did you find anything?"

She raised a small bag dangling from her wrist. "Just this."

He resisted the urge to smile. "That doesn't look big enough for a box of shoes."

"No, but it was on sale and what girl doesn't need a coral bracelet during the summer?"

"Of course," he agreed. He couldn't care less if she bought something in every store in this mall and forced him to work until the day he went to his grave to pay off the credit card bill. A smile flooded her face and life sparkled in her eyes. Anything was worth that, which is probably a truth the credit card companies knew.

"Ready for more or do you need a break?"

She shrugged. "I'm good for now." Taking his hand, she led him from the store and they continued down the walkway.

They hadn't made it very far before she stopped again to look in the jewelry windows at Carlyle & Co.

He looked over her shoulder to see what had caught her eye. A ring sat proudly beneath a small spotlight, which sent beams bouncing off a waterfall of sapphires and diamonds that managed to be eye-catching but not ostentatious. The blue of the stones struck him as familiar and he realized they were the shade of Meg's eyes.

"Isn't that beautiful?" she breathed.

"Comes close to you, but only close."

She shook her head and resumed their walk. "I love looking at things like that in the window, but I don't think I'd want to own something like that."

"You wouldn't?" How could he not know this about her?

"No. Where would I wear that? I'm a mom who plays with Play-Doh or fingerpaints or digs around in the mud and dirt. I don't need to be worrying about getting dirt in my diamonds at this stage of my life. Maybe when we're older and have grandkids and all I do all day is sit and knit."

"You're going to knit?"

"Or quilt, maybe, like Momma. I wish she'd taught me before she passed on."

"You could go to a class. Teach yourself."

"I could, but it would have been nice to learn from her. I was too young, then, to appreciate the quilts she made us."

"I'm sure she knows you appreciate them now."

They passed the turnoff for J.C. Penney's and kept walking. "Do you think, if the tumor had gotten me, that Hannah would have remembered me?"

The very thought of losing her took his breath and he struggled to get it back to answer her. "I — I — what made you ask that?"

"I was just thinking that at least we were old enough to have memories of Momma before the cancer took her. Would Hannah be able to say that about me if I passed on now?"

Thoughts collided in his brain. He didn't want to talk about the tumor or anything to do with the tumor. They'd been having a good day together, a *normal* day together. Why ruin it with the tumor? Why even acknowledge the stupid thing had stolen so much from them? Why muse about how much more it could have taken?

But if she brought it up, she wanted to talk about it. And, today, she got whatever she wanted because he'd be darned if he did anything to wipe that smile off her face.

"I think, even if she had trouble remembering, she has the gift of your scrapbooks to remind her."

Meg stopped short and he fumbled to a stop as well.

"That is the kindest thing you could have possibly said to me, Jamison Fawcett."

He lifted a shoulder, ready to be finished with the whole business of her possible death. She hadn't died and he didn't want to think about the fact that she could have.

She kissed him on the cheek — a light kiss that felt like a feather brushing his skin. He tried to remember the last time she'd given him a kiss like that. Had to be high school. Before they kissed on the lips. He'd been bowled over then.

He wasn't much less than that now.

They continued their walk, coming to the grand entrance of Macy's.

"More shoe shopping?"

She looked across the open expanse to the other side of the walkway. "Hmm, do you need anything to wear to work?"

He followed the incline of her head and noticed they'd come to Jos. A. Bank, the store where he got the majority of his work clothes. "I think I'm good for now. Besides, we're shopping for you."

"I could go next door in Strasburg Children and find something sweet for Hannah to wear to church."

"Again, shopping for *you*. Not me. Not the kids."

"In that case, Macy's shoe department,

here we come."

He followed her into the store, holding his breath for most of the walk through the perfume section. Most of those fragrances probably smelled close to heavenly when used singularly, but coming together in one department wielded by spritz-happy attendants left him walking through a flower garden gone schizophrenic. The crazy kaleidoscope of smells assaulted his brain the second he took in a slight breath.

Thankfully they were through it in only a few steps and over to the shoes. As before, he found a chair and plopped down. Meg barely gave him a second glance. Her eyes, instead, began roving the tables and racks.

He wondered why she brought up her mother. Had she really thought she'd die? He'd barely let himself consider it, much less dwell on it long enough to wonder what the children would remember and not remember. He obviously hadn't been the man she needed him to be or he wouldn't be sitting here guessing her thoughts. He'd know them because he would have asked and she would have told.

Except . . . approaching a woman wearing barbed wire for a mood for eight weeks hadn't seemed a good idea. Best to steer clear until the barbs either wear down or break off.

He thought about going back through the materials the hospital sent home with them to see if this, too, would pass. Did brain surgery patients go back to strong resemblances of their former selves only to then change again?

Who would want to know? Certainly not him. If he only got this day with a cheerful Meg, he'd take it. No sense marring it with the threat of its disappearance. He had to learn — even if it took the rest of his life — to enjoy her one day at a time. Nothing guaranteed him more than this day. The tumor taught him that.

Meg appeared before him a full five minutes later. "Nothing good on sale here. Ready to move on?"

"Did you even try anything on?"

"Nope. But I need a snack and I'll bet Williams-Sonoma has something good to taste test. It's just down the hall."

Allowing her to pull him up from the chair, he snagged the Dillard's bag from where he'd dropped it on the floor. "Lead on, maestro."

Having newly acquainted himself with their kitchen, he had a little more interest in the gadgets in Williams-Sonoma than he'd had in the past. When Meg held up a colander, he nodded because the one they had was dented and ugly. He remembered that from the numerous days he'd spent making mac and cheese.

When she pointed to a navy apron with a red lobster on its front, he decided it was about time they had an apron a man could wear without looking like a cross-dresser and nodded his head.

When she stopped in front of a wall filled with bags bearing names like "Lemon Scone Mix" and "Grandma's Cookie Mix," his eyes grew wide and he went to get a shopping basket. So *that's* how they made all that stuff!

They spent more time in the kitchen store than they'd spent on shoes so far and left the store with a smaller bank account total but a restocked kitchen. "That was productive."

Meg grinned. "I love that store. It lets me pretend I'm like Joy and make three-course meals from scratch every day."

"Joy's marbles are a little out of whack on that front."

"Thrilled to hear that you think so."

Two stores down she tugged him into Brookstone. "Come on. They've got this leg massager I've been dreaming about for two months."

Deciding not to envy a leg massager — after all, there was a slim chance he'd been the one operating it in her dreams (hey, a man could hope) — he dutifully followed her inside. She found a chair with big, boot-like structures in front of it and sat down. Within seconds, her calves were encased in the boots and she had leaned back in the chair, a look of utter bliss consuming her face.

Jamison checked out the price tag . . . and nearly dropped from a heart attack. For that price he'd pay a masseuse to come to their house every day.

"Welcome to Brookstone. Can I help you with anything?"

All day they'd been wonderfully ignored by salespeople, but it seemed their luck had come to an end. Jamison squinted at the name tag and decided "Dennis" didn't mean to be annoying. He was simply doing his job.

"No thanks, we're fine."

"Mmm." Meg's slight moan turned both their heads.

"Don't mind my wife, she just needs a moment alone with the chair."

"We have a few in stock. You could take one home today," Dennis offered with more fake cheer than a mall Santa holding a

169

candy cane.

"I could, but then what would I say to the mortgage guy? I got a better deal from the massage guy?"

Dennis's smile held understanding. Clearly too many customers unwilling to plop down a ridiculous amount of cash had prepared him. "We have an excellent payment plan. I have all the details back here if you'd like to take a look."

Jamison took in the serenity on his wife's face and, for a minute, contemplated going into debt to keep it there. Heck, they might even be able to claim it on their taxes as a medical expense. He opened his mouth to tell Dennis to go get his paperwork, when Meg opened her eyes.

"Okay, I'm done. Thanks for the test drive!" She patted the arms of the chair as if saying good-bye for now to a friend and waltzed out of the store.

Unsure what had just happened, Jamison nodded to Dennis and hurried after his wife. "Um, honey? They've got a payment plan. We could take one of those home today if you want."

She took his hand. "And go in debt for the next two years? No way, buddy. Every time I sat down in the thing, all I'd see on the backs of my eyelids would be the bill and the interest rate."

"It wasn't *that* expensive. We'd have it paid off in a year, possibly less."

"Still don't want it. All I need is a fix every now and then and I'm fine."

Unsure whether to mentally add the chair to his Christmas list, he allowed her to pull him down the walkway. They didn't stop again until they'd returned to the turnoff for Dillard's.

"How about some coffee and a quick bite before we go see what's playing at the movies?"

"Okay, the Food Court is —"

She patted his arm and smiled up at him. "You're such a man."

"What does that mean?"

"It means of course you haven't memorized every square inch of this mall to determine the most appropriate place to park to get to your desired location the quickest."

"And you have?" More that he didn't know about her.

"Of course. That's how I know The Coffee Beanery is on the left right before we get to Dillard's." They turned off the main hallway and she pointed. "See?"

He looked up and, sure enough, there sat The Coffee Beanery. How had he not seen it when they first left Dillard's? Probably because he'd had his eyes fixed on her all afternoon.

"You know, you're pretty amazing, Mrs. Fawcett."

"Why, thank you, Mr. Fawcett. Ready for some good coffee?"

"I'm with you."

Several hours later the moon rose high in the sky like a bright, round beacon and Jamison steered the van back to the interstate. He didn't know which part of the day he'd enjoyed most, only that he wanted to close his eyes and relive every second of it. Too long he'd lived without the Meg he married; having her back felt better than finding gold or oil in their backyard — oil would be very messy to sleep with and he doubted the cuddle factor of gold would rank much higher.

"Penny for your thoughts."

He drew in a breath. "Oh, I was just sitting here thinking about how wonderful it feels to have you back." As soon as he said it, he knew he'd messed up. Stupid, stupid man. Didn't know when to leave well enough alone.

"Have me back? What do you mean?"

Backtrack, Jamison. Find a way out. "Oh, I

don't know what I meant. I'm too tired to be trusted with words." He turned on the radio. Meg loved music, so there were pretty good odds it would serve as a distraction.

He got three songs before she turned it down. "No, really. What did you mean?"

The choices were to brush her off again, ignore her, or face the music.

He really, really didn't want to face it. Yet it was easier to brush cat fur off a cashmere sweater than to brush Meg off a topic she wanted to address. And ignoring her — well, he'd never in his life been able to do that.

A sigh escaped his lips. "I'm sorry. I shouldn't have said it."

"It's okay. What did you mean, though? I know I haven't been exactly like I was before the surgery, but have I been so odd that I haven't been myself?"

A land mine lurked in that question. Shoot, *twenty* landmines! He proceeded with caution. "You've been . . . different."

"Right, but different how?"

Nope, not going there. "I don't know. Just different."

"Well, different as in spacey? Different disorganized? Different moody? Different what?"

"Moody, I'd say."

"I've been moody?" Her voice had lost

173

some of the joy of the day.

He could hear the joy seeping out of her voice. His chest tightened, making him realize it had loosened throughout the hours they'd spent together. "No, not moody. I don't know the word." Couldn't they talk about something else? *Any*thing else?

"Can't think of it or don't want to say it?" Her crossed arms warned he was headed into a hazard zone.

"I don't want to say anything that will hurt your feelings."

"So you've been thinking bad thoughts about me and you think you're doing me a favor by not sharing them with me? What happened to being honest with each other?"

Why, oh *why* hadn't he read the paperwork from the hospital? If he had, he might have known this was coming. Fine one minute, hostile the next. And how could she *not* know she'd been moody? Was forgetfulness yet another fun side effect? Darkness spread along his heart like oil from a busted can, and he sighed.

"Jamison? Come on."

He almost flinched at the accusing tone that slipped into her voice. *She* was accusing *him?* He'd done nothing but be patient and wait on her to get better, and there she sat throwing words at him like weapons.

Thing was, he wanted to still be patient, to give her space and room and time, but it'd been two months and all he wanted was some semblance of his wife back. That wasn't asking a whole lot. And for her to react this way . . .

"You're angry a lot." He all but spat the words, happy to get them out of his mouth where they couldn't fester in his mind any longer. "And bitter and moody and difficult and hard to please."

He shot a glance at her and the shock and anger on her face made him instantly regret his outburst. Somehow she hadn't known. Or had thought no one else knew. Whatever, now he'd hurt her and ruined their day together.

He tried to reach out to her, but she turned her body to the window so that her voice bounced off the glass and back to him, picking up a hollow sound in the process.

"I'm so sorry I couldn't be the perfect wife while I recovered from *brain surgery.*"

That voice — full of meanness and self-pity and completely lacking any of the warmth and love he'd heard from her before the tumor nightmare — sliced so hard he looked down to see if she'd drawn blood.

Only a shirt there. The scars she caused would stay inside.

For the first time he wondered whether she had scars inside as well. Too late to ask her now. Anything else he said would only cause her more pain.

So, swallowing back his regret and disappointment, he shut his mouth and drove home in silence.

FOURTEEN

Jamison jammed his seat belt buckle into its latch. Why did she have to be so difficult? One second they're having a great night and the next she has to act like a banshee. Could the surgery have made her bipolar? How could someone go from happy to angry that quickly? He'd slept fitfully, fighting dreams of a ranting Meg.

He turned the key in the ignition and jerked the gear shift into Reverse. Refraining from squealing his tires — which would only let her know of his own anger — he backed out of the garage and threw it into drive.

The house disappeared in his rearview mirror and he blew out a breath of frustration that sounded like air whooshing out of a balloon. He might as well be that deflated. Meg took all the wind out of his sails, acting so out of character. It would be different if he had any idea what to do, but he didn't.

And helplessness fit him as well as a tutu on a momma sow.

He pointed the car toward Lindell, prepared to go directly to Tandy and Clay's and pick up the kids. But something in him just couldn't do it. The kids had enough difficulty in their lives already. They needed him to be unchanging in the midst of this chaotic time.

Well, if he went home right now, all they'd see was a dad who was angry, unprepared, and a little scared. They needed that like they needed a pound of sugar before bed. He swung the car onto University and punched the gas. He had no idea where he'd end up, but it was enough that he'd arrive there alone. University ran into Elm and he briefly considered grabbing a sausage and biscuit at the gas station. Unable to come up with a better plan, he clicked the left hand blinker and waited through the red light.

But when he came to the lighted sign, his foot refused to tap the brake. Instead, it pressed harder on the gas. He knew he should pull over and think instead of wasting gas that cost entirely too much, but he'd done enough of trying to choose the right path for a while. Every second of every hour of every day, he struggled to be a good husband, to choose the right response. Now, though . . . he'd had enough. So he shook off that mind-set like a snake shedding its skin, happy to be free of constraints that didn't fit on his best day. He tossed a wave to the gas station and continued down the road.

Soon, as he'd known it would, the two lanes divided into four. Not long after, the lights of the city were just a memory in his mirror. And soon after that, he saw the welcome sign to Greenfield.

Had he ever stopped there before? Maybe once or twice. Having lived in Stars Hill all his life, he should know more about their neighboring town. The extent of his knowledge could be summed up in a short list:

1. It ranked smaller than Stars Hill.
2. The police force loved to give out speeding tickets.
3. There was no bypass.
4. A diner downtown served burgers that rivaled Clay's.

Would the diner be open for breakfast? Probably not, but why not try it out anyway? One turn off the main street and he pulled the car into a space in front of Wimpy's Diner. Did the owner take pride in an old high school nickname? Or was he trying to have the last laugh on a nickname given him by the cool kids?

Jamison cut the engine and stepped out of the car into crisp morning air that smelled cleaner than Joy's countertops. He loved that about small towns — clear air. It was why he couldn't imagine ever moving into a big city. Battling traffic, staring at neighbors an arm's length away, breathing in smog and pollution — definitely not a life he cared to live. An hour's drive left him close enough to go into the city when he wanted to take advantage of its amenities, but far enough away to leave the mess behind and go home to peaceful, clean Stars Hill.

He ambled up onto a sidewalk lined with old timers in plaid shirts, overalls, and hats bearing tractor logos. Stuffing his hands in his pockets, he tried not to look like a businessman, which was akin to a city slicker wandering into Heartland. "Mornin'." He nodded. A few tipped their hats in response. Why had he stopped here?

The door creaked on its hinge when he opened it wide to step inside the eatery. Every stool at the bar served as the resting stop for men who could be clones of those on the porch. Well, nearly every seat. He noted an empty spot of red vinyl at the end and wandered on down.

"What'll it be?" The waitress's thick, blonde ponytail swung when she walked and her smile pushed dimples in on each side of her heart-shaped face.

"Uh, coffee, please. Black." Doctoring the brew would clearly label him an outsider.

She dimpled again. "Sure thing."

He looked for a name tag, but none existed. No matter. He wouldn't remember five minutes after he left here anyway. He glanced down the bar, saw a line of men intent on plates piled with steaming eggs, biscuits, gravy, grits, and bacon.

The waitress set a white mug in front of him, a slight chip in its handle. Again the door creaked, sending a slight breeze down the countertop. The smell of all that breakfast food wafted his way.

"You know, maybe some eggs would be good."

She nodded.

"And, uh, bacon?"

"You asking or telling?"

"Telling. Bacon."

She spun on an efficient heel, took one step before he called out, "Toast or biscuits?"

181

She waved over her head, and he noted her fingers were long, like Meg's. She most likely knew enough about her customers to give them the right kind of breakfast.

Sipping the coffee — which tasted fresh and good — he turned a little on the stool and took in the place. Framed pictures told the story of the past three decades. High school kids in letterman sweaters, football jerseys, homecoming crowns, and prom dresses lined the walls. He thought about getting closer to see the details, but worried his red-vinyl island might become occupied in his absence, so he squinted instead.

The style had changed — long skirts became short on the girls, long hair became cropped on the boys — but the poses generally stayed the same. And, from what he could tell, the backgrounds did, too.

She set down a white plate whose sturdy porcelain matched his cup. Steam curled from a pile of eggs, two biscuits smothered in gravy bearing bits of sausage, a mess of bacon, and a serving of grits.

"I didn't order —"

"Trust me." She walked away with more assurance than a Banty rooster.

Since it wouldn't be worth the trouble to argue with a local — much less one who worked at the most popular business in town — he picked up a fork and dug in. The eggs tasted like heaven in his mouth, slick with butter and dotted with salt. He cut a biscuit and tried not to moan when the gravy made his taste buds sing. The old timers might wonder about a guy in business clothes moaning over gravy.

But had they tasted *this* gravy? Nashville diners better watch out if whoever owned this place decided to take his recipes to the city.

He let the lull of conversation surround him, enjoying too much the ability to sit in silence while others hobnobbed. No one here knew him. Right now, he loved it. No one knew he had a wife at home recovering from brain surgery and three kids whose lives were stuck on a roller coaster. They didn't expect him to come up with answers or hold their hands or tell them everything would be okay — or not, if that's what he thought they wanted to hear.

For all they cared, he could walk out of here and drop dead in the parking lot, so long as he wasn't on Wimpy's property and didn't die from food poisoning. Great satisfaction suffused him.

"*Now* you look like a man ready to face the day."

Her husky voice reminded him of the

actress who played opposite Bruce Willis on *Moonlighting* back in the day. What was her name?

"Feeling better?"

He looked at his plate, startled to realize he'd consumed everything on it. "Much better. Thanks."

"Just doing my job." She took the plate and dumped it onto a stack of others waiting for the dishwasher. Wiping those long, slender fingers on a towel, she leaned one hip against the counter. "You new in town or passing through?"

"Passing through." The words slipped free without hesitation, coming easier than the truth.

She nodded. "On the way to?"

He wondered at her curiosity. Then again, small towns weren't anywhere to hide if you meant to hide long. "Oh, I don't know yet. Guess I'll figure it out when I get there."

Her blue eyes settled on his. Did she know him? Had they run into each other in Stars Hill. Shoot, she might know one of the sisters. "Hmm, I wouldn't have pegged you for a drifter," she finally said.

"Guess looks can be deceiving."

"If you don't look deep enough, they'll deceive you every time."

"Sounds like you've been burned."

"Got the scars to prove it."

He sipped his coffee. Weeks of stillness and quiet in his house had left his conversational skills rusty.

"I'm Karen." She held a hand out to him.

He took it. Felt her cool skin. "Jamison."

"A business name to go with the business clothes." She took her hand back.

He smiled. "Something like that."

"Think you'll be back this way anytime soon?"

"I don't know. You have a recommendation if I am?"

"Just wondering if you'll answer to Jay. A body's got to watch all that effort in syllables, you know. Caffeine will only get you so far." She winked. It went nicely with the dimples.

He found himself returning her smile. "If I'm ever back this way, I'll remember to answer to the right name."

"Glad we've got that settled." She placed a ticket in front of him. "Nice meeting you, Jay."

"You too, Karen." He placed a bill on the table, enough to cover the meal and a healthy tip. He'd have left the money for the conversation alone.

She gave him a small wave good-bye and moved on down the counter to refill a coffee cup. He watched her for a second, noting the admiration in each man's eyes when she stopped and served coffee or a helping of words.

Feeling more ready to face the day with a bellyful of good food and better coffee, he rose and went for the door.

The entire way back to Stars Hill, Jamison wondered at such a strange occurrence. What had driven him to Greenfield? Obviously, *he* had driven him, but what controlled his mind to do such a thing? God? Did God know he'd been about to lose it and point him in that direction?

It had to have been. Not that Jamison had ever subscribed to the whole God literally pushing a person down a path, but he considered now that the idea might have some merit. Meg always said God had shoved him into her path that day at school. He *hadn't* meant to go that way. Her locker was nowhere near his chemistry class. But that day, that hour, he'd walked down that hallway. Seeing her leaning up against a bank of lockers had made him notice a girl who'd been there all along.

So, nearly two decades later, perhaps God decided he needed another push. Did Karen believe in God? If she did, she'd get a kick out of his believing God sent him to that diner.

Not that he had any intention of going back there. But in case God pointed the car that direction again, he'd have a conversation starter ready.

He turned right at the light onto University then left at the next onto Lindell. A block later he parked the car and killed the engine.

Eager to see his kids' smiling faces now that he possessed a smile to return, he opened the door and stepped onto the street. The business day had begun without him. Cars and trucks moseyed up and down Lindell, pulling into spaces and emptying out errand-runners intent on finishing the To Do list before lunchtime. Jamison would bet the thirty dollars in his pocket that many of them ended up at Clay's for lunch before heading home.

He climbed the steps to the apartment over the diner that Clay and Tandy shared. The door popped open before he could knock.

"Daddy!" Savannah threw her arms around his leg. "You came back for us!"

Having never been a child with abandonment issues, he wondered if her doubt stemmed from the changes in Meg. "Of course I came back for you, Sweet Pea." He kissed the top of her blonde curls. "I couldn't leave my little ones to the wolves to raise, now could I?"

"Who are you calling a wolf?" Clay came through the entryway of the kitchen. "We much prefer canine companions around here. Don't we, missy?" He wiggled his eyebrows and Savannah squealed.

"Daddy! Save me!" She reached for Jamison and he scooped her up, shielding her from her "evil" canine uncle.

"I'll save you, Princess!" With energy from eggs, biscuits, and sausage, he dashed into the living room. "Where is your court?"

"Through there!" Savannah pointed to Tandy and Clay's bedroom.

Jamison followed her direction and galloped through the door as best he could with a five-year-old in his arms. He found James and Hannah lying on their stomachs on the bed, chins in hands, eyes fixed on *Finding Nemo.*

"Daddy!" Hannah's squeal registered about four notes higher than her sister's. She scrambled off the bed and clasped her short arms around his knee.

"Daddy's saving me from the evil canine companion," Savannah declared.

Hannah only gave her a quizzical look.

Jamison doubted "canine companion" registered in a two-year-old's mind. He patted Savannah's back and deposited her on the bed.

"Okay, you three. Time for us to get out of Aunt Tandy and Uncle Clay's hair and head home."

"But I don't *want* to go home!" The vehemence that poured from James made Jamison step back.

"Why not?"

James kept his eyes on the screen. "It's no fun there."

Well, he couldn't argue with that. He also didn't think an eight-, five-, and two-year-old would appreciate a lecture that home didn't always serve as the happiest place in the world. But then, why *shouldn't* home be the happiest place in the world? At least for children. Maybe happiness was less important than the security of continuity. Of having parents who wouldn't change even if a kid decided to throw a tantrum or life dealt a serious blow. It ought to be a safe enough place to break down and know Mom or Dad would be there with a smile and the affirmation that everything would work out.

But his children's mother had broken down. And he was left to pick up her pieces and give them a safe place during the process.

The eggs turned to lead in his stomach. Back to reality, which didn't mean he couldn't give the kids a few more minutes of escape.

He stretched out on the bed alongside James. Savannah lay down on his other side, sandwiching him. Hannah crawled atop his back. Kid love surrounded him.

"You know, guys, Mommy's going to be okay. We're all going to be okay."

James looked at him with eyes too knowing for an eight-year-old. The light of hope hadn't been snuffed out yet, though. Jamison saw it wavering in the backs of those gold-flecked eyes that were mirror images of his dad's. "You think?"

"I *know.*"

James nodded. "Okay." He refocused on the movie.

Jamison settled in. Marlin had almost arrived at 42 Wallaby Way in the search for Nemo. James needed to know he would go to the ends of the earth — just like Marlon did for Nemo — to keep the kids safe. So he'd lie here and watch with them. And, afterwards, he'd tell them again that Mom would be okay. That they would all be okay.

And he'd make them believe it.
Even if he didn't believe it himself.

FIFTEEN

"Come on, Tandy, it's Friday night." Clay scooped dinner dishes off their table and carried them to the sink. "Remember when we spent every Friday night at Heartland? We haven't been there in, well, look at our son and count back the months to his birthday."

Tandy pulled the tray off of Clayton's high chair and set it on the table. "Clay, look, I miss our nights out just as much as you do. But we can't take Clayton to Heartland. The music is so loud, it would burst his little eardrums. I can't believe you'd even suggest it." She balanced the baby on her hip.

"I didn't. We could see if Joy can watch Clayton. Or Kendra. Kendra's always telling us she wants to babysit."

"You know as well as I do that Kendra and Darin are probably at Heartland right now. They're not going to give up their own fun so that we can go out. And Joy's busy with Maddie. We certainly can't leave Clayton with Meg. Who knows what kind of mood she's in?"

Clay sighed and squirted dishwashing liquid into the sink. "I feel like all we ever do is feed the baby, change the baby, buy stuff for the baby, play with the baby, sit with the baby, and plan our lives around the baby."

"What did you think it would be like? That we'd park him in a corner whenever we wanted to go out?"

He hated it when she got that tone. "No! Don't talk down to me, Tandy."

"Well, how do you want me to talk to you?"

"I am not a child. There's no cause to speak to me as if you're my parent."

"Unless I'm the only one in this place acting like a parent."

"You think I'm not acting like a parent? What other thirty-year-old man do you know who is at home on a Friday night washing dishes and arguing with his wife?"

"*That's* parenthood?" She slapped her thigh. "How about you come whip off your shirt and offer Clayton your breast for dinner? Or stick a pump to your chest and let it suck milk out while you read a magazine and pretend nothing is trying to disconnect you from a particularly sensitive part of your body?"

"So you're a better parent because you breastfeed? I *can't* do that, Tandy. I'm not exactly equipped for the situation."

"How utterly convenient for you."

He dumped dishes in the sink and began scrubbing. He didn't want to fight with her, he wanted to go out and have a little fun. Like they used to. Before Clayton and all the responsibility of raising a child. He didn't regret having the little guy, not for a second. But they had to find a balance that allowed for fun *and* parenthood.

"Look, I only wanted to see if we could plan for a night out for ourselves."

Tandy closed her eyes. She looked older now. Like an adult. Less like the girl he'd married two years ago. He figured babies did that to people. He knew he'd found wrinkles and gray hair in the mirror lately.

"A night out for ourselves would be good." She planted a quick peck on Clayton's cheek. "I'm not saying I don't want us to spend time together."

"Good." He didn't know what else to say. With all the worry over Meg and all the work over Clayton, he felt like they'd gone from age thirty to fifty in two-point-five

194

seconds. Where did the fun of being married go?

Out the window, along with the joy of sleeping through the night.

Tandy walked out of the room, no doubt to get comfortable in the nursery rocker and feed Clayton the rest of his dinner.

Clay rinsed the clean dishes and set them in the drain board to dry. He knew he'd put them away in the morning, as he'd done every day since Clayton's birth. Having a C-section had taken a lot out of Tandy. It only seemed right to pick up the slack while she recovered and took on the duties like breastfeeding. He couldn't do that, so he did what he could — kept the house clean and the laundry done. He didn't do as good a job as she did, but his military background served them well.

But seven months had gone by. Seven months of dishes and dirty clothes and vacuuming and dusting every waking moment — at least, the moments he didn't spend cooking and cleaning and serving Stars Hill in the diner. And now they packed in taking care of Meg's kids so she and Jamison could have some time together or so she could have some quiet time.

He didn't think he'd asked too much to simply find some time for themselves. Zelda and Jack would have no problem watching Clayton. They only had to halfway hint and Jack would jump at the chance to babysit his youngest grandson.

Instead, here he sat with dishwater hands, while Zelda and Jack probably lived it up down at Heartland. He missed the country dance place he and Tandy had frequented in their dating days. The feel of Tandy in his arms, twirling around a dance floor, had faded almost completely and he wanted that back. Wanted to see her with that copper-colored hair all loose and wild, fire in her eyes and a bounce in her step. Her ready smile didn't come so readily these last few months — worn away, no doubt, from night after night of sleep interrupted by a hungry or fitful newborn.

He felt he'd prepared before Clayton arrived. Read all the books and heeded the warnings. Now he knew — no preparation on earth was adequate for parenthood. It was trial by fire, and if you didn't keep up, the whole thing would burn to the ground.

He put the last dish in the drain board and wrung out the dishrag. He moved to the table, wiped off crumbs, tossed the rag into the sink. Another day's chores done. The moon rose high in the sky outside their living room window.

He moved to the window. What happened to those magical nights of staring at those stars? Of his love- and wonder-filled life with Tandy?

"Hey there, stranger. What are you staring at?"

His arm slipped around Tandy, who appeared at his side, with ease. "Just staring. Where's Clayton?"

Her arm snaked around his waist and her head rested in the crook of his arm. "Lying on his activity mat, staring up at all kinds of shiny, brightly-colored objects. He's good for at least ten minutes."

Clay chuckled, planted a kiss on the top of her head. "I'm sorry I got so upset."

"No, I understand where you're coming from. I'm a little tired of only being a mom, too."

"You are?"

"Yeah. It's not that I don't love the little guy to pieces. I do."

"Me, too."

"But I've been missing you, too."

He squeezed her shoulders, so grateful to have her that he couldn't come up with words.

"We can call Daddy tomorrow. I'm sure he's out at Heartland tonight with Zelda, so tonight is out. But maybe he could take

Clayton next Thursday and we can go out to Joe's. See what new jazz singer he's got these days."

Clay swallowed. "Great idea."

"Yeah, I try to have one at least once a month."

"You're paid up, then, for the next thirty days." He looked down at those beautiful green eyes of hers. The same eyes Clayton looked at him with, though his hadn't turned quite Tandy's shade yet. He slid a finger beneath her chin and pulled her lips to his. "I love you."

"I love you, too," she whispered, meeting his lips.

They didn't kiss like this anymore. Not since Clayton. Not a whole lot since *making* Clayton because her sex drive had taken a vacation for most of those nine months. He reveled in the feel of her lips against his. His hand moved behind her neck, holding her to him so he could deepen the kiss.

She matched his intensity, and he knew she'd missed this as well. She broke the kiss and leaned back slightly. "You know, we could ask Daddy to watch Clayton and just stay home." Her voice was thick with meaning. "I hear there's *great* entertainment around here."

He chuckled. "Not a chance. I haven't

198

gotten to show you off in months and I want to take you out like you deserve. Let somebody else cook dinner, clean up after us, and provide entertainment."

"I don't know." Her other arm encircled his waist as well and he pulled her into a full embrace while she smiled. "I'm really pretty happy with the entertainment here."

He kissed her again. Their conversation took a backseat as sensation traveled through his body with her touch. They'd wasted years apart while he chased his dreams and she chased hers. He didn't want to lose one moment with this woman now that they were together.

Several minutes later he pulled away. "I agree with you about the entertainment here. Maybe we'll just have dinner somewhere else and come on home."

"*Now* you're talking." She started to kiss him again, but stopped at the sound of the phone.

He groaned. "Let's ignore it."

"Yeah, because I'm definitely a woman who ignores a ringing phone." She swatted at his chest and backed out of his embrace. "We haven't drifted *that* far apart have we? That you've forgotten who you married?"

"Never." He watched her hips while she walked across the living room and snatched the phone up from its cradle. "Tell whoever it is we're not interested and come back over here. We've got at least five more minutes before Clayton realizes he's figured everything out on that toy."

She giggled and pressed the phone's Talk button. "Hello."

"Tomorrow?" She arched an eyebrow his way. "I guess I can, sure. I'll have to bring Clayton, though. Clay's got to run the diner."

She waited.

"Okay, see you then."

She put the phone back on the handset and came back to him. He folded his arms around her, loving the way she fit perfectly. "So, where are you going tomorrow and which sister needs you?"

"All of them. We're scrapping at Daddy's tomorrow."

"With Zelda?" The sisters hadn't quite come around to welcoming Zelda with open arms yet.

Tandy shrugged. "I guess she'll be there, yeah."

"You know, she's your stepmother now. You girls should start thinking about befriending her at some point."

Tandy sighed and leaned her head against his chest. Her words came muffled. "We

200

know. It's hard, though. She's so strange. None of us can figure out what Daddy sees in her. She's about the farthest thing from Momma he could have found."

"Maybe that's the attraction."

"Hmm. Maybe."

"Either way, they're married. *Why* doesn't matter so much as the fact that they *are* married. And if I know Zelda, she really wants to have a relationship with the sisters."

Tandy snuggled further into him. "Let's see how it goes and go from there, okay?"

He smiled and tightened his arms around her. "Okay."

He had enough to worry about with adjusting to parenthood and helping Jamison out with Meg. Taking on the Zelda issue — well, he just didn't have that kind of room in his life right now.

Sixteen

Saturday morning sunshine streamed through the bedroom window, lighting the backs of Tandy's eyelids to a burnt orange. She cracked one eye open.

Ugh. Morning comes too early.

She laid her arms across her eyes, but the sunlight only poured itself around the cracks of her makeshift barrier. Turning her head, she noted the time on the alarm clock: 5:58. No doubt Clay had already made his way downstairs to the diner and, even now, stood at the stove scrambling eggs and flipping sausages for Stars Hill's hungry citizens.

She pushed the covers aside and swung her legs over the bed. Might as well get started with the day. If Clayton stayed true to form, she had a good half hour before his morning feeding. Maybe a long, hot shower would give her muscles some energy.

She'd been standing in the water for five

minutes before she remembered — scrapping day. The sisters would be at Daddy's in an hour and she stood wasting time with a list of things to accomplish before she could leave.

Rinsing off faster than Danica Patrick drove the Indy 500, Tandy jumped out of the shower and snagged a towel. Clayton always took at least half an hour to eat breakfast. If she tried to cut him off before he finished, all she'd get for her trouble would be an irritable baby an hour later. She pulled on a nursing gown and walked down the short hallway to Clayton's room.

He slept in peaceful escape beneath the wildly colored mobile, one fist curled up by a tiny ear, the other at his mouth. Love blossomed in her heart, rolling across her as it did nearly every morning that she came to him. He might have turned their entire lives upside down, but he made the adventure worthwhile. She gently scooped him up and nestled him close.

"Good morning, sweet prince."

Clayton cracked one eye open, much as she'd done earlier. A chuckle escaped her lips. "I know. Mornings aren't exactly my thing right now, either." Her feet sank into the carpet as she walked the few steps to a giant mahogany rocker. This and the crib were their big baby splurges. Everything else she'd either made herself or begged one of the sisters to help her make.

Kendra's mural of a circus big top, complete with elephants, lions, tigers, bears, monkeys, and clowns spilling out of a Volkswagen bug, filled one wall. Tandy and Meg had sewn fabric balloon cutouts in red, blue, yellow, and green. Cotton valances of matching colored polka dots hung from the tops of the windows. White café rods split the panes horizontally in the center with striped fabric hanging from them to block out some of the morning light. The white background didn't do a great job of acting as a shade, but Tandy hadn't wanted to create a dungeon. Clayton needed to see the sunshine.

She settled into the rocker and got Clayton in the right position for breakfast. He cooed a bit before latching on. "Oh, you sweet boy. I love you, too." Resting her head against the back of the rocker, Tandy planned her day.

Scrapping this morning with the sisters. And Zelda. Couldn't forget that Zelda would be there. Tandy's shoulders tensed and she forced them back down. She really had no reason to *dis*like Zelda and couldn't quite put her finger on the problem. Maybe

Zelda didn't seem real, even though she and Daddy were married now and Zelda lived in the house Momma had shared with Daddy for decades. Or perhaps Zelda had such a different personality than Momma that Tandy couldn't find room in her life for it.

Tandy sighed and looked at Clayton. If anything ever happened to her and Clay remarried, would she want Clayton to accept the new woman into his life? Oh, she'd want him to be kind and considerate, of course. The sisters were kind and considerate to Zelda. Momma would have nothing to correct them on regarding that front. But Tandy couldn't quite bring herself to believe she'd want Clayton having a close relationship with another Mom figure.

So that was it. Even though she'd denied it to herself, the sisters, and Clay, the problem boiled down to Zelda assuming a Mom-figure place. Momma's presence in that space so filled it that no room existed for another. And being "friends" with Daddy's wife simply didn't feel right; it didn't fit.

Clayton's skin felt silky soft beneath her fingertip when she ran it lightly down his face. Such a wonderful child. What agony Momma must have endured knowing she would soon leave her daughters behind. Tandy nearly couldn't bear the thought of Momma adjusting to such an idea. She wished she had a few more minutes with Momma to let her know they'd all turned out all right. They had their difficulties — Meg especially, right now — but they were making it.

Could Momma see them from heaven? Daddy said the Bible didn't cover that. That meant if she chose to believe Momma kept tabs on them, then there wasn't much if any Scripture to say otherwise.

Tandy took comfort in that, though she knew that believing Momma knew what the sisters experienced on a day-to-day basis was a big reason they didn't have room for Zelda. What would Momma say to that?

Momma, the epitome of Southern hospitality, would have welcomed Zelda with open arms. Tandy pictured her now, dressed in the apron she wore more days than not, arms extended to an approaching Zelda. The sight of Zelda — with her short, spiky red hair and artfully applied makeup and clinking bracelets — climbing a porch to stand beside Momma with her long, flowing locks, fresh skin, and lack of beauty accoutrements . . . Tandy couldn't help it. Laughter bubbled forth. Daddy certainly had varying tastes to find love with two such different women.

She switched Clayton to the other side and went on with her mental planning. Assuming they scrapped the customary few hours, she'd have a couple left before dinnertime to run to Darnelle's for groceries. If only she'd put that pad of paper by the rocker like her parenting magazine suggested, she could make a grocery list right now. No sense making one in her head — she'd only forget it by this afternoon.

Okay, so scrapping, grocery store, then dinner. No time to go by the office and check on Sisters, Ink memberships, which was fine given that today was Saturday and not a workday.

She hummed "When We All Get to Heaven," one of Momma's favorite old hymns, and rocked to the rhythm. By the second round of all four verses, Clayton had filled his belly and turned his head away. Tandy stood and returned to her bedroom to get dressed for what promised to be a long day of activity.

Settling Clayton in his bouncy seat, she punched the button to activate music. Clayton smiled as soon as he heard the notes. Definitely a musical kid. She slid on jeans — no time to shave her legs — and a blue sleeveless button-up top. Her brown sandals completed the look and she had herself and Clayton out the door by 7:45. She descended the stairs and entered the diner through its back door.

Clay stood at the stove where she'd earlier envisioned him, a spatula in one hand. Bacon sizzled from the stovetop and "I Heard It through the Grapevine" poured from the nearby radio's speakers.

"Are you revisiting the wonder years?"

He looked up and grinned. "Needed a little Motown to get me going this morning. You two are out the door early."

"Scrapping at Daddy's, remember?"

"Oh, yeah. Want to take some breakfast to the girls?"

"If I show up without donuts, I'm not sure they'll let me in."

"You know where they are. I'd get them for you, but it's a full house out there and everybody came in craving eggs today."

Tandy walked through the kitchen to the doorway that led into the eating area. "No problem. You cook. I'll steal breakfast."

She left him singing along with the radio and entered the eating area. He hadn't been kidding — every chair was filled. The loud din of conversation filled the room and drowned out Clay's music. Good grief.

What a madhouse! How did Clay present a cheerful face to so many people this early in the morning? She shook her head. Thank goodness that was his duty and not hers. So long as Stars Hill needed food, they'd be able to pay the bills and put a little back for Clayton's Harvard fund.

Sitting Clayton on the bar, she reached under the counter and retrieved a donut box. The glass-domed containers scattered across the bar area gave her good pickings to mollify the sisters. Chocolate-covered, sprinkled, and plain old glazed ought to do the trick. She filled the box, closed the lid, and once again scooped up Clayton. Time to hit the road.

A few customers caught her eye and waved. She nodded and kept moving. No time for chitchat. Scrapping time awaited.

"We're outta here, babe," she said as they walked back through the kitchen door.

"Be careful. Love you."

She planted a quick peck on his lips, careful to keep Clayton on her hip away from the sizzling stovetop. "Love you, too. See ya tonight for dinner. I'm cooking."

He arched a brow. "Was that your warning?"

"Don't get excited. It's spaghetti."

"Ah, one of your two specialty dishes."

"If by specialty you mean the only ones I know how to make then, yes, one of my two specialty dishes."

He smiled. "See you tonight."

She left the diner and entered the bright sunshine outside, which served to wipe away the last vestiges of morning fog from her brain. Drat, she forgot to grab caffeine from the diner.

Daddy better be stocked up in sodas or she'd be making a return trip to town.

"I'm here!" Tandy struggled to get up the steps and in the front door with her arms laden down by Clayton, the donut box, and a bag of newly purchased scrapping products.

"Oh! Let me help you." Zelda took the donut box from her hands.

"Thanks. I wouldn't have made it much farther."

"You were doing a fine job."

What was up with this new, helpful Zelda? Tandy tried to get a look at Zelda's face but couldn't.

"The other sisters are already here and upstairs. How about I trade you the donuts for Clayton and get him settled on the floor with some toys while you go get to scrapping?"

Momma taught them all to never look a gift horse in the mouth, so Tandy ignored the clanging bells in her brain warning her that someone had traded Zelda in for some look-alike, and handed Clayton over. Despite Tandy's inability to bond with the woman, Clayton always went willingly into Zelda's arms. Maybe the plethora of shiny objects kept his interest. Or the craziness of the hair. Either way, Clayton reached out for Zelda as soon as Tandy leaned him in her direction.

"Hello, cutie," Zelda greeted the seven-month-old.

Clayton gurgled back, making Zelda and Tandy laugh.

"Are you the cutest little thing in the world?" Zelda held Clayton up in the air, turning him side to side. "Just the cutest little thing ever?"

Clayton responded by jamming a fist in his mouth and sucking.

Zelda lowered him to her hip and smiled. "I'll take that as a yes."

Since Clayton seemed to be in capable hands, Tandy said, "Thanks, Zelda," and went for the stairs. As she came into the scrapping room, she saw the sisters already gathered around the scrapping table working intently on their layouts.

"Hi, girls." Tandy bounded across the room to the supply shelf, pulling down her supplies while the sisters greeted her.

Kendra shoved photos around with one long purple fingernail in an attempt to get the best layout arrangement. "Where's Clayton?"

"Downstairs with Zelda. I'm telling you, I don't know what kind of spell she has over that kid, but he thinks she's the best thing since sliced bread."

Kendra looked up. "It's the jewelry. All that shiny stuff." She went back to her photos.

"Hmm. That's what I thought."

Joy slid a completed page into a page protector. "Or perhaps Clayton recognizes someone who functions at his level."

"Joy Lasky! I can't believe you'd say such."

Joy raised a delicate shoulder. "A spade is a spade, Tandy."

Tandy carried her supplies over to her spot at the table and settled in. "Still, you never speak negatively about someone."

"Well, Mother wouldn't be pleased with me saying it aloud, but she would agree to the statement's truth."

Tandy cast a glance over at Meg, unsure if her silence came from a difficult mood or particularly focused concentration. Seeing

Meg's lip gathered between her teeth, she assumed the latter. "So, what's going on with everybody? We haven't gotten together in so long and I'm out of touch."

"That's 'cause you're stuck in Mommy World," Kendra mumbled.

"Hey, I can't help it if my seven-month-old requires more time than my adult sisters," Tandy shot back, stung by the accusation and reminded of her conversation with Clay from the night before.

Kendra gave her a curious glance. "I wasn't accusing you of anything, T. Just making an observation."

"Yeah, well —" Tandy shifted on her seat — "observe somebody else."

"Motherhood a touchy topic?"

"Something like that."

"Is Clayton sleeping through the night?" Joy pulled photos from a photo box and began sorting them.

"Some nights. Other nights he thinks every time the hour turns over he should wake up and announce it to the household."

Joy nodded sympathetically. "I know. Maddie lulls us into happiness with three or four nights of full sleep and then it's a week of nighttime fussiness."

"Do you ever think about tearing your hair out?"

"Only around four o'clock every morning following every hard night."

Tandy chuckled. "I hear you on that, sister."

"I remember those long nights," Meg said. "Jamison and I thought we'd never see a full night's sleep again. Ever."

"How old was Hannah when she finally slept through the night?"

Meg pouted her lips. "A year and a half."

Tandy threw her arms on the table and plopped her head down. "I don't think I can survive motherhood."

"Now who's the drama queen?"

Tandy turned her head to look Kendra in the face. "You're not allowed to be mean until you have children of your own."

"Then we could be waiting a while. Or forever."

"You and Darin aren't going to have children?" Joy ran a tape runner down a photo.

"We're not sure."

"Oh, Kendra, you must have children."

"Not in this country. We're free to be just the two of us all our lives if we so choose. Ain't America grand?"

"But there's nothing in the world like motherhood," Meg protested. "I can't imagine my life without my kids."

Kendra shrugged. "I'm not sure I'm made to be a mom."

"Do you have a uterus?"

"Ha ha. Very funny."

"What do you think you're supposed to have to be a mom?"

"Compassion? Patience? Understanding? A hole in my head?" Kendra tapped her head.

Tandy sat back up. "You get that stuff when they put the baby in your arms." She held up a hand and stopped Kendra's retort. "No, I'm serious. Would you have labeled me a patient person before I gave birth? Of course not. You develop whatever you need when you figure out a little being is depending on you completely."

Kendra tilted her head and looked at the ceiling. After a moment, she nodded. "Okay, I'll give you that. But don't you miss the things you and Clay used to do? Darin and I haven't seen you at Heartland or Joe's since Clayton was born."

"I know." Tandy shifted again. "And I'm not saying that's easy for us. We were barely married before we got pregnant. But dancing on Friday night isn't the entirety of our marriage."

Kendra shook her head. "Maybe not. Doesn't mean it shouldn't be a part. It was a big part — a regular part — before baby came along."

Tandy shut up. No argument existed for her to combat Kendra's words. Clay had said the same things to her last night, and both of them were right. That didn't make it any easier, just more real.

She envied those Hollywood celebrities who jetted all over the country with their kids — and nannies — in tow. What would it be like to have a nanny? Someone to help with the laundry and the meals and the house. Or even take care of Clayton for a few hours every day so that she could focus on the business, Clay could focus on the diner, and they could focus on each other?

Not that their budget would ever allow such a thing, but the thought was entertaining.

"What are you thinking about?" Kendra pushed her thick hair out of her face. "You've got that smile on your face."

"Oh, nothing."

Kendra's knowing look came a second before she opened her mouth. "Um hmm. I'll bet it's nothing."

Tandy sighed. "Okay, since you don't know how to let something go, I was thinking about how nice it would be if we had a nanny. Not a full-time nanny, but someone part-time. You know, to watch Clayton so I can run to the store or spend a few hours at the office or be with Clay."

"A nanny." Joy sat back on her stool. "*That's* what we need."

"Yeah, and what our budgets can't afford."

"Jenny might want to do some nanny work," Meg offered. "She's done an excellent job on our house and gets along great with the kids."

"Jenny?" Tandy raised an eyebrow. "Jenny who?"

"Wow, you *are* out of the loop," Kendra teased. "Meg went and got herself a housekeeper."

"Meg did no such thing. Meg's *husband* went and got himself a housekeeper."

"You have a housekeeper?" Tandy shoved her photos away and rested her arms on the table. Propping her chin on her hand, she gave her sister a wide-eyed look. "Do tell."

"It's Jenny Sanders. You know her."

"I do! I didn't know she cleaned people's houses."

"Yeah, we heard she had been looking for some work along those lines and Jamison had just about had enough with cleaning, cooking, taking care of the kids, and working, so we hired her. It's not as if I could take over the duties."

Tandy refrained from asking why. Meg had two months of recovery behind her. When would she begin to assume her role in the house again? Or had she found a convenient way to quit?

"So, she does a good job?"

"She does a *great* job. I'm sure we won't have her around forever. I know I'll get back into the swing of things soon, but she's a godsend right now."

Tandy sent a silent thank-you heavenward for Meg's intention toward the future. "Do you know how long you'll need her?"

Meg shook her head. "There's no way to know for sure. I'm betting a few months, maybe four. I don't know when this leg will let me make it up and down the stairs easily enough to do the cleaning and chase the kids. We've started thinking about selling the place and getting a one-level house."

Joy's head jerked up. "You're thinking about selling your house? Since when? You did not mention that to me."

"I didn't?" Meg's forehead wrinkled. "I could have sworn I did."

"You did not. I cannot believe you would sell that house. You've lived in it for ten years. The children have never known anything else!"

218

"They've also never had a mother whose leg didn't work right." Meg's voice took on a steely tone. "We all have to adjust as we can."

Joy abruptly shut her mouth. Tandy watched, but it didn't take an Einstein to see, where Meg's recovery was concerned, Joy wouldn't be pushing boundaries anytime soon.

Tandy cleared her throat. "Well, whenever you no longer need her services, please let me know. Clay and I could use some help. I don't know if we can afford her, but I'm willing to try."

Meg nodded.

They heard clomping on the stairs and turned. Zelda's red hair appeared a split second before her face. "Hello, girls. How's it going up here?"

"Fine," they chorused.

"Everything okay with Clayton?" Tandy said.

Zelda waved a hand. "Oh, he's fine. Fell asleep on me, so I laid him down on your old bed and put pillows around him."

"Thanks."

"My pleasure. I wanted to let you know, though, that I'm headed out. There are a few garage sales over in Greenfield I wanted to check out."

"Oh! Okay. Searching for anything in particular?"

"Not really. I like looking through everybody else's junk, though. Never know when you might find a treasure." Her eye took on a gleam.

Tandy smiled. The hunt for a good bargain was something all the sisters shared. "Good luck, then. And thanks again for watching Clayton."

"Anytime." Zelda made her way back down the stairs.

"You sure seemed friendly," Kendra said.

"We're *supposed* to be friendly, Ken. She's our stepmother."

Kendra reared her head back as if she'd been slapped. "I don't need to be told that."

"Ladies, calm down." Joy, ever the peacemaker, cut in.

"Well, she made it sound like I'm a kid who needs to be told how to act instead of a grown woman with the right to act however I want, whenever I want, toward whoever I want."

"*Whom*ever," Tandy corrected.

"No, it's *who*ever. I don't even think *whomever* is a word."

Both turned to Joy, the Grammar Queen, for a decision, but Joy shook her head. "No, I will not."

"Oh, come on," Kendra whined.

"No. Look it up for yourselves. That way you'll remember it next time."

"*Now* who's acting like a mother?" Tandy said.

Kendra went back to her work. "Ugh."

Tandy let the matter go. She'd started the weekend by fighting with Clay. She didn't want to fight with her sisters, too. What was wrong with her these days that so many conversations became fights? Maybe everybody was on edge because of Meg's surgery. But that had been two months ago and, looking at her now, the only evidence Tandy could see was Meg's handkerchief-covered head where long blonde hair used to be. Meg seemed fine today.

She prayed that didn't mean tomorrow would be different. According to Clay, Jamison now lived with a woman who went from high to low before he even knew she'd been happy. That must be horrible to live with, even if it *did* come from the ever-affable Meg. Actually that probably made it harder. If Meg had been temperamental before — say, like her or Kendra — then the change wouldn't be so drastic.

But poor Jamison had married a woman who always saw the glass as half full. The fact that she could now see it as not only empty but of never deserving a fill-up of anything but coal or sand had to make for a big adjustment in their marriage.

Tandy pulled her materials back and picked up a piece of paper. "So, how are things with Jamison?" The words didn't come out quite as lighthearted as she'd intended.

"They're fine." Meg squinted at her. "Why? Did he say otherwise to Clay?"

"No, suspicious one. You just hadn't talked about him lately, so I thought I'd ask."

"You haven't talked about Clay, either. How's he doing?"

"He's exhausted and needing a break from fatherhood, thanks for asking."

"Well, Jamison's exhausted and needing a break from husbandhood, thanks for asking."

Kendra stood and walked over to the towers of paper lined against the supply wall. "A break from husbandhood? What does that mean?"

"I'm not positive." Meg set her tape runner down. "But if I had to live with me for the past two months, I think I'd be about ready to throw in the towel now."

"Why?"

"Let's just say it hasn't been an easy recovery."

Kendra selected a few sheets of patterned paper and returned to the table. "Again, why?"

Meg took in a deep breath. "I'm an emotional wreck all the time. I know I am. I know I'm irrational and moody and difficult, and even though I know it and I know when it's happening, I also can't do much about it. It's like my body just takes over and reacts however it wants without consulting me first."

"Has he said anything to you about it?" Tandy slipped a piece of paper into her cutter.

Meg shook her head. "No, not really. He tried once, but I got mad — I couldn't stop it! — and he hasn't brought it up since. But I know it's wearing on him. I looked at him yesterday and wondered how he'd aged ten years since I looked at him last. Then I realized *I* put those new wrinkles there."

"Hey, you can't help that you got a brain tumor. It's not like you were out one day and said, 'I know. I'll pick up a brain tumor on my way home. See how that changes things up.' "

"Oh, Tandy, thanks for that." Meg closed her eyes. "This whole thing — we weren't

223

prepared for it. We didn't see it coming and it hit us broadside. We're floundering around like somebody dumped us overboard . . . and we're not sure if we remember how to swim."

Tandy wished she had some words of comfort, but this was out of her league. She and Clay had a hard time dealing with something as normal as the birth of their first child. What if one of them had to go through what Meg went through? "I wish I knew what to tell you to make it all better."

Meg gave a laugh laced with a touch of bitterness. "We'll figure it out at some point. He seems happier these days, a little less tense since he went back to the office. I think being away from me, getting back to his old life, helps."

"Men like to be needed —" Joy reached for one of her photos — "That's what all the books I've read say. He probably feels needed at the office, and those are needs for which he has answers. The needs at home — I'm guessing here, but they're likely ones that he isn't as familiar with and maybe doesn't know how to handle. That wouldn't be easy for anybody, but especially for Jamison who likes to do for everybody."

Meg considered that a second. "You're probably right, but there's nothing I can do about it. I don't know what to ask him to do or be because I don't know myself who I am anymore or what I want to do anymore. I mean, imagine waking up and not knowing if you like chocolate ice cream or vanilla. If you prefer brownies to cake. If you want to dress in cotton or silk."

"Mmm, a blank slate," Kendra mused. "That could be nice."

"It's not nice, it's horrible. Not knowing yourself? Your own likes and dislikes? Before the surgery, I loved Jamison. I remember loving him. I remember our good times together. I even remember our bad times together. But now he gets on my last ever-loving nerve."

"How?"

"In a million ways. Like having a toothbrush that turns on and won't shut off until he's brushed a full two minutes."

"Good dental hygiene annoys you?"

"The inability to bend a rule annoys me. You should see this man get a slice of bread out of the bag." Meg mimicked his actions. "He untwists the tie, lays it just so on the counter, removes the heel — which he knows he doesn't like and which I'm still undecided on — lays it on a napkin. Then he takes out the piece he wants, sets it on *another* napkin, and replaces the heel on the top of the loaf. Then he twists the top of the bag, making sure to get every single molecule of air out that he possibly can, and replaces the twisty tie with as many twists as it had before. Now I ask you, is that not a little neurotic?"

Tandy whistled. "I had no idea you were married to such a freak. Call a psychiatrist, quick."

Meg bristled. "Go ahead, make fun. I'm sure I found his quirks adorable before, but now I just want him to get two slices out and put the dang bread bag back so I can make some toast before lunchtime."

Kendra pushed a brad through her paper and opened its ends to secure its position. "So the fact that Jamison is obsessed with details, cleanliness, and order annoys you?"

"Something like that. But he isn't obsessed with order and cleanliness all over the house. You should have seen the place before Jenny came. Dirty clothes heaped in the baskets, lined up outside the hall by the laundry room. Dirty dishes piled in the sink. I could write my name on the dust of the coffee table before he finally found the Pledge can.

Tandy went to get the blue ink pad. "And *he's* the one who hired Jenny to clean the house, right?"

"What's your point?"

Tandy pulled the pad from its slot next to fifty other ink pads. "Just that he couldn't figure out a way to keep the house as clean as he wanted and, instead of harping at you to do it or going batty, he found a solution and hired it. I don't know why you're upset."

Meg opened her mouth, then closed it.

"Did you think he hired Jenny for some other reason?"

Kendra's question drew Meg's attention. "I assumed it was because he didn't feel like cleaning the house anymore."

"And you got mad at him for hiring someone to do a job you've done for years, probably assuming he thought he was too good for said job?"

Meg nodded faintly. "Something like that."

Kendra tapped a fingernail on the table. "Might want to start giving the man the benefit of the doubt."

Meg didn't respond and Tandy wondered if they had taken the right tack here. Could Meg handle correction right now? Wouldn't she figure this stuff out on her own eventually? Or did she *need* them to point this stuff out to her?

She swallowed a sigh. Between Clayton

and Zelda, Tandy had enough change in her life to handle. What she didn't need was a sister who didn't act like the sister she'd always known.

But she knew better than to say *that* out loud.

Zelda saw the "Welcome to Greenfield" sign and instinctively slowed her speed. The police in this town took particular glee in handing out tickets for those breaking the ridiculous 40 mph limit. Zelda didn't know how they got away with even posting that given that this was a divided, four-lane highway, but that was small-town law enforcement for you.

She checked the address of her first garage sale of the morning and kept an eye out for Morningside Drive. With Jack busy honing his sermon at the church for tomorrow morning, the house all picked up, and the laundry done, she had nothing to do but go run errands or find some good garage sales.

She'd thought being married to Jack would give them more time together, but she spent an awful lot of time on her own. The church demanded many of his weekly hours, and when he wasn't attending to the congregation's needs, he was tending their land. That left her with time on her hands.

What she needed was a hobby. She'd tried to take up scrapbooking to be closer to the girls, but it didn't interest her — and the girls definitely didn't seem interested in making room for her at the table.

So she tried the standby old woman stuff that she never thought she would age enough to consider — knitting, quilting, crocheting, ceramics. So far, she'd dropped them all. There had to be *something* out there she could spend her time on. Maybe a charity needed a volunteer. She should look into that.

Spotting Morningside Drive, she turned the car down the lane and counted house numbers to 225. Several cars lined the curb already. Zelda parked and walked up the grassy incline to where tables full of mer-chandise stood at attention down the drive-way. She perused the goods, picked up a blue glass vase, then put it down. Something else that would need cleaning every week. Pretty, but not worth the effort.

She chuckled. That could be said of a lot of women she knew.

Women in Naples, anyway. Because, de-spite being in Stars Hill for two years, she hadn't yet found the kind of girlfriends she had in Naples. The women here looked at her as if she'd stolen their prize horse.

Which, come to think of it, she had when she'd snagged Jack's heart. If he'd wanted any of them, though, he could have had them in the ten years of singleness between Marian's passing and Zelda's coming to town.

Her eyes roamed over faded paintings, mismatched sets of China, VHS tapes, and a Thighmaster. Not a thing here she needed. She turned and headed back for the car. The other sale that had sounded interesting was located on the other side of Greenfield. She debated ditching it and going home, except that the girls were no doubt still scrapping, and she'd rather not be ignored in her own home.

Opening the car door, she returned to its still-cool interior and started the engine. Morningside Drive dumped her back out onto the highway. She turned left toward town, careful to knock her speed further to the posted 30 mph. Absolutely ridiculous.

At least 30 mph left her eyes free to check out the scenery. Who needed to keep their focus glued to the road at this speed? She came to the red light and flipped her blinker. It'd be her luck to obey the stupid speed limit and then get pulled over for a traffic violation. When the light turned green, she still looked both ways before tapping the gas and crossing the railroad tracks.

Wimpy's Diner sat on the corner, and Zelda gazed at the line of men sitting on its porch. She noted the parking lot was full and began considering a late-morning sausage biscuit when a familiar face made her slam the brakes.

What was Jamison doing in Greenfield? If he wanted breakfast, he could go down to Clay's.

Zelda's suspicious nature kicked in and she pulled the car into the parking lot. Jamison obviously hadn't seen her as he was now waving to the men on the porch as if they knew him as he walked in the front door. Did he come here often?

Maybe he had clients from Greenfield. That would make sense. Greenfield might not be big enough to have a CPA, so its townsfolk would go over to Stars Hill for that. Zelda considered the possibility of Jamison meeting a client and began to feel stupid for being so sneaky.

Then again, life had taught her that most people weren't trustworthy. They wanted to be and they tried to be, but at the end of the day the cold, hard truth hit them in the face.

So she parked the car and got out. If Jamison saw her, she could simply say the truth

— she was out at garage sales and wanted a sausage biscuit. The men on the porch tipped their hats to her and she smiled her thanks, then went inside.

It took a second for her eyes to adjust from the bright morning sunshine, but she managed to spot Jamison sitting on the last stool at the bar. He and the waitress — nearly a dead ringer for Megan — were engaged in lively conversation. While Zelda watched, the blonde threw her head back and gave a throaty laugh. Zelda saw Jamison's eyes travel the length of the woman's throat. When appreciation glinted in them, she knew her suspicions weren't entirely unfounded.

If she'd seen Jack enjoying a woman like that, she'd feel cheated.

Now desperately wanting to avoid being seen, she turned on one heel and reached for the doorknob. But she needed to be sure. She couldn't go running to Meg saying she saw Jamison getting breakfast and sharing a laugh with the waitress. Meg would first want to know why she'd been following Jamison and, given the fact that she didn't have a close relationship with Meg or any of the other sisters, she doubted Meg would believe this was a chance encounter.

Not that she even knew if there was anything *to* tell Meg.

This left her needing more information. She took her hand from the doorknob and instead took a seat in the booth closest to the door and front window. She'd rather have more distance between her and Jamison, but this was as far as she could get.

"Morning!" A high-school girl — judging from her T-shirt that read, "Go Yellowjackets!" — approached the table with order pad in hand. "WhatcanIgetcha?"

Zelda envied the girl with her shiny brown hair and wanted to tell her to enjoy it while it lasted. By sixty, that hair would be brittle and gray. That smooth face would be lined with wrinkles.

"Ma'am?"

Zelda blinked. "Oh! I'm sorry. Having a little trouble getting started this morning."

The girl gave her the universal "You-poor-old-person" look, which Zelda chose to ignore. "I'll just have a sausage biscuit and a cup of coffee, please."

"No problem."

Zelda watched the girl walk away, her step light and bouncy. When had Zelda's steps become less than that? She remembered being the happy, optimistic girl in high school and college. People often said she was the bright spot to their day. When did she become this stodgy old woman who tried to take up knitting?

Pushing the thought from her mind — she could analyze herself later — she focused on Jamison, who was still talking to the blonde. Didn't that woman have other customers to wait on? Even as Zelda watched, though, the woman kept up her conversation with Jamison while filling coffee cups the length of the counter. The appreciative glances her customers gave went unnoticed since the blonde's eyes stayed on Jamison.

And his eyes didn't seem inclined to go anywhere else, either.

Zelda clamped her lips shut. The man had a wife at home recovering from brain surgery and three children relying on *him* for stability and he was over here in Greenfield flirting with a waitress? That couldn't be right. Jack had given her the skinny on all the girls and their men — well, she knew Clay from before — and he'd said Jamison was the steadiest of them all.

But dealing with medical issues could put a strain on the healthiest of marriages. Everybody knew that. Everybody with any sense, which, judging by the rapt attention Jamison now paid to that waitress, didn't include a certain stepson-in-law of hers.

She considered going over to him to say good morning. That'd reveal his intentions quicker than anything else. Zelda had always been able to read a person's character by looking in his eyes, Would Jamison's fill with guilt if he saw her?

If they did, Meg had a whole lot to worry about.

Zelda sat back in the booth to think. Her high-schooler waitress came back, a cup of coffee in one hand and saucer laden with sausage biscuit in the other. "Here you go, ma'am. Can I get you anything else?"

Even her *voice* sounded young. Ugh.

"No, thank you." Zelda's sounded like it came from a coffin somewhere. She didn't realize until this moment that even voices aged.

The waitress nodded and went to check on her other customers. Zelda watched the sway of her long ponytail and tried not to feel three decades older than her actual age.

Hearing Jamison's deep laugh, she remembered the mission at hand and turned her eyes. The blonde was shaking her head in that flirty way Zelda had used a couple million times in her younger years, though this woman didn't look any younger than Meg.

Must be a life-long single to still have that

kind of flirty move in her repertoire. And it hadn't been wasted on Jamison, who leaned forward and said something. The blonde slapped him playfully on the shoulder, then turned and picked up plates from the window through to the kitchen.

Zelda noted that Jamison watched her every move. If he paid that much attention to Meg, maybe he wouldn't be here. But evidently a wife whose feet were firmly planted on the long, tedious road to recovery couldn't interest him like this waitress could right now.

Zelda understood, even as she wanted to go over there and hit him so hard he fell off his stool. Jack would do that the second she told him about this. And she didn't think she could *not* tell Jack about this. Who knew how far into things Jamison had crawled, but it was further than a married man should be and that meant it could go even further if it hadn't already. At some point this would come to light. The family would find out somehow — people always found out in small towns, even if the stuff to find out happened in the next small town over — and when they did they better not know that she knew ahead of time and said nothing.

Then again, this would *not* be welcome

information coming from any source, much less their daddy's second wife.

This gave her another reason to tell Jack. Let him break it to the girls. They loved him more than they loved life itself. They'd know he wasn't trying to be mean, as they would no doubt assume about her. They'd understand he was trying to do the right thing.

The fact that she knew they wouldn't give her the same benefit of the doubt rankled, but reality did that a lot and ignoring it didn't make it go away. Enough years had gone by to teach that lesson many times over.

She dug some cash out of her purse and tossed it on the table, eager now to get out before Jamison saw her. Did it even occur to him he might be spotted?

The second garage sale forgotten, Zelda got in her car and pointed it toward Stars Hill. This would not be an easy conversation to have with Jack, but she'd be darned if she would hide Jamison's secret. Let Jack handle his "sweet" girls. If they'd deigned to offer her friendship, she might be inclined to walk with Meg through this. Heaven knew she'd had some experience with it with her first husband.

But Meg and the others were happy in

their private little kinship. So Jack could deal with it.

SEVENTEEN

A crack of thunder woke him up. Jamison turned to look out the bedroom window, blinking his eyes at the bright lightning.

Great. We make it to the weekend and the bottom falls out of the sky. He closed his eyes. Would Hannah or Savannah be scared by the storm enough to come to their bedroom? Not really a question of if, he amended, but of who would arrive first. He clicked on the lamp and picked up a book.

He didn't have to wait long before Hannah came through the door, her pink polka-dotted elephant under one arm. "Hey, sweet girl, did the storm wake you up?"

Hannah nodded and hugged the elephant closer. "It's loud outside."

"Yes, it is, sweetie. Would you like to come up here with Mommy and Daddy?"

He barely had the sentence out before she climbed up the side of the bed and snuggled down between him and Meg. Meg barely stirred.

Before the surgery, one of their kids could sneeze in the next county and she'd be running out the door with a Kleenex. Now Hannah could crawl up in bed and even carry on a conversation with him, and Meg's breathing didn't miss a beat.

He realized now how many nights her sleep must have been interrupted before he began waking up with the kids. Thank heaven Hannah was two and Savannah and James had their sleeping habits down well. How did Meg ever get them through to this age? No wonder she'd had a brain tumor; her brain probably went on mutiny after all she asked it to do.

After all he'd *made* her ask it to do. Lately more and more thoughts crowded in. He couldn't deny their convincing number. He'd been a pretty lousy husband thus far. He looked across at the sleeping forms of his wife and youngest daughter, their faces bathed in lamplight. Meg had given him three beautiful children, a warm and loving home, and her constant support while he built his career. How did he repay her? By spending more hours at the office than he had to, rarely if ever thanking her for anything she did, and generally taking her for granted.

In some ways, he owed the tumor a debt of gratitude. If they'd continued on the way they were, would Meg have gotten fed up at some point and left? Not until the kids were grown and out of the house, he felt certain. But would he have awakened the day after Hannah's eighteenth birthday to a lonely bed? To a closet half-empty?

Too many other guys told the story of a wife who stuck around until the kids were grown, then split. Until the past few weeks, he'd never considered he could become one of those men.

He'd give nearly anything now to have that warm, loving, solid woman beside him. Instead, every new morning brought the familiar question. Which Meg would open her eyes beside him? Loving Meg? Angry Meg? Volatile Meg? Frustrated Meg? Resigned Meg? Patient Meg?

On the days he got glimpses of the old Meg, hope blossomed. Would today be one of those days? He set the book back on the nightstand, convinced by the passage of enough time that Savannah must not have been roused by the storm's thrashings outside.

"Trouble sleeping?" Meg's soft voice drew his attention.

"Storm woke me up."

Meg glanced back to the window where rain poured down in rivulets. As she watched, another flash of lightning sparked. Thunder rumbled a moment later. "Goodness, it's coming a gully washer out there."

"Yeah, forecast said it would blow over by morning though. Good thing we're getting it. This will give the farmers a good crop."

"When did Hannah join us?"

"Not too long ago, a few minutes maybe."

Meg smiled. "I can't believe I don't wake up for this anymore."

"I've decided it's about time you got a break, anyway."

She propped her head up on one elbow. "A break?"

"From the middle of the night stuff. I'm telling you, Meg, I don't know how you did it. And I should have told you long before now, but I'm grateful and honored with everything you've done to make a family and home with me."

Alarm jumped when tears filled her eyes. Maybe early morning wasn't the best time to try for an emotional and honest conversation.

"You're welcome." She leaned across the sleeping Hannah and kissed him.

Sleeping child or not, he returned the kiss.

Who knew when Meg would be in such a loving mood again? He inwardly sighed, wishing Hannah had slept through the storm. The way his luck ran these days, though, it made sense that Meg would finally open up to him when they had a two-year-old lying between them.

Meg broke the kiss and leaned back into her pillows. "Since we're both awake, you up for some conversation?"

Conversation with Meg. Oh, how he'd missed it. Even if he hadn't slept for seven straight nights, he would have found a way to stay awake.

"Sure. Something on your mind?"

"No, not really. How are things at work?"

"Fairly good. We got some new business in while I was away, so I'm trying to get up to speed on that. Otherwise, things were pretty much as I left them."

"Paperwork still stacked to the ceiling?"

"Would it be my office any other way?"

She chuckled. "By the way, I don't think I ever thanked you for hiring Jenny."

"She's working out well?"

"She's a godsend. Why didn't we hire her years ago?"

"Because I'm a moron who didn't see how much his wife did around here."

"Oh, well, as long as we've figured out the

reason."

He winked. "Trust me, we figured it out."

"Hey, I was thinking about getting up and making us some pancakes this morning. Think you could help?"

Meg wanted to fix breakfast? He'd do backflips in the living room and deliver plates on his feet while walking on his hands! Maybe, just maybe . . .

Things might never be normal in his house again. "Absolutely!"

"Don't get too excited. I'm not talking special recipe pancakes or anything. Just some Bisquick, egg, and milk."

"Honey, you could probably throw water on sawdust and these kids would eat it. I'm afraid my culinary skills have lowered the bar of taste bud requirements in this household."

"Your spaghetti was good."

"Thank Tandy. She told me her way of doing it was idiot proof. Guess she was right."

She crossed her ankles. "You asked Tandy how to cook?"

"No, I griped to Clay about how I couldn't make anything but hot dogs and mac and cheese. He had mercy on me and told Tandy to call with easy fixings. He started out telling me about his dishes, but I got lost after,

244

'Find a big bowl.' That man's talents aren't appreciated in this town. He's over there flipping burgers when he could be a chef somewhere."

"Yeah, I wonder sometimes if he shouldn't have gone to Orlando with Tandy instead of her moving here. He might be working in some four- or five-star restaurant by now."

"Bite your tongue, woman. If he left, he'd take all those burgers with him."

"Not to mention Clayton."

"That, too."

She ran a hand down Hannah's hair. Hannah slept on. "I'm glad Tandy moved back here. I missed her those years she was in school and then Orlando. I'd about resigned myself to never having her back and then, just like that, she decides Orlando isn't the place for her and a life here in Stars Hill with Clay fits her dreams better. Just goes to show you, you think you know a person and then they surprise you."

The irony of her words cut deep. Meg had been nothing if not a constant surprise for two months.

She caught his eye and read him more easily than the front page of a book. "I'm sorry I'm so difficult these days."

"Honey, you're not difficult," he lied.

"Oh, stop. I know I am just like I know

245

I'm as sick of this whole situation as you are. But I'm getting better. I *feel* a little more like me right now than I have since the surgery."

His hopes rose further. She *acted* more like her right now, too. "I'm glad."

Meg swung the covers off her legs. "I'm going to get a shower and get started on breakfast."

"Wait," he checked the clock, "it's barely six. How about I put Hannah back in her bed and we spend a little more time in here? Just the two of us."

Her smile made his breath catch in his throat, for it was the smile he'd known and loved since high school. He quickly picked Hannah up and turned toward the door. Storm or not, Hannah was about to learn how wonderful her own bed could be.

Thankfully the sleeping child's breathing barely changed rhythm when he slid her into bed and pulled up the covers. The storm outside hadn't lit up the windows in at least five minutes. He prayed the worst had passed and he'd have the next hour or so with Meg before the kids stirred.

Aching with a need to hold her and listen to that voice that melted his heart, he hurried back to the bedroom.

She lay where he'd left her, now holding

his book.

"Find some interesting reading?"

She looked over the top of the book at him. "Your bedtime reading is Dean Koontz? How do you calm down enough to sleep after reading this?"

He shrugged and joined her in bed. "I don't know. At some point my eyelids start going down and I can't keep them up. I put the book aside and fall asleep. Why? What do you read at night?"

"Mmm." She put the book on the nightstand and rolled onto her side to face him. "Romance."

For the next half hour, he forgot about books. He forgot about the storm. He forgot about everything. Nothing mattered but this.

Reconnecting with the woman he'd loved for as long as he could remember.

Jamison woke the second time to a sunny room and a snoring wife. Remembering what they'd shared before falling asleep together, he smiled and kissed her cheek. The clock warned him the morning outside was well underway and he wondered why the kids hadn't come barreling into the room by now.

Oh well. No need to borrow trouble. He

slipped out of bed and headed for the shower.

He'd just gotten the shampoo into his hair when the door opened.

"You know, it's not good manners to leave a woman alone in bed."

He turned to her, a smile automatically stretching across his face. "I'm so sorry for the error. Allow me to make it up to you." His lips met hers and he pulled her into the shower. They stood beneath the spray like they'd done before everything went crazy. Things *would* work out.

Maybe he wouldn't go visit the diner on Monday. If Meg was back to normal, then he had no need to see Karen anymore. She'd wonder why he didn't come around, but Karen had served her purpose. He'd found a source of conversation and happiness that allowed him to maintain his sanity while giving Meg her space.

He mentally patted himself on the back for having worked such a neat solution to the dilemma he'd been facing. As beautiful and wonderful as Karen was — and he had enough honesty to admit that to himself, at least — she didn't hold a candle to Meg when Meg was . . . well . . . *Meg.*

Twenty minutes later he and Meg stepped

from the shower and toweled off. "Do you still want to try making pancakes or do you need to rest a while?"

"Thinking pretty highly of yourself, aren't you?"

He grinned. "No, babe. I was thinking of your leg. Thought it might need some rest after all that exercise."

She leaned over and gave him a quick peck on the cheek. "Thanks for the concern, but I'm fine right now. I still need your help, though. Who knows when this thing is going to give out and I go sprawling across the floor?"

He placed his arms around her and pulled her close. "I promise to pick you up."

"Thanks."

They looked into each other's eyes a minute before she pushed him away and continued drying off. "Okay, no more fun for you this morning. The kids need pancakes and I intend to make them."

"You'll get no argument from me." He made short work of his hair and threw on the first pair of shorts and shirt his hands touched. Today didn't demand high fashion, just his presence. Because today he and Meg would make breakfast together for their children. Had they *ever* made breakfast for the kids?

He paused a second to think about it but couldn't come up with a single instance in which he and Meg had come together in the kitchen to make a meal. What a wealth of missed opportunity. No time like the present to remedy that situation.

"You coming?" he called.

"Be right down. Will you go on and wake up the kids?"

"I'm on it."

"Put them in front of a VeggieTales and tell them pancakes will be ready before it's over."

"Will do."

He nearly danced out of the bedroom, his soul light and outlook finally bright.

EIGHTEEN

Elation stayed with Jamison the rest of the weekend and greeted him Monday morning like a kiss. Meg's mood had held. Were they finally past the worst of it? Since the doctor's warning advised they could have been waiting a year for this — or even more — he felt particularly blessed that Meg bounced back after only two and a half months.

Careful not to wake her, he left their bed and began his morning preparations for work. He briefly considered calling in just to enjoy the day with Meg, but too many clients needed his attention after his month-long absence. As much as he wished he could spend the day with her, he needed to make sure they kept their source of income.

He showered and shaved, picked khaki trousers, a white oxford, and his brown sport coat, and set about finding his shoes. It took a few minutes before he remembered he'd left them in the study downstairs where he'd sat with Meg watching *Battlestar Galactica* reruns and polishing his shoes on Sunday night.

He dropped a kiss on her cheek — she smiled through her slumber — and left the bedroom.

Downstairs Jenny came through the front door as he crossed the foyer.

"Good morning, Jamison."

"Morning, Jenny."

"Did you have a good weekend?"

"We did. And you?"

"Pretty good myself. Anything in particular you'd like me to do today?"

He cast a glance up the stairs. "Check with Meg when she gets up, please."

"No problem."

He continued on to the study. Jenny would go about cleaning the house or doing the laundry or whatever chore she could find until the rest of the house stirred and Meg decided Jenny's tasks for the day. Thank heavens for Jenny Sanders. Where would they be without her? Surrounded by piles of dirty laundry and dishes.

His shoes lay right where he'd left them and he managed to get them on in a matter of minutes. With one last thought to the wish of staying home all day, he walked through the kitchen and out the garage door.

At the end of the driveway, it occurred to him he hadn't grabbed any coffee. This did not bode well for the day. The mountain of paperwork awaiting his attention *required* caffeinated sustenance. Attempting to conquer such a Mount Everest of paper without caffeine would be worse than leaving on a road trip to Mexico with no gas.

He could run to Clay's, but Greenfield wasn't that far away and he should do the polite thing and let Karen know he wouldn't be coming around much anymore. He hadn't talked about Meg much with Karen — enough to let her know he had a wife and they had hit a rough patch. Karen didn't need to know anything else. Their discussions were blissfully free of anything requiring hard thought or negative feeling. Instead they talked about movies they'd seen or places they'd visited or exotic lands they wanted to see.

Before he realized he had fully made up his mind, he found himself steering the car toward the Greenfield Highway. Arguments competed in his brain the entire way there. He wasn't doing anything wrong, just going to get some coffee. Sure, he could have turned around in the driveway and gone back inside for some, but that ran the risk of waking up the kids, which would force Meg out of bed and he didn't want to do that to her.

That didn't rule out Clay's as an option, but Clay would want to talk about how Meg was or something and Jamison didn't feel like having that kind of conversation right now. No need to jinx the fabulous situation at home by talking about it.

That left Wimpy's as the coffee place of choice so, really, he had no other option. He wasn't going specifically to see Karen, though telling her his marriage had come out of the rough patch was the right thing to do. He'd complained a bit to Karen about Meg, feeling guilty at the time. Now he could make that right by telling Karen they'd pulled out of it.

Thankfully the drive only took a few minutes and before he could become completely schizophrenic he parked the car and headed for the door. A quick nod to the old timers on the porch and he was inside, taking "his" spot at the last stool by the counter.

Karen came through the kitchen. He noted the way her eyes lit up when she saw him there and felt a sharp pang of loss. He soothed it with the image of Meg's smile this morning.

"Good morning, Jay." She poured his coffee and rested a hip against the counter. "Big plans for the day?"

"Oh, you know. Same old, same old. Numbers to crunch and all that jazz." He'd told her what he did for a living, just not that he owned the firm.

She smiled sympathetically. "Long day in front of you?"

"Judging by the mountain of paper I left stacked on my desk on Friday, yes. Unless some paper fairy came in during the weekend and magically made it all disappear."

"I think we should move to mandatory three-day weekends in this country."

"A slogan that will get you elected for sure."

She filled the cup next to him and the old timer smiled. She nodded, then came back to the conversation. "I don't have time to run for office. This place keeps me hopping."

"You know, you're in here every time I come in. Do you ever go home?"

Her blue eyes traveled around the room. "This *is* home."

"Well, it's a great place and the company is exceptional, but when do you go home, put your feet up, relax?"

"See the posted hours on the door? Add one minute to closing time and you'll know when I start relaxing."

He couldn't quite believe what he heard. "You mean you're here every minute the doors are open?"

"Yep."

"But . . . but why?"

Laughter filled her eyes and he felt like the butt of a joke he hadn't known had been told. "Jay, what do you think I do here?"

"Wait on the customers."

"Hmm, true." She walked down the counter, picking up empty plates and refilling coffee cups along the way. She did it all with an expert touch that he'd realized from day one made her the world's most perfect waitress. "I'm a little bit more than the waitress, though."

The older gentleman sitting by Jamison's side looked up. His face had more wrinkles than a used piece of aluminum foil, but kindness shone through his watery green eyes. Jamison smiled back.

"You think Karen's the waitress?" the old timer asked.

"I'm gathering she might be a little something else."

The grandpa chuckled. "Oh, she's something else all right."

Jamison looked toward Karen for explanation, but she'd escaped to the kitchen. He could see her back through the pick-up window. "What else is she?" Did he really want to know? Hadn't he come here to end things? Now here he sat learning more, getting in deeper, rather than cutting the tie that bound him here.

"Karen's owned this place for years. Ever since her daddy up and had a heart attack mowing the yard one day. Karen came in here, whipped up a batch of pancakes and the best pot of coffee anybody'd ever tasted and that took care of all the questions about what would happen to Wimpy's."

"How old was she?"

The watery green eyes turned to the ceiling as he put a finger to his chin. Jamison waited.

"Oh, 'bout eighteen or nineteen, I guess. We all knew she would have headed out to college if her daddy hadn't passed like that, but he did and she made the best of it. That's little Karen for you. Always making lemonade outta life's lemons."

Jamison turned wide eyes toward the kitchen. "She took over this place as a *teenager?*" He'd respected her before, but now Karen began to take on mythological proportions in his mind. "Where was her mother?"

"Oh, Carrie was tore up with grief, that one. Didn't come out of her house for a year after Paulie passed, 'cept for the funeral. The womenfolk all tried to get her back into the land of the living, but it's like I told my Trudie, sometimes a body's got to be left alone to grieve. Most folks thought Carrie'd grieve herself right into an early grave, but she pulled it together in the end."

"Does she work here at the diner?"

"Nope. Hasn't set foot in the place since Paulie's death. She's happy to leave things to Karen and Karen's happy to have it that way." The old man leaned into Jamison and lowered his voice. "Never a whole lot of love lost between Karen and Carrie — Karen was a Daddy's girl from the time she knew she had opinions."

Jamison could see that about her. The way she responded to the grandpas who came in here, like she was their long lost grand-daughter eager to wait on them hand and foot — he should have seen that before now. And no wonder she could hold her own in a conversation. She'd had to learn to think on her feet at eighteen. What a burden for a kid. At eighteen, he'd been head over heels in love with Meg without a clue what to do about it.

Thank the good Lord above, they'd figured it out, but he couldn't imagine being handed an entire business to run fresh out of high school. His estimation of Karen continued to rise.

"So, all my dirty laundry been freshly aired now?" Karen's voice held laughter and her eyes glinted when she teased.

He took a sip of coffee, appreciating more how good it was than he had before he'd known it as the recipe of a teenager. "Aired, folded, and put back in the closet. You've been holding out on me."

"I haven't. What did you expect? I'd sit a newcomer down on a stool and say, 'Let me tell you my life history'?"

"No, but that's some history you've got."

She shrugged. "It's the life I got dealt. Just like you, I handle what I can and hope the rest doesn't kill me."

"That's why I came in here today, actually." Might as well get this over with. If he stayed to learn too much more about her, his heart might get into trouble and the last thing he needed was an iffy relationship when Meg had finally come around.

"Oh?" She set the coffee pot on its burner and gave him her full attention. "More troubles at home?"

"Actually, just the opposite. My wife and

I had a great weekend together and it looks like maybe things are turning around."

She stared at him for a minute. It took only that for him to know that, for Karen, what he'd shared with her went beyond a passing friendship. He swallowed hard. Had she ever thought there might be something more between them?

When he met her eyes, he had his answer.

"That's good to hear." Her tone was low, no longer the playful voice he'd grown accustomed to hearing. "I guess, then, this is your last cup of coffee?"

Did it have to be? His soul said yes and, though he wanted to argue, he knew he'd better stop this while he still could. He nodded.

"I see." She reached behind and retrieved the coffee pot. Filling his to the brim, she said, "We'll miss seeing you around here, Jay."

He wrapped his hands around the warm mug and decided to be truthful. "I'll miss being around here."

NINETEEN

Meg woke to the songs of bluebirds and sparrows outside her window. For a moment, she felt like Snow White walking through the forest with birds trilling all around.

Then she looked at the clock.

Good grief, the kids needed breakfast an hour ago. How in the world had she managed to sleep this late?

Memories of the night before with Jamison flooded her brain and she felt a blush creep up her cheeks. It had been a long time since they'd shared that kind of intimacy and she'd been a little awkward in the beginning. But Jamison had given her a safe place to figure even this part out again. She felt a rush of gratitude for such a patient man.

Quickly tossing off the sheets, she left the bed and hurried to get into the shower. Jenny had probably come by now, which explained why three children weren't in her bedroom clamoring for breakfast. If they got too hungry, Jenny would take care of it. Knowing Jamison, he'd told Jenny to let Meg sleep as long as she wanted.

Jamison, sweet Jamison.

She stepped into the shower and turned on the water, recoiling at the shock of cold before it warmed up. As she slid the soap bar over her skin, thoughts of what she and Jamison had shared played across her mind. She felt joyously alive. Her life was coming back! She'd beaten back a brain tumor and endured her taste buds turning off and her sense of smell taking a vacation and even the loss and restoration of her driver's license, but she still had her life and her kids and her husband. Life was good!

Rinsing off, she reveled in the flow of warm water for a few more minutes, not quite ready to trade the wife hat for mom hat yet. It'd been a long time since she wore the wife hat and putting it back on had been wonderful.

She'd definitely be wearing it again to-night.

Finally stepping from the shower, she toweled off and padded into the bedroom. Jamison had probably made it to the office by now and she wanted to tell him good morning, to hear his voice one more time before going about her day.

She dialed the familiar number and waited until the receptionist answered the phone.

"Jamison Fawcett's office. This is Amber. How may I help you?"

"Hi, Amber. It's Mrs. Fawcett. Can you put me through to Mr. Fawcett, please?"

"Oh, hi, Mrs. Fawcett! How are you feeling?"

"Wonderful, Amber, thanks for asking."

"Oh, shoot. Should I have asked that? I shouldn't have asked that. It was rude."

Meg held her laughter in. "No, Amber, it was a very polite and considerate thing to do." They still had quite a bit to teach the young girl about reception work. "Is Mr. Fawcett in, please?"

"Not yet, but I expect him here any minute."

Meg must have just missed him. Evidently he had needed to sleep in as much as she. "All right. Will you tell him I called, please, when he arrives?"

"No problem, Mrs. Fawcett."

"Thanks, Amber." She hung up and thought about calling his cell. No, it'd be nicer to have him call her.

She dressed in shorts and a T-shirt and left the bedroom in search of the kids.

She found them at the breakfast table, hands and faces covered in syrup. Otis sat beneath Savannah's chair, waiting on her to drop a bite.

"Good morning, Meg," Jenny greeted her. "Feeling better?"

"Much, Jenny, thanks." Meg moved to the coffee pot and fixed herself a cup. "Thanks for getting breakfast ready."

"It was nothing."

"Well, thanks all the same." No doubt about it, they should have hired Jenny years ago. Not that she fancied herself one of those women with hired help, but if anything good had come from the surgery, it was having a valid reason to hire someone for the household stuff. Meg was free to enjoy the kids and focus on getting better now. She'd felt a little guilty at first — after all, why spend money on someone who did what they were perfectly capable of doing themselves? — but the value of having free time to heal and play with the kids and be with Jamison put a stop to the guilt in short order.

Besides, Jenny needed the money so this could even be seen as a good deed. Didn't the Bible say everyone should work for his wages? Here was Jenny, willing to work and needing a job. Their need of help coincided nicely with her desire to work.

Meg sat down at the table with the kids. "Hey, kiddos. Anybody got any ideas for what they want to do today?"

James chugged his chocolate milk, then wiped off a milk moustache. "Can we go to Aunt Joy's and swim?"

Savannah quickly joined in. "Oh, yeah! Can we, Mommy, please?"

Hannah, not too sure what they were talking about but clearly not wanting to be left out, said, "Me, too!"

Ever since Joy and Scott got an inground pool four years ago, complete with waterfall and slide, Meg had spent half her summer in their backyard. She and Jamison visited the idea of getting a pool of their own every year when the thermometer hovered at 75 degrees, but they'd never gotten one. Why deal with the hassle of it when she could run over to Joy's and play in hers?

"I'll call Aunt Joy and see if she's busy today."

A chorus of cheers rose from the table and Meg went to the phone on the kitchen wall. She dialed and waited through two rings, knowing Joy wouldn't answer until her caller ID had a chance to work.

"Lasky residence."

Which didn't mean she'd break decorum

for a second. "Hi, Joy. It's Meg, though you knew that from your caller ID."

"I've told you before, I don't trust the thing. It may have said Jamison Fawcett and meant entirely something else."

Meg chuckled. "In all your years of caller ID, has it ever once malfunctioned?"

"Well, no."

"And yet you still don't trust it?"

"That's right."

Meg shook her head. "You know you're a nutcase, right?"

"Yes, but you love me anyway."

"That I do. And, because *you* love *me,* I have a favor to ask."

"A favor precipitated by a reminder of love. Lay it on me, I'm sufficiently prepared."

"Would you mind if the kids and I came over for a swim?"

"Mind? Oh, sister, I wondered just this morning how I could drag you over here. Gather up those kids and come on."

"Really? You didn't have plans for the day?"

"You know I don't go into the salon on Mondays. Come on over! Can you stay through lunch?"

"Actually, I was thinking we'd come around lunchtime if that's okay."

"Sure. We'll see you then."

"Thanks, Joy."

"No thanks needed."

Meg hung up the phone, counting her blessings again for great sisters.

"Good news, kids! We can go over to Aunt Joy's to swim in a few hours."

"Not right now?" Jamison pushed another bite of pancake into his mouth.

"No, right now you have a bedroom that I'm certain needs some attention and you, too, Savannah."

"Me, too!" Hannah echoed.

Jenny's laughter sounded behind Meg. "Yes, you, too, Hannah. How about you help Mommy with the laundry?"

"Oh I can do that, Meg," Jenny said and Meg turned to her.

"I know, but I'm feeling great this morning and thought it'd be nice to do a little laundry again. I haven't done a lick of it since I got home from the hospital and I've got to get back into the swing of things at some point."

"Okay." Jenny couldn't hide a small frown.

"Don't worry." Meg laid a hand on Jenny's arm. "I have no intention of taking on everything again anytime soon. I'll probably get one load started and decide I've had enough and leave the rest to you."

She was rewarded with a grin. "All right, then, I won't complain about one less load of laundry."

Meg nodded and headed for the laundry room. "Jamison, Savannah, get started on your rooms as soon as you're finished with breakfast. Remember, the longer you take, the longer before we leave for Aunt Joy's."

The sound of chairs scraping against tile made her smile. She'd lay dollars to donuts their rooms would be spic and span — well, at least as spic and span as an eight-year-old and five-year-old could do — in a matter of minutes.

The laundry room smelled like fabric softener. Meg inhaled the familiar scent. Laundry had always been her favorite chore in the house, probably because she could dump the mess in a machine and walk away. Come back thirty minutes later and — ta da! — no more mess. If someone ever invented a washing machine for dogs, she'd snap one up in a second.

She doubted Otis had been treated to a bath since the last one she gave him. Did Jenny do dog baths? She'd find out.

Three baskets of laundry sat neatly by her upright washing machine and dryer. Looked like Jenny had already gathered up the dirty clothes for her. Man, that woman was efficient. Meg had slept through the entire thing.

Knowing the whole family's penchant for leaving things in their pockets, she began going through each pair of shorts and pants before putting them in the laundry. She pulled a marble from James's blue-jean shorts, then a Barbie shoe from the front pocket of Savannah's T-shirt dress. Hannah's pockets all came away clean. She picked up the last article of clothing, Jamison's gray pants.

It was truly amazing how many clothes she could wash at one time in these upright machines. Jamison had given them to her as a Christmas present three years ago. At the time she'd wondered if that said something about their relationship. But having the ability to stuff a gazillion things in the washer had cut down on her laundry time enough to make her grateful for the gift.

Slipping a hand into the pants pocket, she encountered paper. Jamison and his receipts. This one came from somewhere called Wimpy's. Meg thought she'd heard of the place before but couldn't remember where. Then she remembered. Wimpy's, the burger joint in Greenfield. Kind of their equivalent of Clay's, though she doubted anyone could make a burger better than Clay's.

What was Jamison doing over in Greenfield? Must have a new client or something. She checked the receipt.

Nope, coffee and a breakfast platter, whatever that was. Jamison drove all the way to Greenfield for breakfast? The thought struck her like a rain shower in sunshine. As far as she could remember, he hadn't mentioned going to Greenfield for breakfast. Had he not thought it important enough to mention or was he hiding something from her?

Come to think of it, was this why he hadn't been in the office when she called? She shoved the pants in the machine, added detergent, and punched buttons to start it up. Then she went to find Jenny.

Jenny was attacking the entertainment center in the living room with a rag and a can of the antibacterial Pledge that left such a clean smell behind.

"Jenny?"

"Hmm?"

"Were you here when Jamison left this morning?"

"I came as he was leaving, yes." Jenny didn't turn from her cleaning.

"Do you know what time that was?"

Now Jenny stopped and looked at her. Meg felt dumb not knowing what time her husband had left for work. Would Jenny think the question odd?

"I left the house just before the national news came on, so I got here a little after seven."

And she'd awakened at 8:32. She remembered checking the clock. That left him plenty of time to get to the office except that he hadn't gone directly to the office from here.

He'd gone to Wimpy's for breakfast. Maybe.

She had to keep a level head here and not jump to conclusions. Even if he *did* drive to Greenfield for breakfast, there was nothing wrong with that. Maybe he preferred Wimpy's eggs to Clay's. Maybe he needed a little alone time in the morning to get mentally prepared for work.

"Meg?"

Jenny's voice startled her and she realized the woman still stood waiting for her next question.

"Oh! That's all, Jenny. Thanks."

"Everything okay?"

"Everything's fine. Just trying to figure out my morning is all."

Jenny gave her a quizzical look but didn't

question the explanation. Instead, she went back to her dusting.

Meg returned to the laundry room, needing a quiet place to think and knowing the kids wouldn't bug her in here. The last time they had she'd put them to work. She sat down on the stool in the corner and stared out the small window to the backyard. Why did it bug her so much that Jamison had breakfast out of town? She knew he'd never in a million years cheat on her and the kids, so it wasn't a suspicion of that.

Of course, probably half the women in the world who'd ever discovered their husbands cheating would have said their husband would never do such a thing. She let herself consider the idea that Jamison could have an affair.

At first her mind refused to allow the possibility. But then she thought about how difficult things had been the past few months — not just while she recovered from surgery but even before that, when she'd had headaches all the time. She and Jamison hadn't exactly been close and intimate for a long while until this weekend. And a man had needs. Had Jamison gone elsewhere to get them met?

The thought sat like a boulder in her mind. No, this must be a figment of her surgery-riddled brain. If the receipt had been for dinner somewhere, then maybe. But it was clearly for breakfast, and she did not envision Jamison running off for a quickie before work with some floozy. She was being ridiculous. All her brain hadn't quite returned to normal.

Jamison merely went somewhere for breakfast. He probably wanted to eat where he didn't have to cook the food or clean up after himself. Not that he had to do either of those things now that they had Jenny. Hmm, that didn't completely explain things either, then.

Why did this bug her so much? She'd already decided he wasn't having an affair. Why did it matter where he ate breakfast?

The deception. That had to be it. She felt like he'd hidden something from her and, in all their years of being together, they'd never hidden things from each other. Not intentionally. There had been times when they forgot to share something and it came up later, but neither of them had deceived the other on purpose for anything other than a surprise gift or party.

The idea that Jamison could deceive her about something as silly as his breakfast locale didn't sit right. Had her behavior during recovery pushed him to hide a part of his life from her? To need time away from their home every morning?

Not that she had any proof he went to Wimpy's every morning, so she shouldn't assume such a thing.

She'd just ask him about it when he came home. She slapped her hands onto her legs, her mind made up. Marriages ran into trouble when partners became suspicious of each other for no good reason. All she knew was that Jamison had breakfast at Wimpy's and didn't tell her. Not a big deal. She'd ask him about it this afternoon, he'd give her a completely honest explanation, and life could go on in bliss.

A few hours later Meg settled into a chaise lounge by Joy's pool and sighed. "Ah, this is the life."

"Isn't it, though?" Joy agreed.

"Should we call Kendra and Tandy to see if they want to come over?"

"Already done." Joy poured lemonade for them from a pitcher covered in painted orange and lemon slices. Of course Joy would have designer poolside dishes. "They'll be here later. They're wrapping up some things at the Sisters, Ink offices."

"Speaking of which, how's the business going? I know we said we'd be silent partners, but I think we should know what's going on, don't you?"

"From everything I've seen, it's growing by leaps and bounds. They get more membership requests every week from scrapbookers wanting to connect at the local level. If we want a formal report, I'm sure Tandy would draw it up for us." She offered a glass to Meg.

Meg took it and shook her head. "No, if you say things are going well, then I trust you. I have no desire to read through a report, and I'm sure Tandy wouldn't enjoy writing one."

"You're right about that."

They watched while James and Savannah played together in the shallow end of the pool. Hannah, her arms outstretched and encased by floatie wings, giggled alongside them.

"This is great. They'll be so worn out by the time we leave, bedtime will be a breeze."

"Happy to be of service. So, how are you feeling?"

"I think I turned a corner on Friday." Meg shared with her some details from her wonderful weekend.

"My, you *did* turn a corner."

"It feels so great to be familiar to myself again. I mean, I know that's a weird statement, but it's like something clicked in my brain finally, you know?"

"I can't say that I do, but I'm happy for you nonetheless."

Meg sipped her drink, enjoying the sugary sweetness. Giant puffy clouds filled the sky and sunshine streamed down through them in small patches. She couldn't have asked for a more perfect day after a happier weekend, but here she sat brooding about that dumb receipt.

"Joy?"

"Hmm?"

"Does Scott tell you when he goes out of town to eat?"

"What?"

"If Scott went to, say, Gleason or Dresden and had lunch, would he tell you when he came home?"

"Probably not, unless he told me all about his day. Sometimes when he gets home I'm so tired from running after Maddie all day, I just hand him the parent reins and escape to a bubble bath. If he went out to eat on one of those days, I wouldn't know if he sold four mansions, much less went somewhere for food."

Meg considered that.

"Is something going on?"

Meg set her glass down. "I don't think so."

"You don't *think* so? Details, please."

"I found a receipt in Jamison's pocket from Wimpy's."

"The burger place in Greenfield?"

"Mm hmm. It showed he'd had coffee and the breakfast platter. And I just wondered about it because he hasn't mentioned driving all the way to Greenfield for breakfast."

"I doubt it means anything. He probably met with a client or something."

"Well, that's what I thought, but the receipt was for one. Jamison always picks up the tab when he's eating with a client or even a potential client. So he had to have been there by himself."

"Are you looking for trouble? Because I'm not seeing anything sinister at work here. Jamison had breakfast without you. What's the big deal?"

"I think it's that he didn't tell me. Jamison and I tell each other everything."

"Everything?"

"Yeah. When he comes home from work, I ask how his day went and he tells me."

"You've done that every day?"

"Well . . . not so much since the surgery."

"There you go. He probably went on a day you didn't ask him how his day went, so there was no point in bringing it up."

"Maybe." Meg sat back, uneasy. Was she making a mountain out of a molehill? "I'm being dumb, aren't I?"

Joy crossed her delicate ankles. "I don't know about dumb, no."

"Who's dumb?" Tandy came up behind them and plopped a beach bag down by another chaise lounge. She readjusted Clayton on her hip.

Meg held up her hand. "I am."

Tandy sat down and began pulling out arm floaties for Clayton. "Why are you dumb?" She found the floaties and slid them up his arms, then began blowing them up.

"Because I'm a suspicious, overly inquisitive wife."

"You? No way. What happened?"

Meg explained again about the receipt, beginning to feel a little ridiculous for ever thinking it could mean anything but that Jamison had breakfast.

"Hmm, I wonder why he didn't say anything to you?" Tandy moved to the other floatie.

"That's what I wondered."

"Has he told you when he's gone out to eat in the past?"

"Yeah. Always." The butterflies in Meg's

stomach took up flight again. "You think something's up?"

Tandy stood up and carried Clayton to the pool. "I think it's worth asking him about. I don't think I'd be jumping to any conclusions, though. It's not like you found a receipt for flowers or dinner or something."

"Man, get out of my head."

Tandy chuckled and waded into the pool with Clayton. He gasped when his little feet and legs hit the cold water, but Tandy kept a tight hold on him. It didn't take long before he was slapping his hands into the water, laughing at the resulting splash.

"He sure seems to like the water."

"Yeah, I'm hoping it holds. Clay wants to take a trip to Florida soon and Zelda's offered us her house in Naples if we want it for a week or two, so I think we're going to go."

"Zelda offered to let you stay in her house?"

Tandy nodded. "She and Daddy came in the diner last night and we got to talking and Clay busted out with, 'I think we need a vacation' and of course I told him we didn't have a budget for a vacation right now since we didn't exactly plan for this little guy, and next thing I know Zelda's offering to let us stay at her place. Said it's not doing anything but sitting there vacant anyway, so someone should get some use out of it."

"Hmm." Joy tipped her head. "Did it come with strings?"

"None so far, but she did say something weird — or, weird for her."

"What?"

"She kept asking when we'd like to go down, like she was eager for us to leave. I finally said, 'Are you trying to get rid of us?' and she said 'No, I just think it's important to always work on your marriage.' "

"To work on your marriage? What does that mean?"

Meg pushed her sunglasses up on her head. "Are she and Daddy having trouble?"

Tandy shrugged. "Beats me. They looked fine. He had his arm around her after they finished eating and I didn't sense any animosity from either of them."

"So why the sudden need to work on marriages?"

Tandy shook her head. "I have no idea, but it's weird, isn't it?"

"Very." Meg pulled the sunglasses back down over her eyes. "And I don't like it when she starts acting strange. It's bad enough she's so distant all the time."

"She *is,* isn't she? Such a cold fish. I don't know *what* Daddy sees in her." Joy poured Tandy a glass of lemonade.

"Well, regardless of what he sees in her, he married her, which means we're stuck with her for life," Tandy reminded them.

Joy huffed. "And isn't that a fine mess of worms we've got. I have tried and tried to befriend that woman. I've taken pies and cakes and helped her get the house in order when she and Daddy got home from their honeymoon — you should have seen the disorganization Daddy lived in — and even taken her clippings from my hosta outside. But does she do anything other than give me an insincere 'thank you'? No. When we were over there scrapping, I checked and didn't see hosta anywhere. I think she threw out my clippings." The outrage in Joy's voice could have rivaled the Queen of England's in finding a fork out of place on the royal table.

"I didn't know you were trying so hard with her," Meg said.

"Like Tandy said, Daddy married her and we're stuck with her. I thought it might be a more pleasant experience for us all if we could forge some sort of friendship. But the woman simply has no manners, no good graces, that I can find. She just blunders through life, spouting off opinions and stories like everybody around her should hang on every word and covering her ears with those turquoise earrings and appearing in public wearing those boots with spurs on them." Joy's mouth turned down. "I thought she'd trade them in for sandals when summer hit, but I heard she was at Heartland Friday with them on."

"She was." Kendra waltzed onto the patio. "Darin and I asked her where she got them and she said an old friend gave them to her years ago."

Joy harrumphed. "I'd say her debt of gratitude has been more than paid."

"Maybe if we got her a new pair, she'd chuck the old ones and start wearing the new ones," Meg offered.

Joy pointed a finger Meg's direction. "Now that's not a half-bad idea. Though if it goes anything like the hosta did, we may simply be wasting money on a pair of boots."

Kendra spread a blanket on a chaise lounge and slipped her T-shirt off. "So, who called the pool day? Because, if I have a vote, I say we do this all summer instead of scrapping day, then spend all the cold weather time in the scrapping studio."

"Another great idea!" Joy leaned back in

her chair. "We're on a roll here."

"It's the sunshine. Gets the brain flowing." Meg adjusted the back of her lounger so it lay back at a greater incline. With Tandy in the pool, she didn't have to keep such a close eye on Hannah, and James and Savannah were fine since they both knew how to swim.

She let the conversation of the sisters roll over her and the sunshine warm her face. After the worry of the morning, what she needed was a nap.

It didn't take long before she had her wish.

James's bubbly laughter brought Meg back to consciousness. She opened her eyes and sat up, noting that the sun had moved further down in the sky. "What time is it?"

"About 3:30." Kendra popped a tortilla chip in her mouth. "Have a nice nap?"

Meg stretched. "Mmm, I did." She checked the pool. "Where's Hannah?"

"Needed a nap as much as her mother. Tandy got her down about half an hour ago."

James's head plopped back into the water. A snorkel tube rose up beside his face. The kid loved swimming. "And Savannah?"

"We thought she might need a break, too, so she's watching *Madame Blueberry* in the living room with Joy and Maddie. Joy says that video puts Maddie to sleep every time."

Meg sent up a prayer of thanks again for her wonderful sisters. Her stomach grumbled. "Can you pass me some chips?"

Kendra brought over the bag from which she'd been eating. "Don't tell Joy we were eating straight out of the bag. She'd have our heads."

"My lips are sealed." Meg retrieved a chip and crunched into it, remembering the receipt from Wimpy's and the drama of her morning. She didn't feel like talking it over again, though, so she stayed silent.

"I need a new bathing suit." Kendra picked at the material across her stomach. "I bought this one for our honeymoon in the islands and I think I may have worn it out with all the time we spent in the water down there."

"Sara might still have some in stock."

"Yeah, want to run down there with me?"

"Right now?"

"No time like the present right?"

"Hmm, I *do* need some new clothes." She hadn't purchased one thing for the summer, having spent all of it so far recovering from surgery.

"It's settled then. I'll see if Joy or Tandy minds staying with the kids. Be right back."

Meg watched her go, then turned back to the pool. The sunshine danced along its rippling surface. She enjoyed the feeling of relaxation that had seeped into her bones while she slept. The faint scent of honeysuckle came to her on a breeze and she breathed deeply, taking the fragrance into her being. Summer in the South might be full of humidity, but it also came with the sweet scent of flowers and — in Joy's yard, anyway — lush leaves of plants. Not to mention lemonade and the laughter of kids at play.

Summer might be her favorite time of year, if she thought about it long enough. Winter was great, full of Christmas tradition and sweaters and mittens. But all those mittens and boots on kid hands and feet left quite a wake of snow through her house. And spring came with rain and mud puddles — fun for jumping in, not so fun for the person having to wash the muddy clothes afterwards. Then there was fall, with the rich-hued trees and piles of leaves, but someone had to rake those leaves and the roads stayed clogged with farm machinery on the move while farmers went about their harvests.

No, summer took the prize as her favorite.

"Okay, Tandy's asleep in one of the guest

rooms alongside Hannah, so she's staying here. Joy said she had some things to catch up on, so she doesn't mind staying here with the kids while we go shop. Come on, sister, let's hit it!"

Meg swung her legs over the side of the lounger and stood. Thankfully, her leg continued to obey. "I'm right behind you."

TWENTY

Jamison powered down his computer and leaned back in his office chair. Good grief, this had been a long day. If he didn't look at one more number the rest of the week, he'd be a happy man. Sometimes, when he got this tired, the numbers took on a life of their own. When he tried to concentrate on them, they simply swam all over the place like psychotic minnows.

"Mr. Fawcett?" Amber cracked the door and stuck her head around it so that she looked like a floating, sideways decapitated head. Jamison blinked. He really needed to go home. "I'm going to head on home, if that's okay."

"Sure, Amber. See you tomorrow."

The floating head nodded and disappeared. Jamison gathered up his things, hoping Meg's good humor had lasted the day. His bones ached he was so weary, which left him ill prepared for moodiness right now.

He left the office and got in his car, slipped the key into the ignition . . . then paused. A Wimpy's burger would taste pretty good right now. But he'd been there just that morning. Now that he'd told Karen things were better at home, he had no need to go.

So why this longing to do so?

He pushed the longing away and started the car, turning it toward home. The drive, never long, seemed particularly short tonight. He pulled into the garage and killed the engine but made no move to get out. This was why some men stopped at a bar on their way home from work. It was less about the drink than about the downtime between office and home. Sort of a detox, ironically enough.

He sat until the details of the day's work gave in and left his mind. Only then did he realize Meg's van wasn't in its place beside his in the garage. All this time he'd been sitting here and the house was as empty as Jesus' tomb.

Chuckling, he snagged his briefcase and headed inside. Otis greeted him at the door, his curled tail wagging as best it could.

"Hey, boy." Jamison bent down and

scratched the dog's ears. "Need a trip outside?"

Meg must have left earlier in the day because not one light greeted his entry. She'd have left a light on if she thought she'd be out until dark. He briefly worried something had happened, but his cell phone hadn't rung, so all must be right with the world.

He opened the back door for Otis and watched the dog run off into the fenced-in backyard. Snagging an apple from the refrigerator, he bit into it on his way up the stairs to get more comfortable clothes on. It took only a few minutes to get out of the button-up and into shorts and a T-shirt. Still no sign of Meg and the kids. His stomach rumbled and he went back to the kitchen to see what Jenny had prepared for them that night.

A casserole sat on the top shelf with a Post-It note of instructions for heating. He pulled it out and turned on the oven to the recommended 350 degrees. Tapping his fingers on the countertop, he thought about waiting until everyone else got home before heating up dinner but another stomach growl convinced him they'd understand. He slid the casserole onto the middle oven rack and went to the living room.

Might as well watch some television until they returned. He flipped through the channels, but the only things on were local news and a bunch of home shopping shows. Neither caring about the events of the day nor that he could get a genuine Diamonique ring for only three payments of $233.97, he turned the set off and sat in the dark.

He couldn't remember the last time he'd sat in this house and heard silence. Always one kid was running through or yelling or laughing or Meg was by his side. He never spent time alone here. They spent all their time together.

Stretching his arms along the back of the couch, he breathed deeply. The house smelled of cleaning products. Jenny's touch, no doubt. He noted that every surface gleamed and only two toys lay on the carpet. If it meant they could never afford to go out again, he decided he'd keep Jenny on. He'd never say it to Meg, but Jenny kept the house even more spotless than Meg had. And the kids seemed to adore her.

He leaned his head back and relived the happy weekend he'd shared with Meg and the kids.

Please, God, let her still be in that frame of mind. How long would it take before he quit having that thought? Before he quit worrying that he'd come home to the Wicked Witch of the West?

Not that he expected Meg to be in a happy mood every minute of every day. No one lived that way. But the hatefulness that invaded her after surgery — *that* he could live without for the rest of his life.

His gaze traveled to the clock. Was Karen still at the diner? Probably. They stayed open for the early dinner crowd, according to the hours of operation posted at the door. He tried to imagine her at eighteen, fresh out of high school and faced with her dad's death and the responsibility of running his business but couldn't do it.

Oh well, he didn't need to be thinking of her anyway.

A new thought occurred then, one that made him lift his head and straighten his spine. What if he introduced Meg to Karen? They had a lot in common — that's why he'd enjoyed the verbal sparring with Karen in the first place. He bet if they met each other it'd be one of those situations where instant girlfriends were born.

Then again Meg would want to know how he knew Karen, and he couldn't lie to her. Couldn't act like he'd never been to Wimpy's and this was a chance encounter. He and Meg didn't lie. They didn't hide things from each other. Well, until this. He'd not told her about his trips to Wimpy's, but there really wasn't anything to tell, so it didn't count as a deception. Not a real deception.

He relaxed his head back onto the couch. No, introducing them required too much planning and too high a possibility of needing to lie. With everything finally going great again in his marriage, he had no desire to jeopardize things by letting Meg think he'd done something wrong.

Even though he hadn't.

He heard the garage door go up and rose to greet his family at the door. Clicking on lights along the way, he came into the kitchen and glanced at the stove's timer. Perfect. Ten minutes before it was ready.

James was first through the door. "Hey, Dad!"

Jamison held out his arms, but James completely bypassed him on the way to the living room.

Savannah came next, a small beach bag on her arm. "Hi, Daddy!" He snagged a hug from her before she could pass him for the living room as well.

Hannah and Meg came through together, one little hand tucked inside Meg's, the other holding her pink elephant. "Hi, honey."

Meg looked tired but happy. His heart lifted at the sight of her and he rose to come to her. "Hi, yourself." He kissed her — a kiss that let her know there would be more later, if she wanted, then took the shopping bag from her hand. "You went to Sara's, I see."

"We started out at Joy's swimming, but then Kendra wanted to shop and I may have found a few things for myself."

Jamison knelt down to Hannah, whose eyelids drooped. "Did you go swimming at Aunt Joy's?"

She nodded her little head. "I swept with Aunt Tandy."

He smiled. None of the kids had been able to make the "l" sound at first. "You did? Did you have sweet dreams?"

"Uh huh."

He picked her up and went to deposit her on the couch with the other two. "I'll be right back," he said over his shoulder. "Dinner's in the oven, be ready in a few minutes."

"Oh, thank goodness. I'm starved."

The kids' faces were lit by the blue glow from the television screen.

"Check it out, Dad." James bounced

around the couch, excitement lighting his eyes. "They're playing the movie about the snow dogs on TV tonight! And we made it home in time!"

He set Hannah down in the recliner. "Then I think it's definitely a dinner-in-front-of-the-television night."

"YAY!"

"Okay, okay, calm down. I'll bring your dinner in here. You can watch so long as you eat, got it?"

"Got it."

Jamison returned to the kitchen, where he found Meg with the oven door open.

She looked up at him. "What is this?"

"A casserole Jenny left us. I think the note said chicken and chives."

"Sounds good." She shut the oven door. "Actually, anything neither of us has to make sounds excellent."

He came and slid his arms around her waist. "I'll amen that." Her lips met his and he forgot about the kids in the next room and the stresses of work that had plagued him all day. All he cared about right then was her kiss, which she gave with abandon.

"Careful, Mrs. Fawcett, or I'll get ideas."

"Oh? What kind of ideas?"

Oh, how he loved the way her eyes twinkled at him. He kissed her again, using actions rather than words to convey his answer.

"I think I like your ideas," she murmured.

He pulled back and looked into her eyes. "I missed you all day."

"That's good since I found myself missing you a good bit of the day as well."

"Just a good bit? I'm wounded."

"Big baby. There was a part of the day I worried about you."

He let go of her and went to the cabinet to get out the glasses. "Worried? What about?"

"I decided I'd do a little laundry today."

Hearing she'd taken on a house chore cheered his spirit further. "You did? That's great!"

"Well, it was until I found a receipt in your pants pocket from Wimpy's. Since when do you go to Greenfield for breakfast?"

His hand stilled on the glass. He felt caught but didn't know why since he hadn't done anything wrong.

"I've gone a few times. It's a quick drive and they make a mean breakfast platter and one excellent cup of coffee."

"Yeah, but you go all the way to Green-field? Why not Clay's?"

He shrugged. "I don't know. I went for a drive one day to clear my head and ended up in Greenfield. I was hungry, so I stopped at Wimpy's, discovered the amazing coffee, and thought I'd go get some the next time I woke up wanting breakfast but not wanting to make it." *And wanting fabulous conversation when you couldn't give it to me.*

He dismissed that thought. He hadn't *replaced* Meg, just found a substitute until she could get back to her old self.

He looked up to find Meg's gaze steady on him. "Jamison, we don't keep things from each other." Her voice held an undertone of warning. "Are you keeping something from me? Because it feels like you're keeping something from me."

He was. He knew he was. And he knew what . . . or, more to the point, who. But telling Meg about Karen would be like throwing water on a man who'd just recovered from a near-drowning. Cruel and completely unnecessary. Besides, Meg stood on dry land now. No need to throw water around. "No, honey, I'm not keeping anything from you." Meg let out a breath and he set the glass down and went to her. "What did you think?"

"I didn't know what to think. It just felt so weird that you were off somewhere eating without me and now I find out you've gone several times and it feels . . . strange.

You've been having breakfast somewhere and I didn't have a clue. It makes me wonder if there are other things I don't know and I've never had that thought about you. About us."

"Oh, honey, there's nothing else you don't know." *That you need to know.* "I went off for breakfast. No big deal. Really. Please don't question us. We're fine. We're *good.*" He took her hands in his. "I promise."

Her blue eyes met his and he held the gaze, praying honesty shone in his gaze.

"Okay," she finally said. "But please don't start keeping things from me. I know we've had a couple of hard months here, but that's no reason to start hiding stuff from each other."

"Absolutely. I didn't mean to hide this from you, it just never came up."

She nodded and sniffed.

His heart twisted at the sound. She'd shed plenty of tears these past weeks but, so far as he knew, none of them because of him. He hated bringing tears back to her eyes. He pulled her arms around him and then put his around her. "I love you."

"I love you, too."

He held her for a minute, watching the seconds count down on the oven timer and dreading the buzzer that would break their embrace. But, inevitably, the clock hit 0:00 and the buzzer sounded. She left his arms and turned toward the stove. He didn't get a glimpse of her face before she turned.

"Go tell the kids it's time for dinner."

"I told them they could eat in front of the television tonight. James is watching that movie about snow dogs."

"Oh, I forgot. He's been talking about it all afternoon. He saw a commercial for it and has been waiting." She took the casserole from the oven and set it on the stovetop. "I guess we get to dine alone, then."

He wiggled his brows. "I'll find the candles and put the ice in the glasses. You get their plates ready. K?"

"Okay."

Her voice didn't hold quite the level of energy and happiness he'd heard this morning, but she also didn't sound mad, so he chose to focus on the positive. He went to the dining room and took the candlesticks from their place on the large table. He didn't want to eat with her eight feet away from him. The round breakfast table would be better.

Carrying the candlesticks in each hand, he came back into the breakfast room and set them on the table. He went and poured

298

three cups of milk, then carried them into the living room.

Hannah was close to sleep. "Hannah, wake up, sweetie. Dinner's ready."

"Okay," Hannah mumbled.

He doubted she made it through dinner, much less the movie. Setting the cups down on the end table, he looked around for the TV trays. They rested against the far wall. He no sooner had them set up over each child's lap than Meg entered with three plates of casserole.

"Here we go, kiddos." She placed a plate on each tray. "Daddy and I are eating in the breakfast room, so yell if you need anything, okay?"

"Mm hmm," Savannah responded.

James, engrossed in the movie, barely acknowledged her. Jamison found the remote and pressed mute. That got the little boy's attention.

"Dad!"

"Your mother was speaking to you."

"What, Mom?"

"I said to yell if you need anything."

"Okay, already. Can we watch the movie?"

"You can watch the attitude or I'll turn the movie off." Jamison had known the day would come when James would develop an attitude. He just hadn't expected it to start

299

at eight years old.

"Yes, sir."

The kid must really want to watch this movie.

"And remember, if I come in here and you're not eating, I'll turn the movie off and bring you all to the table."

"Yes, sir." James picked up his fork and dutifully took a bite of casserole.

Satisfied the children would at least put forth an effort to eat, he took Meg's hand and left the living room.

"They're really worn out."

"They should be. They spent hours in Joy's pool and you know how the water wears them out."

"So, are we okay?" He didn't want to bring it up, but he needed to make sure the issue had been put to rest.

"We're okay."

"Good."

"Oh, Kendra and I are going garage sale shopping with Zelda this weekend. Can you watch the kids all day Saturday?"

"Sure. But you're spending the day with Zelda? Since when do you want to spend time with your stepmother?"

She spooned casserole onto two more plates and carried them to the table. He brought their water glasses and sat down next to her.

"Kendra and I talked about it while we were out shopping, and we think maybe we should be making more of an effort to be friends with Zelda. I mean, it makes sense. Now that Daddy's married her, there's no getting rid of her so we might as well make the best of the situation, right?"

"Sounds logical."

"Well, Joy has tried to be nice and it didn't work. Kendra and I thought maybe Joy was a little too, um, *proper* for Zelda and that we might meet with a little more success if we try."

"But garage sale shopping? You haven't done that since James was a toddler."

"I know, but I liked it then and Zelda went last weekend, so we know she likes to go. It's a chance for us to find some common ground with her."

He lit the candles and enjoyed the glow reflecting on her face. "Hey, I'm not trying to dissuade you." He put the lighter on the table. "I think it's great that you're willing to try."

Meg sighed. "I wish I could say I'm looking forward to it. I'll try to have a better attitude about the whole thing by Saturday, though."

"I'm sure it will be fine."

"I hope so."

They ate in silence for a bit, simply enjoying each other's company. He continued to watch the dance of the candle's glow on her smooth skin. He'd heard that everyone always looked better in candlelight — probably why it was used in so many romantic movies — but Meg looked like a goddess. Even with her head covered in that handkerchief — she didn't like the shortness of her hair now that it had started to grow back — and the exhaustion of the day clear on her face, she was beautiful. His beautiful wife.

"You're staring," she chided gently.

"I don't think I'll ever get tired of looking at you."

Her eyes widened. "Really?"

"Of course. Have you looked at yourself? You're the most beautiful woman I've ever seen."

She gave a half laugh. "I used to hold my own, but not these days. Maybe when my hair grows back in." She rolled her eyes up to the handkerchief.

"I like your short hair. I miss running my fingers through your long hair, don't get me wrong, but with your hair gone I see your face better." He ran a finger down the side of that face, stopping under her chin. "And it is a gorgeous face."

She smiled. "Thank you, though I think you might be blind."

"Nope, 20/20 vision." He let her face go. The cinnamon scent of the candles surrounded them.

They chatted over dinner. He told her about his day — leaving out the fact that he'd driven to Greenfield just that morning. He knew he wouldn't be back, so no need to arouse worry in her again. She shared stories with him about the sisters. Before he knew it, an hour and a half had passed.

He picked up his glass and drained the last of the water there. "I've missed doing this with you."

"Having dinner?"

"Sitting and talking. I think that's what I missed most after your surgery. Remember when we'd sit up all night and talk?"

She nodded. "We'd look at the clock and try to figure out where the time had gone."

"Right. We didn't do that for a long time before your surgery. And then, after, well . . ." He let his voice trail off.

"It was hard to hold up my end of a conversation for a while."

"I know." He reached across the table and took her hand. "I didn't mean to make you feel like I was complaining. I'm just happy to sit here and share dinner with you again."

She squeezed his hand, then let it go and pushed back from the table. "How about we put these dishes away and get the kids to bed?"

The gleam in her eyes told him all he needed to know. "I think that's an excellent idea."

TWENTY-ONE

The week passed by in a blur and, before Meg knew it, Saturday morning dawned clear and bright. At first she didn't remember what she had planned for the day, only that she'd planned something.

Then she glanced at her alarm clock and it came rushing back to her. This was her morning to bond with Zelda. Meg groaned. Why couldn't Zelda like doing something in the middle of the day? Must the woman choose something that required a person to get up early on the weekend and present herself to the public?

Shaking her head, Meg got out of bed and headed for the shower. She needed the smell of soap and shampoo to wake up her senses and prepare her for the day.

An hour later she pulled the car into Kendra's driveway. She'd considered taking the van, but Jamison might decide to take the kids somewhere and that meant he'd need the van. So she drove along in his car, breathing in the scent of his cologne, which permeated the car's interior.

Kendra came outside before she'd even cut the engine.

"Wow, look who's on the ball today."

Kendra pulled the visor down and flipped open the mirror. She folded the scarf in her hands once and began arranging it around her hair. "I cannot believe we agreed to do this. Did we lose our minds?"

Meg backed the car out of the driveway and into the road. "Yes."

"Well, that's what I thought."

Meg turned on the radio, hoping for some music to lift their moods and prepare them for the day ahead.

"There isn't enough music in the world, sister." Kendra finished with her hair and put the visor back into position. "Only an insane woman gets up at this hour on a Saturday to go looking through things that other people have the good sense to throw out."

"Not throw out. Put up for sale."

"Because they hope to make a little money before they throw it out."

"I'll grant you that."

Kendra's hands flew all over as she talked. "And yet we think we should haul ourselves out of bed and go meet a stepmother we don't even like all that much to go do this. I ask again, have we lost our minds?"

"Yes." Meg looked across the seat. "But we've got to befriend her sometime, and I for one am sick and tired of feeling awkward about scrapping in my own mother's studio. So let's put on our happy faces and get this done."

Kendra crossed her arms and stuck out her lower lip. "I don't get why Tandy and Joy got out of this."

"Because they're obviously smarter than we are."

Kendra's laugh overrode the music. "You'll never get me to admit that in their presence."

"Me, either. You tell them I said it, I'll tell them you're a liar."

"Deal."

They arrived at the white gates with a black *S* on the front and Meg turned down the drive to the family house. She wound down the gravel path, noting the bare fields. Daddy must have harvested the winter wheat. Time to plant some corn.

Zelda sat in a rocker on the front porch, looking like a countrified Buddha. She was dressed in a white button-up shirt — the buttons, of course, turquoise — and blue jeans. Big, silver hoops dangled from her earlobes. They matched the circles on her wrists.

"*What* is with her turquoise obsession?" Kendra hissed.

"Remember, we're being nice today. Trying to make friends."

"Yeah, yeah. I'm with you."

Zelda came down the porch steps and had the back door open before Kendra could get out of the front.

"Oh, I'll move back there, Zelda."

"Don't you worry yourself, Kendra." The car rocked as Zelda got in. "I'm fine back here. Get to pretend like I'm being driven around all over town by hired help."

Meg decided to take that for a joke rather than a snub. "In that case, where can I take you, Mrs. Sinclair?"

Zelda's laughter rang out. "Oh, honey, let me check the paper again." Meg heard the rustle of the newspaper and adjusted the rearview mirror to keep an eye on her step-mother.

"I think we should start over on K Street and work our way through town. Then, if we have time, there are a couple of sales over in Greenfield that sound promising."

"Promising how?" Meg steered the car back down the driveway and onto the two-lane country highway.

"They've got antiques and Depression glass. Generally speaking, anybody with Depression glass has some good quality furniture and knickknacks to go along with it."

"All right then, let's hit the ones in Martin and see if we need to head on down the highway."

For the next hour and a half Meg and Kendra tagged along behind Zelda, hitting yard sale after garage sale after yard sale. By the time they'd finished the ones in Stars Hill, Kendra knew she needed either caffeine or a bed.

"Uncle!" she said, getting into the car after the tenth sale.

Zelda buckled her seat belt. "What?"

"She's crying uncle," Meg explained. "It means she gives up. And I'm with her."

"You girls in need of a break?"

Meg directed the car toward Clay's. "I just need some caffeine and I'll be fine."

"Me, too." Kendra cut her eyes at Meg.

Meg clearly read the message. What were they thinking? Zelda's enthusiasm for yard sales rivaled the sisters' enthusiasm for scrapbooking. Oh well. Once they got inside Clay's, they could "realize" they were hungry and order accordingly. They shared no further conversation until Meg parked the car outside of Clay's.

"Y'all go right on in, I'll wait here."

Meg twisted in her seat. "You're not coming in?" Thoughts of a plate piled with eggs and bacon went flying out the window.

"No, by the time I get these old bones in there, you two can have your caffeine and be back in the car, headed to Greenfield. If you'll be so kind as to bring me a cup of coffee and a couple packets of sweetener, I'll be fine."

Meg dared not look at Kendra, knowing her sister had probably intended to eat breakfast as well, not just grab a cup of go-juice. "Um, okay, then. Be right back."

The sisters left the car and went into Clay's.

"I don't think I've ever been homicidal, but I'm getting there," Kendra said. "How many sales did she say there were in Greenfield?"

They wove their way among the tables to the bar. " 'A couple,' whatever that means."

"A couple better be two or less. I think we picked the wrong way of bonding with Zelda."

Meg went behind the counter and fixed Kendra a Diet Dr Pepper and herself a Coke. "I think you're right."

"Hey, what are you doing behind my counter?" Clay came through the swinging door to the kitchen.

"It was either this or die of exhaustion in your dining area. I thought you'd prefer this."

He nodded. "Ah, yard saling didn't go well?"

"It's still going." She put Kendra's drink in front of Kendra and went to get Zelda's coffee.

"You're not done?"

"No. We're going to Greenfield now. Kendra and I needed a jolt, though, to keep up with her."

Clay threw back his head and laughed.

"Hey, this is not funny, mister," Meg grumbled.

"Yeah, you tell him," Kendra agreed.

"That woman is three decades older than the both of you and she's running circles around you. I'm sorry, ladies, but that's funny in my book."

Meg put a lid on Zelda's coffee. "Get a different book."

Clay clamped his lips together, but the mirth still lit his eyes. "Yes, ma'am."

Meg picked up her Coke and headed for the door. Kendra slowly followed her.

"Next time we take her to the movies,"

Kendra said.

"Definitely."

They walked back into the bright sunshine of the day and got into the car. Meg thought about the different ways she could get out of going to Greenfield. She could claim a headache. Given her recent history, they'd believe it in a heartbeat. Or she could say she was simply too tired. They'd probably buy that, too.

But both of those required her assuming the identity of the recovering surgery patient again and she'd just gotten out of that mode last week. She didn't feel like reassuming the role, even if it would get her out of going to Greenfield to paw through a few more people's junk.

She drove down Lindell and turned right on University. Ferns and petunias dotted the porches of the various houses along the way. Summertime in Stars Hill — what a gorgeous sight to behold.

Turning left onto Elm, she said, "So, Zelda, Joy told me she brought you some of her hosta. Did you have any luck with them?"

"I sure didn't. Planted those cuttings she brought over in the backyard. I knew I shouldn't have planted them at all. No offense, honey, but Joy presented those things

312

to me like they were the Queen's jewels themselves. Should have told her thank you but no thank you because I could tell they meant a lot to her. But I tried anyway and, wouldn't you know it, a week later they shriveled up and refused to grow. I had to dig them up and throw them out before Joy could see I'd killed her prized plants."

Meg cut a look at Kendra, whose eyes had gone wide.

"You mean they *died?*" Kendra said.

"Deader than a doornail, and for the life of me I don't know why. I had your daddy look at them and he didn't have a clue, either. And you girls know as well as I do that your daddy can grow a rosebush in the Arctic. You ask me, those hosta had gotten used to the fancy soil over at Joy's and went into shock when I plopped them down into our everyday dirt."

She had a point there. Meg doubted the dirt in Momma's old flower beds had been tended to since she died. Daddy spent all his outdoor time working on the farmland, not the land up by the house. He'd always said that was Momma's territory.

That meant that, no matter what Zelda plopped into the ground there, it would more likely than not die. Poor Zelda hadn't had a chance from the get-go with those plants.

"Have you tested the soil?" Meg looked in the rearview mirror to gauge Zelda's reaction.

"Tested the soil? What does that mean?"

"You know, sent in a sample to the ag boys and asked them to tell you what it needed to prepare it for planting."

"I didn't know such a thing existed."

"Oh, yeah. And it's not expensive either. I think it's around five dollars. They'll come out and get the sample themselves then, a week or two later, bring out a report and tell you what to add to the dirt to make it a heaven for plants."

"Well, I'll be. I sure wish I had known about that before I put those hosta in the ground."

Meg laughed. "I'm sure Joy will understand if you tell her what happened. She may even offer to bring you more cuttings once the dirt's been prepared."

"I'm not about to tell that woman I killed her plants."

"Uh, Zelda," Kendra cut in. "I'm fairly certain she knows."

They rode for a moment in silence. "Said something to you, did she?" Zelda finally said.

Meg heard the longing in Zelda's tone and frowned. Maybe Zelda really did want to be friends with the sisters. "She may have mentioned that she hadn't seen the plants around the house anywhere." Meg wished now she hadn't brought it up. She didn't want to make things difficult between Joy and Zelda. Especially if Zelda had made such an effort. But being honest was always the best policy, right?

Zelda's hearty chuckle put Meg's worries to rest. "I might have known she'd check. Thank goodness she didn't come over and see them lying dead in the ground. I think that might have been the death knell for any chance at a friendship."

Zelda's voice once again told Meg that her stepmother seemed to be after a real relationship with the sisters. She resolved to try a little harder to befriend the woman. "Probably." Meg took a long drink of her Coke. Joy took her plants as seriously as she did everything else in her life. From the high-end artwork carefully selected and placed throughout her home to the choices of flooring, molding, and light fixtures, Joy researched everything to death and did her dead-level best to settle on the best of whatever it was. Meg used to think she did it for show — to let the rest of them know she was somehow better than them. She'd since figured out Joy just cared a whole lot about quality and would rather do without than make-do with something less.

Meg swallowed. So things between Zelda and Joy might not be the best right now, but the sisters had to start somewhere in forming a relationship with Zelda. If the past few weeks had taught her anything, it was that families had to love each other no matter what they thought of each other. Heaven knew she hadn't exactly been the Meg they all loved before the surgery. Yet the sisters still showed her grace and love, and she doubted any of them had even thought of pulling away from her forever.

Daddy had made Zelda family. She was Daddy's choice. That meant the sisters needed to try to love her and befriend her even if she wasn't the person they'd have picked. And the bridge-building might as well start with her. "Okay, we're coming into Greenfield. Which way to the first sale?"

"Go through town and turn left at the red light. Then it's four streets down and turn right, fifth house on the left."

"Red light, left. Got it." Meg tapped Kendra on the leg. "You awake over there?"

Kendra lifted her head from where she'd rested it against the window. "Yep. Ready and rarin' to go."

Meg looked at her sister's heavy-lidded eyes. "Oh yeah, you look it. Drink your DP."

Kendra obediently took a drink and swallowed.

Zelda leaned forward to better see Kendra. "How about you sit in the car for this one, finish that drink, and you can join us on the next one?"

Kendra didn't hesitate. Her head came back to the window and her eyes closed. "Good idea."

Meg stopped at the red light and looked in the mirror to meet Zelda's eyes. "That was nice of you."

"I have a moment every now and then."

She started to respond but stopped when Zelda's eyes widened — first with surprise, then something that might have been panic.

"You know, now that I think about it, this first sale doesn't sound as promising as I thought. How about we skip it and go to the next one instead?"

"But we're already over here near it. Just a few streets away." Meg looked through the windshield, trying to find whatever it was that had made Zelda's expression change. "Is something —"

And then she saw it. Wimpy's. One block over from them. Sitting like a giant blinking sign in the parking lot — her van.

A thousand questions collided in her mind at once. Was that really *her* van? It couldn't be, even though her license plate was clearly on the front of it. But if that was her van, where were the kids? Who was watching them while Jamison came over here for breakfast? And what was he doing here? He said he came over during her recovery, but that was over. Besides, they had Jenny now. No reason in the world for him to be at Wimpy's, she didn't care *how* good the coffee tasted.

Had he brought the kids with him? They didn't drink coffee. *Okay, that's a dumb thought. Get a grip, Meg.*

A horn honked behind her and she jumped. The light had turned green and here she sat like a frightened statue over . . . what? Nothing. She was jumping to conclusions and she knew it.

She turned left and then right into the Wimpy's parking lot.

"Oh, honey, I don't think this is such a good idea."

There was a note in Zelda's voice . . . Meg looked at her, saw the worry pinching her brow, and it dawned that Zelda knew something — which meant there was something to know.

Meg let the engine die, then turned in her seat. "Zelda, do you have something you should tell me?"

Zelda looked like a rabbit who'd run out into the middle of a freeway. "Um . . ."

"Please, you need to tell me whatever it is."

"Look, let's just go on back home. I don't need to go to these yard sales, I've got enough junk —"

"Zelda Sinclair, spill it or you'll be *walking* back to Stars Hill."

Her stepmother turned to look out the window. Meg watched her debate with herself, the war playing out clearly on her facial features. A tick even began to jump above her left eye.

"Come on, Zelda. If *I* knew something, I'd tell *you.*"

That did it. Zelda's eyes held tears when they came back to Meg's. "I'm sure it doesn't mean a thing, Meg."

"Then it won't matter if you tell me."

"I came over here a couple of weeks ago. To go to a yard sale. The day y'all came over to scrapbook. Remember?"

"Sure."

"I came down here, just like we did, and I saw Jamison going into Wimpy's. It struck me as odd — you know, why would he come all the way here for breakfast when he can get it at Clay's — so I stopped and went inside."

"And what did you see?" She'd deal with the fact Zelda had spied on her husband later.

"He sat at the end of the bar, drinking coffee and talking to the waitress."

Meg was fine until the waitress part. "What do you mean 'talking to the waitress'?"

Zelda's gaze went to the floorboards and her shoulders slumped. "I mean what you think I mean. They were laughing it up and carrying on and I felt like they knew each other somehow, or were sure enjoying each other's company."

Meg struggled to maintain a stoic exterior. It wouldn't do for her to break down here in the middle of the parking lot in front of Zelda. Besides, all Jamison had done was talk to a waitress. Big deal.

But it hurt like the dickens. The most special part of their marriage was their ability to talk to each other, to have long conversations. He'd been sharing that with someone else?

No wonder the receipt Meg found had been for one. The other woman worked here. Of course she wouldn't have to purchase something to spend time with Jamison.

Then again, Meg *had* been pretty awful to live with for a while. She didn't even like herself during those weeks of recovery. It made perfect sense for Jamison to go elsewhere for conversation and laughter. He certainly couldn't get those things at home. She couldn't blame him for doing this.

But she sure as the sunrise *could* blame him for not telling her. For creating a situation where she could find a receipt in his pants pocket and have to question him.

And now she *really* blamed him because she'd been herself for a week and he was still coming out here. If the reason had been for good conversation, then he had that at home now. At least *she* felt like they had it. They'd talked and talked and reconnected.

Evidently he didn't do as much connecting as I did. She let the idea slide away, not sure her brain or heart could handle it. She hadn't been very involved when Kendra had that thing with a married man last year. Now she wished she'd paid attention.

She considered waking Kendra for some advice, but she looked so peaceful leaned up against the window, lightly snoring. Better to go in there and find out if she had anything real to worry about. Her heart was convinced she did — but she wanted to be sure. Wanted to give Jamison the benefit of the doubt. Owed that to him after all their years together.

Just like he owed me honesty.

"Meg?" Zelda's voice broke her thoughts. "I think it's time for a breakfast break, don't you?"

The blood drained from Zelda's face. "Oh, no. I'm not hungry at all. You're hungry? Let's go on over there to that gas station. I'm sure they have a sausage biscuit or something."

"Zelda, I'm going in there. You can stay in the car if you want. But I'm going to find out if I have something to yell about before I take my husband's head off."

Zelda paused, then her chin came up and her shoulders squared. "All right, then. This isn't what I'd recommend, but it's your marriage and your call. If you're going, I'm going in with you."

"Oh, you don't have to do that, Zelda. I doubt I'll be staying very long."

Zelda patted her spiky red hair and adjusted her earring. "No way I'm letting you go in there alone. It's both of us or neither of us."

Meg took a deep breath. She'd really rather not have Zelda witness what she felt certain would be a scene, but she also wouldn't mind the support if things got ugly. "All right, then. Let's go." She cast a last glance at Kendra, who slept on in blissful ignorance. No help coming from there. Kendra could sleep through a bomb blast and wake up wondering what knocked down all the buildings.

Meg opened the door and stepped out. Yep, the van still sat in the parking space. If the attraction really was coffee, he could have gotten it to go and been halfway home by now.

Older men lined the porch. They tipped their hats to her and Zelda. "Ma'am," a few of them greeted. Meg hoped the look she gave them was kind, but she wasn't sure if her facial muscles were obeying her wishes. A lot of her felt frozen, like she was an iceberg drifting along with the current, unable to determine a course or direction, helpless against the forces at work.

The door squeaked on its hinges. She registered that somewhere in the back of her mind. Took in the pictures covering one wall and the people sitting in every available seat. But, really, only one of these people mattered enough for her to register his presence completely.

Jamison sat at the last stool at the counter.

He wore the shirt she'd given him for Christmas last year. It looked as good on him as she'd envisioned when she picked it off the shelf at the mall in Nashville.

Except . . . he hadn't worn it for her. She knew that when she lifted her gaze a fraction of an inch to the left, where a woman who could have been her sister stood talking to her husband. Meg's feet glued themselves to the floor.

Dumbfounded. She hadn't understood the word fully until now. Now she knew it in every fiber of her being. Each bit of her had gone dumb, unable to register the sight presented to her eyes.

The woman's laughter carried the length of the counter. Jamison's beloved rumble mixed with it. Together they made a pleasing sound that hurt Meg. It shouldn't have been that pleasant. It should have been disconnected, inappropriate, unacceptable.

But it sounded nice.

Meg recoiled.

Zelda's arm came around her and Meg had enough sense to be grateful for a stout stepmother.

"Come on, Meg. Let's just go."

But she couldn't turn away. It was like standing at the railroad tracks, watching a car stall while a train bore down. Nothing could be done to halt the inevitable crash, but still a person watched. As if watching could somehow stop the coming disaster.

The blonde laughed again and put her hand on Jamison's arm. He didn't pull away. Made no move to indicate this was anything untoward or unwelcome. If anything, his smile grew.

Meg gasped. *Her* Jamison?

"Meg, you've seen enough. You know, now. Let's go."

Some of the diners had begun to stare at the two women standing frozen in the entryway. Meg could see them from her peripheral vision. Saw them begin to talk in low voices or behind their hands, just like Stars Hill folks did when they were talking about someone in the room.

She was the someone.

She couldn't find it in her to care.

Surely Jamison would look up soon, see her standing, and come to her. All she had to do was wait.

But seconds ticked by and he only had eyes for the blonde in front of him, not the blonde he'd married. A woman who looked like her. Her height, her build. Her hair.

Except Meg's hair resembled a blonde version of Zelda's now, not the long, wavy locks Jamison loved. Did he come here because the woman's hair reminded him of hers?

Another dumb thought, Meg. You're losing your grip here.

Well, what was she expected to do? In the space of three months she'd had a brain tumor discovered, had brain surgery, recovered from that, and found out her husband —

What? What should she call this? It hurt like an affair, but she couldn't believe Jamison did anything but see this woman here at Wimpy's. That wasn't an affair, was it? Did she even have cause to be mad? Or was she being one of those waspish women who followed their husbands around or hired detectives to spy on them and used every little thing to start an argument or question the man's commitment?

Abruptly she turned and exited the diner. Zelda said nothing, just walked behind her to the car. Meg listened to the clink of Zelda's jewelry, focusing on that instead of the thoughts that wouldn't slow down enough to be heard in her brain.

They entered the car. Kendra slept on, oblivious to the fact that Meg's world had just shifted farther than the San Andreas ever could. Meg grabbed onto the steering wheel — a woman caught in a tornado, grasping for a plumbing line. Everyone knew plumbing lines went deep into the ground — deep enough to give you a fighting chance for survival. Not like in that movie about tornadoes. Too much of that had been Hollywood computer effects. People here in the world of real tornadoes laughed at portions of that movie.

But the plumbing line was true. Momma had said.

So Meg held onto the steering wheel and waited for the internal storm to stop buffeting her. Waited to find a calm place to stand and think. Waited to wake up from a nightmare she couldn't comprehend.

Zelda placed turkey slices onto hoagie rolls, shaking her head. "I know it sounds incredible, Jack, but I also know what I saw with my own two eyes. Twice now. He may not be having an affair in the traditional sense of the word, but he's definitely cheating on Meg. You should have seen him today with that waitress, laughing and talking up a storm. Her hand on his arm. Him looking up into her eyes like he can't get enough of her. A man isn't supposed to be that way with any woman but his wife."

Jack swiped a slice of cheese and tore off a piece. "Tell me again what you saw." He put the piece of cheese into his mouth and chewed.

Zelda related both encounters at Wimpy's. "I wasn't sure it was something bad until I saw Meg's face while she watched them today. That woman felt betrayed. It was all over her face. She had that look of a woman who just found out her husband isn't quite the man she thought. I've seen that look on so many military wives' faces I could spot it a mile away."

Jack ate more of the cheese and Zelda stayed quiet to let him think. Sometimes Jack needed a little while to mull over something before he was ready to talk about it. She hadn't expected him to come up with an instant plan. She just needed to tell him about Jamison and let him figure it out.

Heaven knew *she* didn't have any idea what to do. Well, that wasn't exactly true. She had an idea or three, but none that would be helpful to the situation unless Meg wanted her husband severely maimed for life. Zelda had no patience for men who strayed. No reason in the world for a man to go outside his vows and have his needs — any needs — met by another woman. Any respect she may have had for Jamison and how he'd weathered this tough time with Meg went out the window faster than money from the offering plate in hard times.

She slathered mayonnaise on their sandwiches and set them on paper plates, then went to get the potato chips. She and Jack didn't eat fancy most nights. Neither of them had a whole lot of energy or inclination to fix the kind of three- and four-course meals Joy prepared for her family. Did Joy still keep up that kind of meal schedule now that they had Maddie?

She doubted it.

Putting a handful of chips on each of their plates, she nudged Jack's side. "Come on, old man. Bring your thoughts to the table."

He picked up their glasses and followed her into the dining area.

"So, do you have a grand plan yet?" Zelda bit into her sandwich.

Jack started in on his chips. "Not completely, no. I'm thinking something along the lines of a sermon on fidelity — of all types. What do you think?"

Zelda considered that. Meg would know Zelda had told Jack about what they'd seen. Surely Meg assumed Zelda *would* tell Jack, but they hadn't talked about it. In the end, though, having Jamison hear truth about his behavior mattered more than if Meg got mad at her for talking to Jack. Meg should assume Jack knew everything Zelda did. If she didn't assume that, then tough on her.

"I think it's a good idea." Zelda chomped on her sandwich.

"Good. It's settled, then. I'll be up late tonight revising the sermon. I'd planned to preach on sin, so most of the Scripture references will stay the same, I just need to put in some marriage-related material."

Zelda looked at Jack. She hadn't considered the work he'd have to put into his sermon on such short notice. "Maybe you should wait until next weekend. I hate for you to stay up. You know how you get when you don't have your sleep."

Jack shook his head. "No, if Jamison's allowing another woman to give him the kind of friendship he should only share with Meg, then I'm not going to let another week go by without doing what I can to address the situation."

"You could skip the sermon and go directly to him."

"I considered that, but it occurred to me that if somebody like Jamison can do this, then I don't have a good idea of who else in the congregation might be struggling with the same thing. Maybe God allowed me to know about this purely so I'd preach about it and a few would hear. I'm not sure why, but I do know that preaching about it is the right thing to do."

"Then I'll go put on a pot of coffee. You're going to need it to burn that midnight oil."

He snagged her hand as she passed him. "Thank you, Zelda."

She smiled and patted his hand. "My pleasure."

TWENTY-TWO

Thunder rumbled outside and fat raindrops splatted against the window pane. Jamison looked toward the mess Mother Nature graced them with and groaned.

"Any chance of skipping church this morning?"

Meg came out of the bathroom, toothbrush in hand and an odd look — wariness? — in her eyes. "Why?"

Jamison waved a hand toward the window. "You want to drag three kids out in that?" They'd all look like drowned rats before they made it to the church door. He hated rainy Sundays.

"Oh, buck up. It's just a little rain."

Another roll of thunder sounded.

"Just a little rain, she says." Jamison was teasing, but Meg didn't smile. "And some thunder and lightning and wind gusts up to thirty miles an hour, but that's nothing."

"Exactly." She flounced back to the bathroom. Shortly he heard the sink's faucet come on. What was *with* her?

If he fought her on this, she'd probably give in. He didn't think her idea of a good time was schlepping three kids through the rain, either. But she hadn't been to church since the surgery and, now that she felt like going, he didn't want to be the one to douse her enthusiasm.

Groaning, he got out of bed and joined her in the bathroom. "All right, but we're putting the kids in rain boots and slickers and I don't care if that's not dressy enough for church."

She cut her eyes at him and snatched up a brush. "Yes, sir."

"And no white dresses."

"Mm hmm. Anything else, King of Grouch?"

"Yeah —" he pulled her close — "good morning." He breathed in the fruity scent of her shampoo. With her hair so short, he wouldn't be able to smell it once her hair dried but now, with it still wet from the shower, he could inhale that familiar fragrance that had been Meg's for years.

She tensed, then hugged him back. "It *is* a good morning."

Unsure of her hesitation, but knowing he'd rather not get into it with her, he let her go and stepped into the shower. The warm water felt good, but he knew he'd better lather up, shave, and get out. Meg rarely left enough hot water for anyone to have a full-length shower after her.

That used to irk him, though he'd long ago told himself that Meg looked and smelled the way she did because she faithfully ran the water heater out of its supply. Most of the time he'd wait for the tank to heat up another round of water before taking his shower, but rainy Sundays required way more time to get out the door and to the church.

Yet another reason to skip church during storms.

Not that Jack hadn't preached about just this thing plenty of times. He called those able-bodied individuals who skipped church when it wasn't convenient, as in when it stormed outside, fair-weather Christians.

Jamison didn't consider himself a fair-weather anything, just a man who knew enough to stay in out of the rain.

The water cooled and he turned it off with a smile. *Meg.*

By the time he'd dried off, combed his hair, gotten dressed, and made his way downstairs, Meg had the kids at the breakfast table in their pajamas.

"Morning, everybody."

"It's storming, Dad. Look!" James pointed to the French doors where rain pounded everything between the sky and the ground.

"Yeah, pretty bad out there, isn't it?"

"But we're safe inside, right, Daddy?" Savannah turned big eyes to him.

Jamison knelt down to her level and took her face in his hands. "We're absolutely safe." He stood and walked over to Meg, who was in the midst of pouring batter into the waffle iron. "Which is why smart people stay home from church when the weather is nasty."

She closed the lid on the batter and turned to face him and the kids. "That's just a little wind and rain, kids. We're going to eat these waffles, then get ready for church."

"But I don't *want* to go out in the rain!" Savannah yelled. "We'll melt!"

Meg laughed and Jamison turned to share it with her, only to realize she hadn't looked at him since he'd entered the kitchen. "No, we won't. Unless someone here is the Wicked Witch of the West and I don't know about it."

"I'm not a Wicked Witch," James said. "That's just a dumb movie."

Savannah pointed to her chest. "I'm not a

335

Wicked Witch, either."

"Me, either," Hannah said, not to be out-done.

"Then we're all perfectly safe to go to church, rain or no rain." Meg went back to the waffle iron and raised the lid to reveal a perfectly golden waffle. "James, get everyone forks. Savannah, get the butter from the refrigerator. The waffles are ready!"

With a minimum of fussing, they managed to get the kids into the van — with Jamison thanking the Lord aloud for garages that were attached to the house and Meg studi-ously avoiding eye contact with him. Before long it was back out of the van and up the church steps.

By the time Sunday school ended, they'd mostly dried out. Meg and Jamison gathered up their things in the Sunday school room and headed toward the sanctuary for, as the kids called it, "big church."

Jamison looked through his bulletin while they waited the final few minutes before service, refusing to contemplate the reason behind Meg's bad mood. Probably just another round of hormones or after-effects of the surgery. He liked two of the five songs they were singing today. Better than noth-ing.

The music minister stood and greeted them, then the music of the morning kicked off. Jamison sang along, half of his mind on the song and the other half on his conversation with Karen yesterday. He still didn't know why he'd gone back. Karen had been as surprised as he. But something drew him back there and he decided he'd better go find out.

The conversation, as always, had left him cheerful. He'd picked up the kids from his mother's and been back home before Meg returned from her garage sale shopping with Zelda. He'd thought to mention to Meg that he went to Wimpy's, but that would have made it seem like there was something to tell. And there wasn't.

The tempo of the music changed, leading the congregation into the second song selection. Jamison followed with the ease of a lifetime of singing these songs. He could do the Sunday morning routine in his sleep. He knew it shouldn't be a routine, but some days it felt that way. Like today, when he'd rather be at home with his family instead of running between rain drops and showing up looking like a wet cat.

When offering time came, he passed the plate, but his thoughts remained on Karen. Their verbal sparring had been particularly fun yesterday. He hoped Meg would be back at that level soon. While her current recovery level thrilled him to the core, she hadn't quite gotten to where they were before. He didn't know if she ever would but had made peace with it if she didn't. He could always go see Karen if he needed a real verbal matching of wits.

Before he realized they'd been through the songs, Jack took the pulpit and opened his Bible. Jamison prepared to tune in. The songs were Meg's part of worship, but the sermon was his.

Jack cleared his throat and stepped up to the podium. He heard the shuffling of church bulletins and Bible pages as the congregation readied to hear his sermon. Would they be receptive to the message he'd been up all night preparing?

Would Jamison?

No time to think about that now. This wasn't the first time he'd felt called to talk about an unpopular, potentially messy topic. And it probably wouldn't be the last.

Placing a hand on either side of the pulpit, he began. "Love. Is it fantasy, fact, or feeling? I see many couples today with something eerily similar occurring in their marriage: they have 'fallen' out of love with their spouse. I generally ask them if they broke any bones when they fell in love the first time."

That got a few chuckles.

"You get the humor in that much better than most of these folks. Usually they respond by telling me they simply do not love their spouse anymore. I wish I could be surprised by that, but I've heard it too much. Without fail I always ask them, 'If you don't love your spouse any more, how much *less* is your love?' I get a whole lot of deer-in-the-headlights looks to that question."

He dared a glance over to Jamison, not surprised when his son-in-law didn't meet his eyes.

"Seriously though, what does it mean to fall in love? Were you just walking along on life's pathway and all of a sudden — *boom* — you were on your backside looking up, wondering what hit you? Had you fallen before you had time to think about what you were getting into? Was it a kiss or maybe just a look from that special someone that sent the warm fuzzies running all over your body and made you think this must be love?

"In the Book of Revelation, chapter 2, Jesus speaks of those who have left their first love. They called 'em AWOL in the army,

Zelda tells me. That means 'Around here but With Out Lights on,' for those of you wondering." As laughter rippled through the congregation, Jack sought his wife's eyes and was warmed at the support he saw in her gaze.

"If you have your Bible, turn with me and let's see what God has to say to us."

Those who hadn't already turned to the passage printed in the bulletin responded to his command. He paused so they'd have time to find the Scripture, then began reading.

"Scripture says, 'To the angel of the church in Ephesus write: These are the words of him who holds the seven stars in his right hand and walks among the seven golden lampstands: I know your deeds, your hard work and your perseverance. I know that you cannot tolerate wicked men, that you have tested those who claim to be apostles but are not, and have found them false. You have persevered and have endured many hardships for my name, and have not grown weary. Yet I hold this against you: You have forsaken your first love. Remember the height from which you have fallen! Repent and do the things you did at first.' " (NIV)

Jack didn't usually read that much Scripture aloud, but they needed to hear the meat of the Word before he expounded on it. Besides, he loved the last part of the next verse. "And in verse 6: 'But you have this in your favor: you hate the practices of the Nicolaitans, which I also hate. He who has an ear, let him hear what the Spirit says . . .' "

He laid the open Bible on the pulpit and paced to the right. Looking out over the congregation, he saw a couple hundred sets of eyes gazing back at him. It only took a glance to confirm Jamison's eyes were in that group.

Meg doodled a flower on the notes section of her church bulletin. If anybody looked at her, she'd appear to be a woman taking notes on a sermon — rather than a wife worried about her husband's response to her daddy's words. She shaded in the round petals while considering the timing of this particular sermon topic.

Zelda must have said something to Daddy.

Unsure how to feel about that, Meg drew a house beside the bed of black ink flowers. As she sketched in windows and a chimney, she almost felt the vibrations of stress coming off Jamison. Did he know how loudly

341

his body language spoke to her? Did he think — after all these years of marriage — that she *wouldn't* be tuned in to him?

Did the rest of the congregation know that her husband had let himself strike up an inappropriate friendship with a woman in Greenfield? Meg raised her head and glanced around. Most eyes were fixed on Daddy, some were focused on laps or bulletins. None seemed to be throwing fiery darts in Jamison's direction.

Meg heaved a sigh and went back to her drawing. The home coming to life underneath her pen was picture-perfect.

Like her life used to be.

Jack scanned the crowd, making eye contact with a few. "Now, I bet you're scratching your head, wondering how in the world can he get a message about love and marriage from this passage? Well, you're not alone. When God sent me to this passage last night, I thought He wanted me to preach a message on church attendance or coming to love Him more. I already had a couple of those prepared and it wouldn't take much time or effort to fix a sermon for today. I argued with Him for a while — ever tried that when God's speaking to your heart?"

A few chuckles met his question. He

smiled and shook his head. "Sounds like some of y'all know the craziness of fighting with the Eternal One. Well, as He always does, He eventually won. He's just like that. So I didn't get the sermon I went looking for. Kind of like I went to a calf sale and came back with a sow.

"See, I got the distinct impression that God was telling me that a lot of marriages were mirror images of some of the churches He was speaking of here in Revelation 2. They started out in a big way, lots of pomp and circumstance, bells and whistles and all. And then something happened on their journey to spiritual bliss and they fell out of love with what He called their first love. For the sake of this message I would like you to think of the term *first love* the same way you would generally think of marriage, okay?" Heads nodded. "Now, let's go back and lay some groundwork for what ol' John is writing about here in Revelation."

Several of those in the congregation were scratching notes in the designated space on the bulletin. Questions to throw at him later? Maybe. Could be this lesson hit home for more than he wished.

"In Acts chapter 19 we find Paul teaching at the church in Ephesus. He taught for nearly three years there. It had to be a

Baptist church, cause that's about the average stay for most Baptist pastors at one church today."

More chuckles. Good. They were still with him.

"Anyway, it was in Ephesus that Paul first introduced the baptism of the Holy Spirit to disciples of John the Baptist. Man oh man, I bet he had to do some tall teaching to keep them folks from changing denominations.

"It was in Ephesus that the Bible says many miracles were done, extraordinary ones the Bible called them. So much so that even handkerchiefs and aprons that had touched Paul were taken to the sick." He adopted the tone of an old Southern revival pastor, yelling out loud and strong: *"And their illnesses were cured and the evil spirits left them!"* He pounded the podium. Those who were falling asleep twitched awake and those who'd been paying attention smiled or chuckled.

Jack went back to his normal voice. "It would seem that a great tent meeting had broken out among them Ephesian folks. Why, lookit, one of the first book burnings took place there. Guess they got serious about their religion real fast.

"Now, before Paul preached Jesus there,

many of the Ephesians had practiced sorcery and witchcraft. After becoming believers in Jesus, they brought all their books on sorcery and spells and all to the town square and burned them for all to see, so caught up in their devotion to this Jesus. Man, were they worked up or what? Sounds a lot like the first couple of years — or months, depending — of marriage, doesn't it?"

Jack let his gaze rest on a few of those sitting before him. "Remember what those first few months, hopefully years, of marriage were like? Spending time with that special someone every night. Not really wanting to go to work. Just longing to lie in bed or walk around the house or apartment and look at each other all day."

He shot another look Zelda's way. She winked at him.

"Ah, but eventually reality sets in and we begin to shift our attention to other things in life, like a career or maybe starting a family. And sooner than we can realize it, we're spending more and more time at the office or in the field trying to get ahead or when the family starts on the journey of becoming the next super star in sports and one of the parents has to drive them all over the place. Time begins to slip away from us and then one day — *wham* — someone new walks into our life."

Jamison settled his right heel on his left knee. *Be calm.* But the self-direction wasn't working. The longer Jack preached, the higher his blood pressure rose. Whatever happened to preaching about hellfire and brimstone? To telling the stories of all the Bible characters — Abraham, Isaac, Jacob, David, Joseph? Did they really need to focus on Revelation? A book hardly any Christian walking the earth could understand on their best day?

He tapped his pen against the Bible lying open in his lap. He hadn't written the first note. Meg, meanwhile, looked as if she'd decided to write an entire Bible study based on Jack's sermon today. Fabulous. *Just when things are looking up in his marriage, Jack has to rain down judgment.*

And all for something that was completely innocent.

Jamison put the cap back on his pen and settled his back against the pew. *Relax. He'll be done in a few minutes.*

And the second that happened, Jamison would be out of there.

Jack waved a hand in the air. "It all may start kind of innocent-like. A woman says

346

something about how you've been keeping yourself fit since getting married. Or maybe she compliments you, and it kind of just strokes your ego. And you haven't been getting much of that lately from your wife — she's too busy with her own job and the house and kids. Besides, there's nothing wrong with just talking to another woman, is there? Your wife used to tell you how good you looked all the time.

"The same thing happened to Paul. They'd been talking him up everywhere he went, bringing all those sick people to him to be healed. Listening to his every word. Hanging on every syllable. But isn't that what they were supposed to be doing? I mean, after all, he had told them that new converts were to desire the sincere milk of the word — just like newborn babes would have done. Have you ever seen a newborn baby that didn't want some milk to drink? Man, they're always hungry. Feed them until they get full and a few hours later they're starving again. That just what those Ephesian folks were doing — wanting more and more from God's table. How about you? Do you sincerely desire food from God's table? I mean, really hunger and thirst for it, just like a newborn babe does?

"Now I know what some of you hunger

and thirst for. I've seen you fidgeting around in your seat, looking at your watches, can't wait for the service to be over with, right? Right. Because what's on your mind is getting home and feeding your belly and taking the required Sunday-afternoon nap."

Scattered laughter and a few red faces met his knowing smile. Jack had mercy on the latter and went on. "But, back to Paul and his trouble. It took just three years and then reality set in with some of those in Ephesus. It was the money thing. An uproar took place concerning a few folks' ability to make money. It tied back to their old style of worship and that goddess Artemis. And silver. Put simply, greed overcame them. And pride. Their reputation in their province of Asia Minor and the other cities around them mattered to them. Tying their greed to their previous worship was a very good idea. So much so that if we didn't know better, we would think that it might have come from satan himself! Before long, these folks rushed the disciples to overpower them. A lynching-party mind-set had set in. They wanted blood."

Jack paced to the other side of the pulpit, then leaned one elbow against it. Time to bring this sermon home and make the crucial point. "So what, you're asking, does

348

all this have to do with you? Well, lately I've been talking to some friends of mine that are in trouble. Not the kind of trouble you can see from the outside. No, what's got them messed up is an affair. But not just your old garden-variety affair. What's snagged these folks is what's called an emotional affair."

He nodded at the raised eyebrows. "I know, I know. An affair's an affair, right? But these folks assured me an emotional affair isn't as bad as the actual physical thing. 'Sometimes,' they said, 'the other person didn't even know about the crush I have on him or her.' "

Jack straightened. "Say *what?* You'll have to s'plain that one to me, Lucy. I mean what's the point in having a crush on someone if they don't know about it? Wouldn't that be kind of like kissing your mule?

" 'You see,' they continue, 'there's this person in the post office where I go every day and he's always there, smiling at me, talking really nice to me — like Bobby used to do before he started working all that overtime at the factory.' Next thing they knew they started wondering what it would be like to be with this other person. Then they began to fantasize about the person all day and even sometimes at night when they were at home. 'But I would never physically act on it, would I, preacher?' I ask how their relationship with the spouse has been affected by all this fantasizing. 'At first it didn't have any effect. But after awhile, my thoughts of him began to creep into my mind when I was having sex' — notice here they did not say *making love* — 'with my husband. I began to let them take more and more of my time. But it's not like I had a *real* affair, preacher. Right? Besides, Bobby's been acting like a jerk lately — always pounding on that submission thing. Why, if you listen to him long enough, he sounds like he thinks he's God's right-hand man. If he keeps on acting like this, it won't be long before he's gonna want me to bow down when he finally does get home at night. Kinda like I did when we first got married. Why, it almost reminds me of how Dad treated Mom all those years before she left. Humph, maybe she had a *right* to leave! What d'ya think pastor? Do I have that right?' "

A few old-timers shouted out, *"No!"* Jack waited a moment, letting the scenario sink into the minds of the congregants. He'd avoided looking toward Jamison and Meg's side of the sanctuary to this point. Instead,

350

he looked at Zelda, who had her head turned slightly and her eyes cut over to Jamison. Zelda could tell him after the service what impact his words may have had.

He walked back behind the podium and leaned forward. "Know what I think? In the Old Testament, adultery was a very serious sin with some heavy consequences attached to it, up to and including stoning the offending parties to death. Even in the New Testament, when they brought the woman caught in the very act of adultery to Jesus, they wanted her stoned. So you see, adultery carried a heavy penalty with it.

"Jesus, in His teachings we call the Sermon on the Mount, Matthew chapter 5, teaches us a new way of looking at the problem of sin we all carry around. While in the Torah it was the *physical acts* that brought about the consequences for one's actions, in Jesus' new way of looking at things, the problem with sin was taken to a new and higher level. The level of thoughts and motives.

"Jesus said it plain and clear. 'I tell you if you even think about it, it is the same as if you had already committed the act.' Wow! That's some hard teaching. Who could live up to that kind of scrutiny? Even our thoughts are now put on record for our judgment? Lord help us all! Exactly the point!

"So, dear friends, it seems crystal clear to me that there's no difference between the physical act and the emotional. This is why we must guard our hearts and minds from letting these thoughts creep in. Might be why Paul said, 'Whatsoever is good, whatsoever is pure and wholesome, think on these things.'

Jack paused, studying those watching and listening, their faces intent. Should he tack on the ending or did they get the point? Always a fine line between *preaching* and *teaching.* He tried to stay out of making the folks feel preached at. Better to leave them thinking about his words than missing the point because they were mad at him.

Time to wrap it up.

"Take a last look at that Scripture. 'But you have this in your favor: you hate the practices of the Nicolaitans, which I also hate.' According to the early church fathers — such as Ignatius, Irenaeus, Clement of Alexandria, Tertullian, and Hippolytus . . ."

He paused, grinning at the congregation. "Impressed y'all by knowing the names of these fellows, didn't I?" Laughter eased around the room, and he nodded. "According to those fellas, the name *Nicolaitans* referred to those who, while professing themselves to be Christians, lived licentiously. Hmm, let's see . . . self-proclaimed Christians acting and living like the world? Married people acting and living, whether actually or emotionally, as if they were single — or worse yet, sometimes wishing they were? I think I see a correlation here. And the church is being praised for *hating* those practices. What does that say to us if we live our lives on fantasies, dreams, and feelings versus facts based on God's Holy Word?

"Here's a fact you can hang your hat — or eternity — on: God made a conscious decision to leave heaven and come to earth, walk among us humans, die that awful death on the cross to pay the price for our salvation, rose on the third day, and then returned to heaven. What we do with the actions He performed for us is our decision. That's love — not looking elsewhere when the relationship is broken or difficult, but instead finding a way to make the relationship whole." He let his gaze travel the room, careful not to pause when he looked at Jamison and Meg.

Father, please, let Your truth pierce Jamison's heart.

With that plea filling his heart, he turned

and asked Jason Walker to say the closing prayer.

TWENTY-THREE

Jamison fought to control his anger while Meg talked to the other churchgoers. They hadn't seen her in months, so everyone wanted to stop and chat. All Jamison wanted to do was punch something. Instead, he sat in the pew and fumed. Soon he'd have to go get the kids. If he didn't, though, the workers would just bring them to him. Members of the Sinclair clan always got stopped by congregants after service, so the workers had learned to bring the kids out rather than waiting forever.

Someone in the family had to have seen him talking to Karen and told Jack. No way would Jack preach a sermon like that just by coincidence. Had he just been called a *Nicolaitan?*

Someone thought they had something on him, thought they had witnessed him doing something wrong and, instead of coming to him to talk about it, had gone to Jack. He couldn't decide if he was more angry at the someone or at Jack, who could have called him for a private conversation on the phone rather than preaching a sermon on the matter.

And who did Jack think he was, telling husbands they shouldn't have friendships with women outside of their wives? This wasn't 1950. Granted, the values and morals they believed in were timeless, but the way they expressed them changed with the times, right? Right. Which meant what was taboo in 1950 was perfectly acceptable now. Shoot, back then a man couldn't be *seen* with a woman unless he'd declared formal intentions to court her and asked her parents.

These days women had two and three dates in one night! The times had changed, and Jack hadn't changed with them. Harmless flirting happened all the time. Meant nothing. Just a style of conversation in today's world.

Of course, that didn't explain the overwhelming sense of guilt building in Jamison, but he pushed that down and focused on the anger. Twice Jack had looked directly at him during the course of his sermon. And if Zelda had craned her neck any further, she'd have given herself a neck sprain. The entire congregation saw it and, with the way people in this town loved to talk, he knew some of them had put what they thought was two and two together and come up with five. He hadn't had an affair or done anything other than have conversation with Karen.

Conversation you should have had with Meg.

He shoved the thought away again. Conversation was nothing. Words. Just words. A respite for a man whose wife needed time and space to heal. Jack didn't understand. He'd have a nice, long conversation with Jack — when he didn't fantasize about throttling him — and all would be understood. Karen had done him — done them all — a favor.

He saw the kids as they came through the back sanctuary door and pasted on a smile.

"Daddy, look what I made!" Savannah held up a picture.

Jamison peered at it, trying in vain to determine what his daughter had drawn.

"Isn't it the most beautiful giraffe you've ever seen?" The teacher winked at him and Jamison smiled.

"It is, indeed. Good job, sweet girl."

"I made one, too." Hannah pushed a piece of construction paper into his hand.

Jamison held it up, needing no help once he saw the cotton balls glued to the page. "What a gorgeous sheep, Hannah!"

James rolled his eyes but said nothing.

"How was your church, James?" Though too old for the nursery, the church had set up an alternative worship service geared specifically to eight- to twelve-year-olds.

"Good," James mumbled.

Jamison didn't have the patience to draw the boy out right now. When he calmed down, he'd go back and have a conversation with his son.

"Glad to hear it." He turned to the nursery worker. "Thanks for bringing them up, Nancy."

"Don't you worry about it." Nancy walked down the aisle toward the front doors of the church.

"Meg —" he touched her arm to interrupt her conversation with Miss Rose — "you about ready?"

"Stars alive —" Miss Rose placed a tiny, gloved hand on her chest — "here I am rattling on about the weather and you've got your three young ones to get home and fed and off to bed for a nap, I'm sure. Don't let me keep you, hon." She adjusted the small hat on her bed of white curls.

Meg hugged the short, older woman.

"Nonsense. Thanks for stopping to talk. I've missed seeing you."

Miss Rose went the way Nancy had gone.

"Thanks for the rescue." Meg's mood had shifted again, he realized, watching her gather up her Bible and purse. Was *she* the reason behind Jack's sermon?

"Don't mention it. Ready to go or do you want to tell one more person that you're fine, recovering well, and thankful for their prayers?"

"Jamison Fawcett! I *am* grateful for their prayers and I don't mind talking to them. I haven't seen any of them in ages."

"Yeah, well, I'm tired and hungry and ready to get home."

"Add grumpy to the list."

"That, too."

"Everything okay?"

"Fine." He had no way to tell her that her dad's sermon had left him filled with fury. If he did, she'd want to know why and he didn't want to have an argument with her over nothing. Over stupid breakfast in a stupid diner. Or else she already knew and had chosen to go running to her daddy rather than to him.

She looked at him for a second, then let the matter go.

He picked up Hannah and prepared to

race through the downpour still falling outside. Why didn't they just stay home? Smart people stayed home, safe and dry under their rooftops when it rained outside. But, no, they had to not only get dressed but get the kids dressed and drag everybody outside in this mess.

And for what? To be humiliated in front of the entire congregation. At least Meg didn't seem mad anymore, which he hoped meant she hadn't put the dots together. Despite her finding a receipt from Wimpy's, she may not even know there *were* dots to put together.

Because there weren't. There were dots if people with their minds in the gutters wanted to *think* there were dots, but there weren't. And if Jack had just called him instead of preaching that sermon, he would have known that.

They got the kids buckled into their seats as fast as possible, but still dripped with rain by the time they situated themselves in the front seats.

"Don't we look a sight?" Meg laughed. "A family of drowned rats."

"I *told* you we should have stayed home." *Too much anger there. Tone it down.*

Again, she looked at him for a moment, but let the matter go.

360

Maybe the post-surgery Meg had a streak of patience the presurgery Meg had not. Because the old Meg might have let it go once, but she wouldn't stand for his temper without an explanation a second time.

Unless she knew why he was mad. Unless she'd talked Jack into preaching that sermon.

He put the van in drive and left the church, happy to have it in his rearview mirror and certain he'd be happier when he couldn't see it at all.

"You know, I think we should visit a new church soon."

"What?"

"Yeah." He warmed to the idea, surprised he hadn't thought of it once in all these years. "We've gone to your dad's church forever. Maybe it's time we visited some other churches, made a home for ourselves somewhere other than under your dad's authority."

She turned on the radio and soundly ignored him.

Not the right time to discuss changing churches. Shut up, Jamison.

They rode the rest of the way home listening to the radio and keeping their mouths shut. Should he be grateful or suspicious that Meg let his strange behavior go without a comment?

He hadn't decided by the time they'd pulled into the garage.

Better to let it go and pretend nothing happened. Make her bring it up if she wants to.

He unbuckled the kids on his side of the van and went into the house. A good book. He needed a good read, something grand and faraway like *Dune.* A story that had nothing to do with his life or even the planet on which he lived.

Meg and books went hand in hand. He found time for them two or three times a year. But when he needed a book fix, he knew from experience it wouldn't go away until he'd found a fantastic read.

And right now he'd had it with his life and trying to be the right man all the time. Even with Meg better, things were a muddled mess. Thinking it through seemed pointless. He'd *tried* to think it through, for goodness' sake, and had gotten nowhere.

Putting it out of his mind sounded like the best option. And only one way existed to do that — an excellent read.

Maybe Koontz. While Koontz's characters stayed on this planet, they dealt with circumstances not of this world's making. And if he picked up the next book in the Odd Thomas group, he could even have a character with otherworldly powers of perception.

Warming to the idea, he hurried to his study where he knew a Koontz book awaited. He'd purchased it the last time they were up in Cool Springs shopping but hadn't had time to read it since.

Meg watched Jamison all but sprint to his study and let him go without a word. Daddy's sermon had touched a nerve, that was plainer than the nose on her face. But Jamison didn't know how to deal with the emotions the sermon had churned up, and a conversation with an ill-tempered, unsure man was about as wise as wearing control top pantyhose a size too small on a ninety-degree day.

So she went into the kitchen to fix them all some lunch and sent the kids upstairs to play. Hannah didn't want to go — she loved to play in the kitchen — but Savannah got her attention with a Barbie and off they went.

Meg got a bag of frozen chicken nuggets out and dumped them on three plates. The kids would one day tell their spouses that all their mother ever made them were chicken nuggets.

They'd be about seventy percent right.

She punched buttons on the microwave and pressed the big silver Start button. As the machine hummed to life, she got drinks ready for the kids and considered what she and Jamison might eat.

You know what? Let the man get his own lunch. He's been getting his own meals for a while now without you knowing about it.

She finished fixing the kids' lunches and put all their plates and drinks on a tray. They could eat in their rooms today if they wanted. Jamison wasn't the only adult in the house who needed a little space and time.

She got the kids settled in front of a movie in James's room, happily munching away, and went back downstairs. They'd be content for at least an hour. By that time, maybe she'd have figured out what to do about their daddy.

Because she had to do *something*. Letting his behavior go not once, not twice, but three times in the past hour hadn't been easy and wasn't something she planned on continuing. Eventually they'd have to talk. And when they did, she needed to be ready with sorted out emotions and clear arguments.

She wandered into the living room and sank down into the recliner. As she rocked, she considered all she and Jamison had been through in their marriage. Until her surgery, there wasn't much. A spat here or there, the sleepless nights of parenting a newborn, the adjustment each time they added a child to the house — that was it. No threats of divorce, no raging furies, no worry that one would leave the other.

Until now.

Now she'd seen her husband all but flirt with another woman. Admitting it to herself helped a little bit. Gave her a reason for the fear and anger fighting within her heart. The fear made sense — losing Jamison or even having to fight another woman for Jamison filled her once-certain future with uncertainty. The anger made more sense because Jamison's flirting broke the trust they had. It broke *them.* Even if he'd only flirted — and she prayed to God he'd only flirted — he'd still crossed a line.

A line that, until now, it had never once occurred to her that either of them would think of crossing. When they'd stood before God and all the members of Grace Christian and vowed to love each other for better or worse until death parted them, they meant it. They'd just never had that promise tested until a tumor made her someone she hadn't been the day of their wedding.

Did that make his actions understandable? Pardonable, even? Should she be grateful all he did was flirt — please, God, let him have only flirted — and let it go?

No. Not only because he still went there even now, when she had made it to the other side of recovery, but for another important reason. Because when they swore those vows, they also said in sickness and in health. It didn't matter that they hadn't had to experience real sickness before her brain tumor. It only mattered that when sickness struck her down, he went somewhere else.

So it had gotten hard — really hard — for him for awhile there. Did he think she'd been strolling through the park on a vacation? No, she'd been fighting for her very identity. Struggling to figure out where the woman went that she knew and had been happy to be. Anybody could stick to a marriage in the good times. The bad times gave each of them the opportunity to *prove* their love.

It spoke volumes that he chose the dark days to form a friendship with another woman. Had he done this in their sunny times, she might not even have thought twice about it. But he'd chosen another woman to make him smile, to laugh with, while she stayed at home fighting demons in her mind. What kind of husband did that make him? What did it say about their marriage? What did it say about his commitment not only to her, but to their family?

Had he thought of James, Savannah, and Hannah at all while he sipped coffee and shared stories with that woman? Or had he only been grateful to be free of them for a few stolen minutes?

She'd never questioned Jamison's inner strength, always believing they shared an inner core that would come through if ever a day called for such. But that day came and Jamison wasn't the strong husband she needed. No, he pretended strength at home and then drank from another woman's well of happiness to ease the thirst his wife no longer quenched.

She ought to stomp in there and demand some answers, whether he was ready to give them or not! Just walk right up to him and tell him she knew all about his little waitress and what in the world had he been thinking? Seeing the surprised look on his face might help.

Then again it might not.

What was she really after here? Did it matter more that he feel pain or that they make it through this with their marriage intact? Three little ones playing upstairs depended on her to fight for the latter. They needed a mom *and* dad.

She sighed, resolved to wait until Jamison came to her. But when he did, he'd better be ready for the whole enchilada.

Because she was ready for a conversation.

Twenty-Four

Throughout his morning routine on Monday, Jamison fought with himself. By the time he slipped out of the house and into his car, he wondered if he'd become one of those people with split personalities.

On the one hand, he wanted breakfast at Wimpy's this morning. Meg hadn't been to the grocery store in over a week, so they were out of a lot of stuff at the house and he hadn't found anything for breakfast in the pantry other than cereal.

Who would choose cereal when they could drive for a few minutes and be served an entire breakfast platter? Which he could also get at Clay's, of course. He really should go to Clay's instead of Wimpy's. But a part of him wanted — craved — that smile on Karen's face. Hearing her voice and sharing laughs gave him a good start to his day.

Why did he even hesitate? Because of that stupid sermon of Jack's. Because Jack wanted them all to act as if they lived in 1950. Because Jack was out of touch with the current social structure. Because Jack had to share his opinion with the entire church body so that now Jamison worried about church members seeing him at Wimpy's.

Ridiculous. Absolutely ridiculous. Talking to Karen . . . Well, okay, he could admit to a twinge of guilt over not even kissing Meg good-bye before he jetted out the door to see Karen. To get breakfast.

He blew out a breath and turned on the radio. His thoughts were so mixed up he might as well ignore them and listen to the news. Morning Edition on NPR kept him occupied until he pulled the car into the Wimpy's parking lot.

He greeted the old-timers on the porch with a smile and wave and hurried into the diner. His stool sat waiting for him. He ambled over to it, catching Karen's eye on the way. She smiled a good morning, finished her conversation with the customer in front of her, and came over to him.

"Morning." She poured coffee and tucked her hair behind her ear.

"Good morning."

"Got big plans for the day?"

"Just playing around with numbers."

Karen scrunched her nose up. "Not my kind of day."

"And what is your kind of day?"

She tapped a finger on her chin and thought. "Oh, I don't know. A beach, a hammock, a good book, and a glass of ice water would be a good start to it, though."

"Good plan."

"There's a difference between plans and reality."

"What's that?"

"Plans are what you make to get through reality."

He laughed, the tension in his chest easing a bit. See? Easy conversation. Nothing wrong here. "In that case, I'll get to work on a plan."

"Your reality not as easy as you thought?" She quirked an eyebrow. "Is your wife okay?"

The tension coiled once again at the word *wife* on Karen's lips. "She's doing very well, thanks for asking."

"Glad to hear it." An old-timer down the counter raised a finger and Karen nodded. "Be right back."

While he waited for her return, Jamison sipped his coffee. If Meg was doing better, then what was he doing here? If he could answer that question, then life — and he himself — would make sense again.

But he had no answer. Or did he and he wasn't willing to admit it?

He'd begun debating with himself again when Karen reappeared, this time holding a platter of breakfast food.

"You looked hungry this morning."

He picked up his fork. "Famished."

"Dig in, then. Don't mind me. I'll just be over here making plans."

He smiled and picked up the saltshaker.

Half an hour later, with a belly full of good food and a heart full of good feelings, he left the diner and headed to work. He should have been starting *all* his mornings like this. It was just bad timing that he'd found Wimpy's when Meg was in the middle of her recovery. If he'd been coming here before the surgery, it probably wouldn't even be an issue to worry about.

He sighed. Timing. Just his rotten luck that he'd stumbled upon Wimpy's during the darkest days of his marriage. Because he still would have enjoyed the place if he'd found it years ago. He felt pretty sure of that. He might not have hit it off so quickly with Karen. Before the surgery he didn't know any other women existed on the planet except Meg, his mother, and the sisters. He would have known her, and Meg would probably have known her, and it'd be no big deal.

Ugh. Timing.

His cell phone rang and he looked at the caller ID. Meg. He debated answering it, then decided she'd just call the office if he didn't and she'd know he wasn't there yet. He pressed the button to take the call.

"Good morning."

"And good morning to you. You at work yet?"

His guard went up. Was she checking up on him? "Almost there. Why?"

"Just wondering. I'm going to the grocery store this morning and wondered if you had anything you wanted to add to the list but didn't want to interrupt if you'd already gotten that head of yours into the numbers."

He relaxed. "Oh, nope, I'm numbers-free right now except for the stock report on the radio."

"So?"

"So, what?"

"Anything to add to the grocery list?"

"Oh. Um, nope. Whatever you think."

"Okay, then. You all right?"

"Of course."

"You sure? You sound funny."

He swallowed and took a deep breath. "I'm fine, just have a lot on my mind.

Monday morning, you know."

"Well, then I'll let you go get to it. Have a great day."

"You, too." He ended the call and ran a hand through his hair. The boulder of guilt settling on his chest finally convinced him.

Going to Wimpy's either had to stop or he had to make sure Meg was okay with it. He had enough going on in his life without feeling guilty about where he ate breakfast.

Of course, he wouldn't feel this guilty if Jack hadn't preached that sermon. But Meg had heard the sermon and hadn't disagreed with it. At least she hadn't said that she disagreed with it, so he had to assume she agreed. He still thought going to Wimpy's was fine — he hadn't broken any vows or cheated on Meg. He would never be the kind of man who could cheat on his wife.

Then why did the sermon yesterday make you feel like that kind of man?

He pushed the bothersome question aside and made his way back out to the car. It wasn't long before he parked in the office lot and grabbed his briefcase. Time to put all this from his mind and focus on the day's work. His clients certainly didn't care where he ate breakfast. They only wanted their finances handled with intelligence and efficiency. Shoving Meg and Karen and the whole mess into the back of his mind, he resolved to give the clients what they paid for.

An hour later Jamison sat staring at his computer screen.

Every time he tried to bury himself in the numbers — a safe haven he'd counted on for years — thoughts of Meg and Karen kept bobbing to the surface. He'd no sooner make one calculation than he began calculating the costs of talking this over with Meg or of not ever going back to Wimpy's.

Sighing, he focused again on the computer screen and tried to figure out Walter Prescott's quarter earnings. Prescott had a board meeting in one week and needed these numbers a week ago to prepare. His phone call that morning left no doubt in Jamison's mind that another firm would get Prescott's business if Jamison didn't have a report finished by the end of the day.

Jamison stuck his pencil behind his ear and tapped keys on the keyboard. Creating quarterly reports didn't even require his entire brain, he'd been doing them so long. He could finish this one in no time and then have the afternoon free to —

His fingers froze over the keyboard.

To what? Think about Karen? Meg? Since when did he take time off of work to worry over his personal life? Other than the month after Meg's surgery, he'd been as constant at the office as daylight was each morning. What had happened to his staunch commitment to the clients?

He shook his head. The fact that Prescott had even felt the need to call and ask about the status of his reports ought to have been a wake-up call. Jamison was losing his edge here. *Get in the game, man. Focus.*

Karen's smiling face appeared in his mind's eye and, for a moment, he let himself forget the numbers to enjoy it. Then he shoved it away and buckled down. This report *had* to get done, and he'd quit before he let a client down.

Meg ran mousse through her wet hair and scrunched it between her fingers. The brochures had warned her not to expect the hair she'd had before surgery, but she'd hoped they were wrong. If the inch-and-a-half growth on her head was any indication, her thick, strong hair had decided to make a comeback. Which was a great thing since her husband was obsessed with a waitress who had her hair. Or hair that looked like hers. Or something like that.

She shook her head. Thick hair that hung past her shoulders had been one thing. This short do was quite another thing entirely. How did Zelda do this every day? Short hair didn't let itself be thrown up in a ponytail and forgotten on errand day. No, it had to be *styled* if the wearer had any plans to go out in public.

She sighed and scrunched some more until her hair resembled something close to a do. Good enough.

Grabbing her Kabuki brush, she applied powder, then a touch of eye shadow and mascara. Now she looked presentable. Not as good as the diner woman, but she doubted that woman had been through brain surgery lately. No wonder she'd turned Jamison's head. No doubt, she'd been turning it just this morning. That would explain why Jamison hadn't been at the office when Meg called.

A quick glance at the small quartz clock on her vanity told her she hadn't a moment to spare worrying about her husband's devotions. Kendra would be here any minute to watch the kids and free Meg up to go grocery shopping.

Meg didn't understand the thrill she felt at undertaking the mundane task of shopping for groceries except that it resembled a return to her normal life. An assuming of tasks that she competently handled before the surgery.

Finding humor in her own enthusiasm over a grocery list, she went downstairs to see if the movie she'd plopped the kids in front of had reached an end.

She heard Bob the Tomato's voice saying, "So you see, kids," and knew she'd come in the last two minutes of wrap-up. How did parents get anything done before Veggie-Tales?

She came around the corner and stopped at the sight of Kendra sitting in the middle of the couch with kids on either side of her. "Hey, I didn't know you'd gotten here."

"Figured you were upstairs putting your face on, so I came in here with the kids."

"You figured right. Do I look okay?"

"You look great. Think the leg will hold out?"

Meg knocked on her thigh. "Feels good so far."

"Okay, call me if you need me."

Meg would have turned to go, but this whole idea of Jamison falling for another woman had her so rattled that she stopped.

Kendra looked up. "Something you forgot?"

"Can you come in the kitchen a second?"

"Sure." Kendra gently tipped Hannah off her leg and stood.

Meg turned and walked ahead of Kendra into the kitchen, wondering if she shouldn't let the whole thing go. All she'd seen was Jamison talking to a waitress. And, of course, a good suspicion that he'd been back there this morning. Why would he still be going there when things were going so well between them? What allure did the woman have? What hold over him?

She came into the kitchen and turned to face her sister. "Something happened on Saturday when we were out with Zelda."

"I *knew* it!" Kendra snapped her fingers. "For the record, I didn't buy your headache story. You were acting *weird.*"

"Wives do that when they see their husbands flirting with other women."

Kendra froze, her eyes going as wide as a full moon on a harvest night. "Excuse me?"

"Don't make me say it again."

Kendra blinked. "Jamison? *Jamison* was flirting with another woman? Who? Where? You saw him?"

"You know the diner in Greenfield? In the main part of town? Same diner I found the receipt from a few days ago in his pants pocket?"

"Yeah, Whompy's or something like that."

"Wimpy's."

"Okay."

"He was there, drinking coffee and eating breakfast again, except this time I figured out he's not going there for the good hash browns. You should have seen her, Ken." Meg paced the floor. "She had hair like me and looked like me and he sat there on that stupid red stool just staring up at her like she'd hung the sun, moon, and stars."

"Tell me you dumped his coffee on him. His eggs, at least."

"He doesn't even know I saw him."

"Girl, you better be kidding me. You saw your husband flirting with another woman and you did *nothing?*"

Meg threw her hands up. "What was I supposed to do? It wasn't exactly a situation I had prepared for and I panicked. I left so I could think."

Kendra crossed her arms. "I can't believe I slept through all this."

"Me, either. Remind me to call and wake you up the next time we're under a tornado warning. You'd sleep right through the thing."

"I have a weather radio. Wakes me right up."

"Fabulous. Can we get back to the main issue here, please?"

"Right, right. Sorry. Okay, so this was four days ago. You haven't said anything since?"

Meg shook her head, more miserable by the minute.

"Not a word? Not even a mean look?"

"No. And believe me, I should get a Grammy for my performance."

"An Oscar. Grammy Awards are for music."

"Kendra! *Focus!*"

Kendra winced. "Sorry again." She thought a minute. "I guess this explains Daddy's sermon Sunday."

"You think Zelda said something to him?"

"I think that's one weird coincidence if she didn't."

Meg looked at the ceiling and paced some more. "Great. So now Daddy knows. I can't believe he hasn't come over here and yanked a knot in Jamison's tail himself."

"You sure he didn't?"

"I'm sure I'd know if he had."

"Good point. So, what are you going to do?"

"I don't know! Do you think I should even be upset? I mean, all Jamison did was talk with the woman. It's not like he's having an affair or anything."

Kendra's face hardened. "It starts with words. Trust me on that."

Too late Meg remembered Kendra's bout with a married man before settling down with Darin. "Oh, gosh, I'm sorry to bring that up."

"Don't sweat it, really. It's in the past. But learn from someone who's been there and never use the phrase, 'It's only words.' "

Meg nodded, biting her lip. "So you think I should be worried."

"I think if I saw Darin talking it up with some girl and he hid it from me, he'd come home to a couch with a sheet and pillow on it."

Meg fell into one of the chairs and dropped her head into her hands. "Oh, Ken. I don't think I have the strength left in me to deal with this. I just want to pretend it's not happening."

She heard Kendra's Keds squeak on the tile as she crossed the kitchen, then felt her sister's hand on her head. "I know, Meg. I know. I wish I could fix it for you."

Meg let the comfort of Kendra's hand seep into her. It was a gesture they'd all seen Momma do time and time again when life dealt a devastating blow. Meg wanted her Momma more than anything right now. Momma would know what to say, what to do.

Daddy would, too, but it wouldn't be the same. A girl needed her momma when her husband acted the part of a jerk.

Meg sniffed and lifted her head. The understanding in Kendra's eyes nearly did her in. "Thanks, Ken."

"I didn't do anything but have homicidal thoughts."

"If I need to move the body, I'll let you know."

"I'll get to work on escape plans."

Meg managed a smile and stood. "I better get to the grocery store before this leg decides it's done for the day."

Kendra's arms came around her and Meg leaned into her sister's strength. "No matter what happens, Meg, you've got the sisters."

Meg swallowed and took a deep breath. Women had gotten through worse with a whole lot less.

Jamison typed the final word on Prescott's report and pressed the button to save and print the document. He heaved a sigh as he sat back in his chair and ran his hand through his hair. Time to admit the truth that stared him in the face and dogged his thoughts for the past six hours.

He had a problem.

And its name was Karen.

How he'd gotten to this point he wasn't quite sure. Just realizing he'd gotten here left him bumfuzzled. He felt like he'd just roused from a bad dream. Like someone had draped gray netting over his eyes for the past three months.

Now, having taken six hours to do a report that normally took two, the netting had been whisked away. And he was left with a clear image of the truth of what was, yet a murky path to having gotten there.

He ran a hand down his face to wipe away the residual grogginess. Opened eyes didn't necessarily mean a clear path lay at his feet. He couldn't exactly go home and declare, "Hi, honey! I've been driving to Greenfield several times a week to talk to a woman who reminds me of you."

He'd sound like a lunatic.

At the same time, honesty had always served as a cornerstone of his marriage. Even when the truth hurt or would cause an argument, he and Meg gave each other the gift of honesty, no matter what.

Until now.

He couldn't hide this from Meg any longer. She needed to know he'd shared — what? Friendship? Conversation? Interest?

As the printer behind him hummed and spit out Prescott's report, Jamison thought back to Jack's sermon. It didn't take him long to put his finger on the exact point he'd gone wrong.

He'd allowed Karen to meet a need only Meg had the right to meet. The need for conversation, for understanding, for entertainment, for laughter, for the ability to feel liked and wanted. For a sense of being connected to someone.

For emotional intimacy.

He'd turned to Karen for those things when only Meg should be given that right. But knowing what to confess didn't make him rush from his chair to the car. As much as he needed to make this right with Meg — and he needed that like a dying man needed oxygen — he had to have a plan. Without it, he'd go blundering in and hurt her even more in the process of confessing than he did in committing.

At a complete loss, he raked his hand through his hair again and cast about for ideas — any ideas — to present his stupidity to Meg.

Okay, start with the fact that you're an idiot. She knows that already, but it might help for her to know that you know it, too.

He jerked open the desk drawer and snatched up a pad of paper. If ever the time for a list had existed, this was it.

1. I'm stupid.

Tapping the pencil on the notepad, he thought some more. Focus on her? On the fact that he loved her? Since she'd doubt that after his confession, it was probably something he should reiterate up front.

2. I love Meg.

Okay, there. He had two steps. He could do this. He pushed off from the carpet and turned circles in his desk chair. Try as he might, he couldn't get to step three. Ridiculous. He could make an utter mess of his personal life, but he had barely a clue how to clean it up. He was as bad as Hannah with her Barbies.

Worse, really, since Hannah knew where her Barbies belonged.

Recognizing desperation, he thought about calling one of the guys. Did any of them have any experience with this sort of thing? Darin! Not only had his first wife left him for another man, but Kendra had been seeing a married man before she married Darin.

If any of the guys could help him, it was Darin. He pulled out his cell phone and dialed.

"Hello?"

"Hey, man, you got a second?"

"Sure. Everything okay? You sound panicked."

"I am, but I think I can make it okay."

"*Make* it okay? What'd you do?"

"Why do you think I did something?"

"Because Meg's still in the free-pass zone. She can do stuff, but it falls under brain-surgery recovery and she can't be held accountable. You, on the other hand, can be held accountable all day long. What'd you do?"

Jamison sucked in a very deep breath and took the plunge. "I got too close to a woman other than Meg."

Silence greeted his confession. So that wouldn't be the way to go with Meg. Okay.

"Darin? You still there?"

"I'm here." No missing the hard edge in his friend's tone. "And you're calling me for what?"

"Because I don't know how to tell Meg without hurting her any more than she's already going to be hurt."

"Why tell her at all?"

"Because I'm not going to hide things from her. Not any longer. That's what got me in this mess. If I'd been honest with her from the start, I'd have stopped things with Karen a long time ago."

More seconds of silence ticked by. Maybe Darin's wounds were still too raw. "Look, man, I shouldn't have called. I'm sorry to bring this kind of stuff into your life again —"

Darin's long sigh made him sputter to a stop. "Naw, don't worry about it. Guess it's just my lot in life to help folks through it." He sounded weary. "What kind of plan you got so far?"

"Well, I thought I'd start by telling her I'm stupid and I know it."

"Sounds reasonable."

"And that I love her."

"She's not going to believe you, but you need to say it anyway."

"And that's where I get lost."

"Makes sense because that's the part where you tell her what you did. Can't see you jumping into that all eager."

Jamison closed his eyes and tapped his foot on the carpet. "I don't know if I can do this."

"Your call, but I think you've got the right idea telling her."

"You do?"

"Yeah. Honesty's the best policy and all that jazz, right?"

"Right."

"Besides, let's say you don't tell her and she finds out or she already knows and is just waiting on you to say something. Longer you wait, deeper that hole gets."

"No way she knows. She'd have said something."

"Were you sitting in the same church I was Sunday? Sounded like somebody said something to Jack."

Jamison stopped tapping his foot. *Had* Meg asked Jack to preach some sense his way? For a split second, he felt betrayed, but then knew better. Meg wouldn't ask her dad to address an issue in their home. She'd come to him.

Which meant someone else knew.

"Somebody knows," he said out loud.

"Yep."

"Oh, no."

"Yep."

"I've got to get to Meg."

"Yep."

Urgency overtook him. "Thanks, Darin. I've got to go."

"I'll be praying, man. Let me know if I can help."

"Thanks."

Jamison dropped the phone back on the desk and jerked the Prescott report from his printer. He dumped everything on his desk into his briefcase and grabbed his keys, then rushed from the office.

"Amber, please have this couriered over to Prescott's office. I've got to run home."

Amber came up out of her chair. "Is everything okay with Meg?"

"She's fine. I just need to get home. I'll see you tomorrow."

He didn't wait to see if she had a response. He had to get to Meg. Someone could tell her at any moment and that would make her feel even more betrayed.

God, what was I thinking *to carry on that kind of friendship with another woman? Why didn't You stop me? Make me realize what kind of damage that could do to Meg?*

But even as he whined to heaven, he knew the answer. He'd been so caught up in himself that he'd lost sight of his wife.

All the verses in the Bible about loving his wife as Christ loved the church came flooding back. Christ *died* for the church! And Jamison couldn't even get through a few weeks of a bad mood before he went trotting off somewhere else to find a woman to share an emotional intimacy.

Filled with self-loathing, he jumped into the car and squealed tires out of the parking lot. With an eye out for police, he held the speedometer nine miles over the speed limit as he made his way through town. In several minutes less than his usual time, he pulled the car into he garage.

The van sat in its customary spot, so Meg was home. As were his kids. His kids! He hadn't spared a thought for them, either.

He deserved to lose his family. His actions the past two months certainly didn't show he valued them.

Fully awake now from whatever foggy murk he'd fallen into, he hurried into the house, dread filling his mind, fear weighing his heart . . .

And prayers for God's mercy on his lips.

TWENTY-FIVE

Meg's head jerked up at his abrupt entry. She was sitting at the kitchen table peeling potatoes. He saw her strong fingers gripping the knife and potato.

How had he ever gazed on another woman's hands in admiration?

Her eyes widened. "You're home early. Is everything all right?"

How could he say this? How could he stand here and shatter what they'd shared for two decades?

"Jamison? You're scaring me."

"I'm stupid," he blurted.

A shutter came down over her face. She said nothing and stared at him.

"I love you."

Still, she said nothing, though she resumed peeling the potatoes with a calm he couldn't quite understand.

"I — I don't know how to tell you this, but when you were getting better after your surgery, when things were so hard around here, I didn't know what to do. I didn't know what kind of man to be for you and I hated not having any answers for you and I was so stupid that I couldn't handle not being able to handle the situation, so I went somewhere else."

No hint of a reaction. Just simple, calm words. "Somewhere else?"

"To some*one* else. I started a friendship with another woman. It never went beyond just talking together, I swear, but there was a lot of talking. Flirty talking sometimes. And I've been thinking about Jack's sermon, and I know that I had that friendship to meet a need that you were meeting before and that you couldn't while you were getting better and I'm not saying that excuses me, I'm just explaining that I turned to another woman to satisfy something in me that I should only let you satisfy and I need to tell you and I need to know you can forgive me and we can be okay because I swear it will never happen again." He came to a stop and gulped in air. He hadn't meant to dump it all on her like that, but once it started it rushed out like a flood, and all he could do was keep up with the torrent of words as they escaped his mouth.

She said nothing. Just sat there, peeling

potatoes as if he'd said gas prices were going up again.

Darin's words came back to him. Had
Meg known? Had she told her father? He
couldn't fathom the old Meg doing such a
thing, but the new Meg he wasn't so sure
about. The new Meg did things in new
ways, ways he didn't know as well and
therefore couldn't anticipate.

He counted to sixty, giving her time to
respond. When she didn't, he said, "Meg,
did you know?"

Her eyes came to him then, red-rimmed
with unshed tears. Her lip quivered and he
started toward her, but she held a hand up.
"Don't."

A whirlpool of destruction swirled around
him and he couldn't find a way out. "You
knew?" He couldn't wrap his mind around
that. "How long?"

"Four days."

He counted back. Long enough to tell her
dad and have him preach a sermon. "Why
didn't you say anything?"

She threw the potato at him. The old Meg
would never have done that. He wasn't
prepared. Didn't react in time. It bounced
off his shoulder.

"Why didn't *I* say anything?! Why didn't
you? You coward!" She followed up the first

potato with a second. "Jerk!" He learned to duck by the third one. "What were you *thinking?* Or should I ask what you were thinking *with?!* No, I don't have to ask. I know. I've seen her. Get out of my kitchen!"

Jamison's feet were frozen to the tile. He stared at this woman clothed in Meg's skin but saying and acting nothing like his Meg.

Not that he'd acted anything like the Jamison she'd known.

"Get *out!*" Her scream — an ugly, broken sound — terrified him so much that he obeyed.

Fear and anger coursed through Meg, shaking her down to her fingertips, so that when she tried to dial Kendra's number, she messed up the first two tries. Taking a deep, steadying breath, she got it on the third try.

"Hello?"

"It's me. How are the kids?"

"Happily rotting their brains in front of the television and their teeth with a bowl full of M&Ms. Enjoying your afternoon?"

"Jamison just left." Meg told her what had gone down.

"Oh, Meg. Oh, honey. Tell me what you need. A dull spoon for castration? I've got just the thing."

Meg sniffed. "I'm calling a scrapping night."

"I'll call the others. See you at four?"

"See you then."

Meg hung up without any ideas for how to fix the disaster her life had become, but confident that the sisters would help her figure it out. She simply had to hold on until four o'clock.

At a few minutes until four, Meg climbed Daddy's porch steps with feet as heavy as a lead boat. Which was fitting, since she felt certain by the end of the night she stood a good chance of sinking.

The door opened before she had a chance to reach for it.

Tandy's arms came out to her. "Get on in here and let's get this all sorted out."

Meg let herself be pulled into a hug. Thank God she had sisters. Tandy kept her arm around Meg as they made their way through the house. She glanced into the living room and saw all three children lined up on the couch, glued to a VeggieTales video. Paid shot through her heart and she tripped. "Steady sis," Tandy consoled. "We're here." Her feet felt like blocks of cement, but she somehow trudged up the steps to the scrapping studio. Joy and Kendra already sat on their stools, though no scrapping items were on the table.

"We decided to put our whole focus on the issue at hand rather than scrapping for the time being," Joy explained.

Meg had just settled in on her stool when Zelda's face appeared at the stairs.

"Hi, girls."

"Zelda, now is not a very good time," Joy warned.

"Your daddy said Meg called a scrapping night."

"She did."

"Then I think it's a good time."

Meg blew out a breath. She wanted to be a bridge-builder, but also needed to deal with her life before putting herself out there for everybody else. She didn't have the energy to put tact into her next words. "Zelda, look, I'm going through something here and I'd rather talk about it with my sisters than my stepmother, okay? No offense or anything."

Zelda looked at her for a long moment. "I've got a story to tell you and I'd like the opportunity to share it. If you want me to leave afterward, I'll go. But since this is my house, I'd like the respect of being able to at least share this story."

Meg huffed and nodded, motioning a

hurry up signal with her hand. The quicker Zelda got on with it, the quicker she'd leave and the sisters could help her figure out what to do.

"I don't think I've shared this with any of you before, but my first husband, God rest his soul, had one major flaw. He had a problem staying faithful to me when he was deployed."

Meg raised her head. What was this?

"He wasn't the only man to wrestle with loneliness and depression out in the field," Zelda continued, fiddling with her rings, "and he justified it by saying he never strayed when he was home. And he didn't. I believe that. But it didn't make the times he deployed any easier to deal with. In my mind, it was in the hard times that a man proved himself to his spouse, and my man made it pretty clear what he did to manage the hard times. He let another woman meet his needs.

"For a lot of years, I wrestled with it. Most times he wasn't doing anything physical with the woman. He was just having a friendly flirtation for whatever months he was away — getting the looks and small touches from a woman that he couldn't get from me several oceans away."

Meg checked out her sisters' faces; they

all looked as flabbergasted as she felt. Was this why Zelda had seemed so calm and in control in the Wimpy's parking lot? She'd known what Meg was experiencing?

Zelda kept going. "When I brought it up to the other soldiers' wives, they acted like I was an ungrateful wife and un-American. According to them, I should let my husband do whatever he needed to do to serve his country faithfully and stop making such a big deal about him being friends with another woman in his unit.

"For a while I thought they must be right and I tried to follow their advice. But I learned, after a whole lot of prayer and Bible-searching, that those wives were wrong. Like your daddy said in his sermon, anytime a husband gets his needs or wants met by a woman other than his wife, he's crossed the line. Doesn't matter if it's conversation, affirmation, or sex. It all cheats his wife out of something that's rightfully hers.

"When I figured that out, I decided to talk to my husband about it. At first, he took the side of the other military wives, as you might guess. It took him over a year to come to me and ask forgiveness. Our marriage changed after that, we were closer, more intimate. He deployed one more time, but I believed him when he told me he stayed faithful — in the full sense of the word — on that mission.

"Now, your situation is a little bit different, Meg. Your hard time wasn't a military mission but a medical one. Still, I thought you might want to know that I had a blessed, amazing, wonderful marriage for the three years of faithfulness I enjoyed with my husband." She leaned on the table and waited until Meg met her eyes. "Don't write him off and don't shut him out for too long. He's human and made a mistake. Nobody in this family will think anything of you for forgiving him — well, anything other than that you're a strong woman committed to her vows and her family."

Zelda waited a minute longer, then pushed off of the table. "That's all I wanted to say. You still want me to go?"

Meg slowly shook her head. And here she thought she was a bridge-builder. "No."

Zelda climbed up onto a stool. "Okay, then. Let's figure out where you go from here."

TWENTY-SIX

Meg rested her forearms on the table and glanced at the sisters, all of whom were staring at Zelda. She turned back to her stepmother. "Why didn't you share this with me before?"

"Oh, Meg." Zelda's eyes held empathy and regret. "I couldn't decide if I would be dishonoring my husband's memory and if your daddy would be comfortable with me telling you stories about my first marriage. That might be disrespectful to him, and I wouldn't dishonor him for the world."

That made sense. "So you talked to Daddy and he preached that sermon instead."

"Yes."

"Thanks for that."

"You're welcome."

Kendra huffed and waved her hands, her bracelets clanking. "Okay, so what does she need to do, Z?"

"Like I said, your situation is a little bit

different than mine. Raymond was at war, but I'll bet Jamison feels like he's been in a war. He got in over his head and tried to find something that would make him feel like the man he was before the surgery. I doubt he meant for it to become a regular thing and I really, really doubt he's done anything physical with this woman."

"Oh, me too," Meg rushed to agree. "Not that I could see Jamison even sharing conversation with another woman like I saw him doing at Wimpy's, but I definitely don't see him getting physical with someone else." She tried to picture it, but simply couldn't.

"Yeah, but he still shared things with that woman that he should have been sharing with you," Tandy reminded them. "Are you okay with that?"

"No."

"And you don't have to be." Zelda adjusted her giant silver hoop earring. "It's okay to feel hurt and betrayed. I know I did. But you're going to also have to get to the place where you tell him that. And that you forgive him."

What would it be like to forgive Jamison? To let this go? To return to their marriage as if he hadn't done this awful thing? Could she do it?

He'd certainly done plenty for her in these

weeks of recovery, overlooking her mood swings, patiently waiting out her tantrums, shielding the kids from her when she wanted to rage at them for no good reason. When she considered all she'd put him through — granted, she hadn't *chosen* to put him through it, but still — it occurred to her that she might want to afford some grace to this man she'd pledged to love, honor, and cherish until death they did part.

Because, at the end of the day, marriage was supposed to be about loving the other person. Not defending self. Not finding blame or being right.

Loving.

Meg looked up to find the sisters and Zelda watching her. She met Zelda's gaze. "You really forgave him?"

"I did. And I was a better woman and wife for it."

Meg nodded. "I think I know what you mean."

TWENTY-SEVEN

Meg pulled the van into her garage and turned off the engine, her mind whirling with thoughts like a tornado with wood after hitting a barn. The dashboard clock glowed 11:52 because she hadn't yet opened a door and cut its power. Nearly midnight. Time for Cinderella's coach to turn back into a pumpkin?

She glanced around the van. Not exactly a coach, but filled with amenities like leather seats, a DVD player for the kids, and other bells and whistles. Maybe a modern-day coach.

Come on, Meg. You're stalling and you know it.

Of course she was. As soon as she walked in that door, she'd have to wake Jamison up and talk this out. She considered letting it go until morning, but knew she'd never get to sleep with this hanging over their heads.

At least he'd finally said something to her.

The sisters and Zelda kept pointing out that she should be grateful for his confession. And she did feel gratitude. It warred nicely with the betrayal.

But, as Zelda had said, Jamison wasn't the only one at fault here. Granted, she'd been recovering from brain surgery and thus should be given a whole lot of latitude to deal with her life's changes. But in the midst of it, Jamison was who she leaned on for ultimate support.

Not God.

Startled at the realization, Meg let the thought calm her mind and spirit. She had put Jamison in a position to fail. Had expected him to be perfect. To be her salvation. To be, in essence, God. Of course he flailed around like a three-year-old who'd been asked to build a bridge. Being God — what an insurmountable task she'd placed before him.

Not that relying on him was wrong. Zelda reassured her she should have been able to trust Jamison and rely on him as her husband. But that didn't allow her the right to expect perfection from him. To expect him to just take her bad moods and anger with a calm, patient stoicism of one who had the perspective of the ages.

She should have taken all that anger to

God, not hurled it at her husband's feet as if he had a clue what to do with it. She'd expected Jamison to be God. And, of course, he'd failed to do so.

Failed in a pretty monumental way, but that stood to reason given the enormity of the expectation placed on his shoulders. She didn't excuse his behavior, but with Zelda and the sisters talking it through with her she at least began to understand it. And that helped a lot because, when she showed up on Daddy and Zelda's doorstep, she hadn't a clue how her Jamison could have possibly befriended another woman in that way. Could have looked at someone with *that* look she'd seen.

Now she understood. The other blonde probably made him feel like his old self — like the man instead of the God-failure. Who wanted to be reminded of his failure all the time? So he'd gone off to find approval and he'd found it at that diner.

The automatic light clicked off overhead, stirring Meg from her reverie. Time to face the music. She opened the door and stepped out onto the concrete pad of the garage. They'd shared this house for so many years that she hadn't looked at it with fresh eyes in a long time. Thousands of women, if not millions, walking the planet would give their right arm to have the life she'd been blessed with.

And they'd almost thrown it away.

She picked up her pace and entered the house. Through the far side of the kitchen, lamplight fell through the doorway. He'd left a light on for her. He always did that. The sight warmed her now and she walked that direction to turn it off before going upstairs.

When she came around the corner, it wasn't an empty living room she saw but Jamison, sitting in the recliner, a book lying forgotten on his chest. His eyelids were closed in peaceful sleep.

She stopped and leaned against the entry, looking on him. He'd tried to stay up for her. He *had* stayed up, just not awake. She smiled at that.

He must have sensed her presence, because he stirred and those beautiful eyes she'd fallen into as a teenager opened.

"You're home."

"I am. We need to talk." She came into the room and sat down on the couch. Turning to face him, she decided to just take the bull by the horns and get this over with. "Thank you for telling me about your . . . friendship. I have a confession to make, too."

He raised an eyebrow, but said nothing.

She snagged a pillow and toyed with a loose thread on its corner. "I've been thinking a lot about how we got to this point. I'd like to think everything happened because of the tumor, but I think we both know it's more than that. Since my surgery, I've relied on you to be God to me. And, of course, you're not God."

She paused for breath and he said, "No, I do a pretty bad job of being Him. I'm evidently much better at imitating a Nicolaitan."

The thread came loose a little further, so she continued pulling at it. Backing out of the conversation would do no one any good, though all she really wanted to do was run upstairs and bury her head in a pillow. "I know and it was wrong of me to put that kind of expectation on you. We've been together so long that I fell into this idea of you meeting all of my needs, of you handling anything that came our way. When that tumor came, I just expected you to handle it, to handle me. And when you didn't, I got mad at you." She let out a short laugh. "I got mad at you for not being perfect."

Unsure how to continue, she stumbled to a stop and pulled the thread even more. It was coming unraveled as fast as her nerves. The recliner squeaked when he let the footrest down and came out of it. He joined her on the couch and put his hand over hers where it had been fidgeting with the thread. His touch calmed her heart.

"I'm sorry I couldn't be perfect for you," he whispered. Tucking a finger under her chin, he directed her face to him.

Reluctantly she met his gaze. "I'm sorry I expected you to be."

"And I am *so* sorry that I didn't just tell you how at odds I was and started talking to another woman instead. That was foolish, stupid, and hurtful and I still can't believe I did such an idiotic thing. I don't know if I even have the right to ask, but do you think we can get past it?"

A part of her thought about saying no, about defending herself and making herself invulnerable to further hurt by cutting him off. But she reminded herself that the goal wasn't to get mad or get even or defend self. Her goal was to love this man, for better or worse, in sickness and in health, until death parted them. Her dedication was to this marriage. "Yeah, I think we can."

He pulled her into an embrace that felt like home. That reminded her of why she loved him in the first place and why she'd continue loving him until the last place. Jamison, *her* Jamison.

She wrapped her arms around him and settled into that place by his neck where her head fit perfectly. No, he wasn't God for her. But he *was* the one God had created for her to spend her life with. Zelda — of all people! — had reminded her of that.

And as long as she remembered they were in this for a lifetime, they could face anything together. She settled further into the crook of his shoulder. No sense worrying about what *anything* might mean.

EPILOGUE

Jack Sinclair sat on his front porch, sweltering in the oppressive July heat of the South. Zelda sat beside him, a glass of lemonade in her hand sweating water droplets onto the worn oak boards.

"This is a wonderful birthday party, Jack," she said.

"Happy to hear it," he returned. Something had changed between Zelda and the girls. He suspected it had to do with that last scrapping night. She hadn't shared details with him and he'd been happy to be left in the dark. Her assertion that all would be fine with Meg and Jamison was enough for him.

He watched his grandchildren take turns between the Slip 'N Slide and inflatable swimming pool complete with eight-foot-tall water slide. Before Zelda, he wouldn't have thought to purchase such things. He'd have let the kids run through the water hose spray and considered that a fun day. But Zelda knew what kids liked, being a big kid herself in a lot of ways. So, when she dragged him through the aisles at the toy store and pointed to two boxes, he didn't ask questions. He just paid for the items and came home.

After all, Zelda's birthday, Zelda's wishes.

Savannah, Hannah, and James squealed their pleasure with their new grandmother's toys while Clayton and Maddie looked on in wide-eyed fascination. His girls sat under shade umbrellas, mother hens keeping a close eye on their chicks. Their husbands were gathered around the grill discussing the best steak rub.

Jack took it all in under the haze of the summer sun and realized this wasn't the family he'd expected to end up with. He never thought someone would get Kendra to an altar, but Darin's love proved strong enough for her to commit. And after Tandy's and Clay Kelner's huge fight in front of the town, he'd have bet half the farm those two would end up on opposite ends of the globe. But there they were, husband and wife, with a little combination of themselves in baby Clayton.

After years of watching Joy and Scott try and try to have a child, he'd resolved to be content with them giving him no grand-children. But God had other plans. In His infinite wisdom and miraculous plan, He gave them Maddie, who looked so much like Joy that when people saw the child, they commented it was clear she'd gotten her mother's genes. And, he guessed she had.

And Meg. His sweet Meggy, with the sunny disposition and positive outlook no matter what life dealt them. When he'd heard about Jamison's relationship with another woman, he felt as if he'd walked into another universe. Of all the children, Meg gave him the least trouble. He and Marian spoke often of how much easier Joy and Meg were to raise than the spirited Kendra and opinionated Tandy.

But it was Meg who suffered from a brain tumor and Meg who nearly lost her mar-riage. Jack shook his head. Satan's attacks on an unprotected flank never ceased to amaze him.

"What are you shaking that head about, old man?" Zelda teased.

"Careful who you're calling old man, woman. I'm not the one celebrating a birthday today."

She sipped her lemonade, a smile lighting her eyes above the glass.

"I was just thinking about how good God

is to not let us plan out our own lives."

"Ha. I know a few people who might disagree with you on that."

"I'd have been one of them a few years ago, but I'm learning we're not quite smart enough to write the stories He writes. His have twists and turns that we wouldn't know to go after. Take Maddie, for instance. If I'd sat down and planned out Joy's life when we first brought her home from China, I don't think I'd have been smart enough to have her need to go back and deal with things before having a baby girl herself. But God knew she'd need that and that their baby girl would need what she learned along the way."

"Hmm, maybe you're just short on imagination."

Jack set his rocker in motion with a push of his booted foot. "Maybe. But to have that plan for Joy, I'd have had to make her go through the pain of not conceiving and then miscarrying. I doubt any amount of imagination would have made me choose that for her. Even though she's a better mom and woman for it."

"You know, you're a pretty wise old man."

He cut his eyes toward her. "I've got to keep up with you."

She laughed. "Everybody needs a challenge in life. Keeps us young."

"Well, then —" he gestured to the bounty of kids and grandkids in the yard — "looks like we're going to stay young for a very long time."

"Having spent two years getting to know your girls, I'd have to agree with you."

"Are you saying my daughters are a challenge?"

"Never. I'm simply saying they'll keep us young."

He gazed out across the expanse of green grass, seeing the sun play on his daughters' hair and turn his grandkids' skin golden. He listened to their chatter and laughter, and happiness welled up in him so fast and high it took his breath. He turned and took in the peaceful sight of his wife, a woman he hadn't known to want until she crossed his path. Until she woke him up from the loneliness of mourning Marian.

No, not the story he would have written, but a story he felt blessed to be a part of.

"Happy birthday, Zelda," he said, and rocked away the day.

ABOUT THE AUTHOR

Rebeca Seitz writes novels for women and is also the founder of both a literary public relations firm and an event management company. She lives at Storybook Farm in southwest Kentucky with her husband, their son and daughter, and an ever-changing cast of fish, turtles, barn cats, deer, and other wildlife.